ELYSIUM

ELYSIUM

PART 2 OF THE SOVEREIGN TRILOGY

AJ WHITNEY

This book is a work of fiction. Any references to historical events, people, or places are used fictitiously. Other names, characters, places, and events are products of the author's imagination, and any resemblance to actual events, places, or persons, living or dead, is entirely coincidental.

Copyright © 2026

All rights reserved, including the right to reproduce this book or any portions thereof in any form whatsoever.

For information, address:
Blue Handle Publishing
2067 Wolflin Ave. #963
Amarillo, TX 79109

For information about bulk, educational, and other special discounts, please contact Blue Handle Publishing.
www.BlueHandlePublishing.com

To book A.J. Whitney for any event,
contact Blue Handle Publishing.

Cover and interior design: Blue Handle Publishing

Editing: Book Puma Author Services
BookPumaEdit.com

ISBN: 978-1-955058-36-0

*To Tim, who loved a good story
but never got to read this one.*

*And to Mom, who never tried to stop me from writing
one (even when you were probably concerned).*

I could not be more grateful that you found each other.

THE AFTERMATH

Cool mist hung in the chilly spring air, clinging to the freshly tilled earth, the blades of bright new grass springing up, and the dozens of bodies that lay strewn about. It moistened her dark skin as she lay in a heap on the ground, her fallen rifle only inches from her slack fingers. Whatever happened here had left quite a scene throughout the small rural settlement, had anyone been conscious to behold it. Person after person lay on the ground outside, rifles, knives, and other weapons dropped nearby. The village was littered with slumbering bodies, and not one in their beds.

A slight groan—more like a whimper—escaped Maggie's dark lips as her eyelids began to flutter. She reached up and cradled her aching head in her hand. The morning light, dull though it was through the spring fog, was overwhelming even through her eyelids. She flinched against it, squeezing her eyes shut tighter. Her bed did not feel as warm or as comfortable as usual.

Whatever this illness was, she would simply have to fight through it. There were cows who needed milking, eggs that needed collecting, water to be brought in from the pump, and breakfast to be made. The girls would help, of course, but Maggie would have to get herself up and moving.

"John," she croaked, though no discernible sound passed through her lips. Attempting to roll over to her husband, she discovered that her legs were sprawled in odd and painful directions. One arm was pinned beneath her back. She slowly unfolded her throbbing body. Pins and needles spread through her limbs as blood flow returned to them.

She tried to call out for John again, but she simply couldn't activate her vocal cords. She swallowed hard and realized there was nothing there to swallow. Her mouth felt like it had been stuffed with cotton.

Maggie turned onto her right side and, unable to find the edge of her bed, pressed her hands down beneath her to bring herself up onto her knees. Feeling cool soil beneath her fingers, she startled ever so slightly. She opened her eyes a crack and peered through her lashes to find that she was not in her bed at all. She pushed herself upright, but a crack of pain blasted through her skull. She swayed with ferocious dizziness and landed back upon the earth.

This time, she opened her eyes from where she lay. She turned her head slowly to one side and found another man beginning to come to. Turning her head to the other side, she discovered her beloved John, face down in the dirt, rifle discarded. He wasn't moving. She couldn't tell if he was even breathing.

Panic spreading through her bones, Maggie tried again to rise to her feet but failed. Instead, she crawled on her belly until she reached him. She struggled to turn his body through waves of pain and dizziness that threatened to overtake her. In agony, she lay across his silent form, putting her head against his chest, and waited. Finally, she felt his ragged breaths and heard his slow, steady heartbeat. She began to weep into him, wracking tearless sobs that overtook her entire being. He was alive.

Maggie summoned all her strength and brought herself to sitting by sheer force of will. In spite of a rush of vertigo, she remained upright by John's side. Still unable to speak fully, she whispered his name urgently.

"John? John! Wake up!" She shook him lightly at first, but then more urgently. After several minutes of furious jostling, it became clear that a new tactic was needed.

Maggie leaned down and spoke into his ear with whatever small voice she could muster. No response. She placed her hands gently on either side of his face. She lifted his head and kissed his lips. When she still received no response, she smacked his cheeks and even slapped him hard, just once. Still nothing happened.

"Wake up! Why won't you wake up?"

Her pleas went unanswered, at least by John, but she soon became aware of another presence kneeling beside her.

"I'm afraid you can't wake him, Maggie," a gentle voice warned. "This is no natural sleep."

Hesitantly, Maggie pulled her gaze from her slumbering husband and found the kind eyes of their aging healer, Sophie.

"Here, you need to drink. It will help you regain your voice," Sophie directed, handing Maggie a mug of cool water.

Maggie took the cup but didn't drink. "What do—"

"Drink first. Then you can ask your questions."

The healer's weathered hands guided the cup to Maggie's lips and gently tipped it from underneath. Sophie watched Maggie drink, continuing to guide the cup until she was satisfied.

"There now. That feels better, doesn't it?"

Maggie couldn't deny it. Her raw throat was somewhat soothed, and she felt much more confident in her voice.

"So, what do I mean it's not a natural sleep?" Sophie began, taking the question from Maggie's lips before she had a chance

to test her vocal cords.

Maggie nodded dumbly, cradling John's head in her lap. She was accustomed to being the one in charge, but Sophie's presence, though kind and reassuring, dwarfed her and made her feel like a child again.

"Have you had a look around?" Sophie asked patiently, gesturing broadly.

Maggie had been so focused on John that she had not taken the time to look around her or try to understand what was happening. She simply needed her partner to be alive. Now, she saw the bigger picture—men and women lay in heaps in a neat line across the barren field on either side of her. Back toward the town, more dark masses were spread as far as she could see.

"How many?" Maggie inquired, stifling a gasp.

Sophie sighed deeply. "It looks to be everyone, though I've not been awake long myself. I've been trying to find the Elders and the other healers to see who's awake to help."

"What happened? I can't remember anything." Maggie was returning to her businesslike self, preparing to take charge and jump into action.

"It's all a blur. We must've been drugged, though it's not quite clear how. It doesn't seem to be the water supply, or I'd have passed back out after my first drink. I'm not entirely sure how else you drug an entire population."

Maggie put her fingers to her temples, trying to massage away the pain that threatened to crack her skull in two. "I just feel so . . . foggy . . . Nothing makes any sense, and this damned headache makes it impossible to think."

Sophie nodded. "I feel the same. All these symptoms are why I think it's some kind of drug. Whatever's in our systems has some serious side effects. The dehydration doesn't help much either. Who knows how long we've all been unconscious? Are you hurt anywhere?"

Maggie shook her head impatiently. "How do we wake them up?"

"We don't. If they were drugged, it will have to run its course and make its way out of their systems. Everyone is different, and we may have all gotten different doses. Without knowing what it is or how much was given, it's impossible to say how long it will take. All we can do is wait."

"I'm not much for waiting," Maggie replied sourly.

"Don't I know it." Sophie smirked, remembering Maggie's many past attempts to become pregnant again after the child she and John lost all those years ago. "But we don't have any other choice."

She stood then and offered Maggie her hand. "Come on. Let's get started brewing some peppermint tea for the headache. You can watch for John to wake up from your porch."

Maggie let Sophie help her stand. Her legs were shaky and her knees wobbled. The pain in her head got worse, so Sophie helped steady her.

"Put your arm around my shoulders. You'll feel unsteady for a bit. Once we get you in a comfortable chair, I'll give you some feverfew to help with the pain. There's not enough in the storehouse for the whole town, but the Elders and the healers will need it to get things sorted. Everyone else will have to make do with the tea."

"Including John," she added, side-eyeing Maggie.

"Yes, ma'am," Maggie replied, leaning into Sophie for support. The pair hobbled along toward John and Maggie's house, where Maggie swallowed some feverfew extract and recovered on the front porch while keeping a watchful eye on the sleeping settlers nearby.

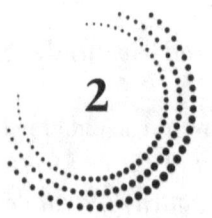

2

WELCOME TO ELYSIUM

"Welcome to Elysium. We're glad to see you are recovering well and are now awake. A staff member will escort you to the Orientation Room shortly. We trust you will remain cooperative. Your new life is about to begin."

That's what the voice said. I'm still not sure where it came from. *What does any of this mean? I have to get out of here!*

I struggle against my restraints to no avail. They're thick and strong, and I'm weakened and confused. No matter how hard I push or pull against them, I simply cannot free my arms and legs. My face feels hot, and tears sting my eyes.

"Mama! Papa!"

The sound of my own voice startles me. It echoes in this bizarrely white room. I'm so hoarse that it doesn't even sound like me. The harder I struggle, the more I cry. The more I cry, the louder I become, demanding my mama and papa.

Are they even alive? I need them to be alive!

Suddenly, the glass wall beyond my feet opens, and two strangers dressed from head to toe in pale blue enter the room before the wall closes behind them. They wear hoods and masks over their faces, so all I can see is their eyes obscured by giant clear glasses. I'm not sure whether to be curious or terrified. I settle on a little of both as I scream at the top of my lungs. My voice cracks, and I'm thrown into a coughing fit so horrendous I fear I'll never breathe again.

A gloved hand offers me a glass of water, but I can't sit up to take a drink. There's an oddly tiny, flexible pipe protruding from the top of the glass. This alien figure places the tube into my mouth and instructs me to drink.

How do you drink from this?

I look straight into the creature's bug-like eyes.

"How?" I choke on my words.

The two creatures exchange looks, and the other says, "They don't have straws there. She doesn't know what you want her to do."

The first blinks and nods. "Sorry, I'm new here," it says to me.

She says to me? It sounds like a woman's voice. My bed starts moving, and a strange humming noise emanates from directly behind my head. I look side to side in a panic, trying to discern what's happening. The hooded figure speaks again.

"Sorry, I'm sorry. I'm just adjusting your bed to help you sit up a little . . . so you can drink."

Definitely a woman. At least they're human. I think.

She puts the glass up to my mouth, and I drink in ice cold water. It feels like the snow we bring in and melt when the pumps freeze in the winter, but it tastes so much better.

How do they get water that tastes so clean?

The second figure speaks. He sounds like a man but young. His voice isn't nearly as deep as Papa's yet.

"Harper, this is Elysium. You're in a special hospital right now to help you recover from the trauma of being taken. I'm sorry about the restraints. We know it can be unsettling to wake up here where everything is different, so we make sure you can't get up and hurt anyone else or yourself before we can explain what's going on."

I'm in a hospital? Like where the healers work?

This doesn't look like any hospital I've ever seen before. Doesn't smell like one, either. Our hospital smells like sickness. This place smells... sharp and weird. I don't know how to describe it. I've never smelled anything like it.

The man continues. "Dr. Tori will be in to check on you soon. We've been monitoring your vitals to make sure you're well enough for orientation. You've been asleep a lot longer than the others. You gave the extraction team quite a bit of trouble—broke somebody's nose and gave yourself a nice concussion."

I must give him a quizzical look because he continues to explain.

"A concussion is an injury to your brain. It happens when you hit your head too hard. We're pretty sure it was that headbutt you gave Corporal Collins. You're going to be okay, though."

These people seem a little friendly for kidnappers. I'm wary, but something inside me wants to trust them. Maybe they're helping me.

"What's all this? Why's this thing in my arm? Are you trying to hurt me? And who's Corporal Collins?"

The woman lets out a tiny laugh, and the man glares at

her. "That's not helpful, Tina," he scolds.

"Sorry, Greg," she says, sounding genuinely apologetic. She looks at me. "I don't mean to be rude. It's just, they told us you might be a little more difficult than the others, but I didn't expect you to ask every question at once."

I stare daggers at her but don't say a word.

"Most people just aren't as curious as you are right off the bat," she offers awkwardly.

"I thought you said you were new here." I eye her suspiciously.

"She's smart, too," Greg says. "The thing in your arm is a flexible needle. It's called an IV, and it puts medicine directly into your bloodstream. We're not going to hurt you. We're here to help."

"What about the annoying beeping noise?" I demand.

"That is a machine that keeps track of your heart and your breathing. It makes sure everything is functioning as it should. Honestly, you probably don't need it now that you're awake, but it lets us know if an emergency is happening so we can help you."

I nod my head thoughtfully. *I guess that makes sense, but...*

"Why is everything so different here? We don't have any of this stuff where I live. This looks like a completely different world!"

"It practically is," Tina replies. "We have a lot of things that you don't have where you came from. That's why it can be such a shock to wake up here. I promise you're safe, though. Dr. Tori will explain everything to you in orientation."

"What's orientation?" I ask.

"It's basically a meeting where they explain everything to you. You'll get to ask as many questions as you want, and Dr. Tori will tell you anything you want to know. There really aren't any secrets. It's just that she knows a lot more and can explain things a lot better than we can."

"If there aren't any secrets, then why don't you know as much as she does?"

Even Greg laughs at this one, and I feel resentment rising in me. It must be easy to laugh at people when you're the only one in the room who understands what's going on.

"Because most of us don't have as many questions as you do, that's all." He shrugs. "She'd tell me anything I wanted to know, but I have a feeling I've never wanted to know half as much as you do."

"Where are my friends? Where's my sister and my mama and papa?" I don't know why I didn't think of it before. Nothing could possibly be more important than that.

"Everyone is fine, I promise," Tina reassures me. "Just let us do our job, and you can ask Dr. Tori your questions in a little while."

I nod my head, deep in thought. I'm so busy thinking about Matthew and Ava that I barely even notice what these new people are doing. The next thing I know, the glass wall is sliding open again, and a tall woman in a long white coat enters the room. Greg raises an eyebrow at her.

"Harper has been cleared of contaminants, Greg. You can take off your clean suits if you'd like. She's not carrying anything contagious or dangerous to any of us."

Elysium

Greg nods and breathes a sigh of relief. He pulls off his glasses and mask and lowers his hood. He doesn't look much older than me. He has long hair like a woman, pulled back into a ponytail, and a little bit of hair on his chin. Tina has removed her face coverings, too, and I see that she has short, straight black hair with a pink streak, and a hoop through one side of her nose.

Who *are* these people?

The new woman moves toward me. She checks some machines and a clipboard she picked up from somewhere in the room. I can't seem to focus on her face because I'm so distracted by her clothes. She doesn't wear the same light blue outfit as Greg and Tina. Instead, she wears a brightly colored button-up shirt with little birds on it and slacks, like a man. I've never seen a woman who wasn't wearing a dress.

"Harper?"

I shake my head and blink. Clearly, she has been speaking to me, and I was so busy marveling at her clothes that I didn't hear a word she said.

"Sorry, what?"

She smiles a kind smile, and her eyes crinkle at the corners. "My name is Dr. Victoria Taylor, but you can call me Dr. Tori. I'm in charge of the hospital here in Elysium."

My brow furrows. "What's Elysium?"

"This is. Elysium is an underground city, not too terribly far from the community where you grew up. Your people call us the Sovereign."

My eyes go wide.

"I assure you we're ordinary people just like you. Your village has been building legends surrounding our city and people for hundreds of years. I'll admit, we must seem very mysterious to them. We've kept our presence mostly secret, but some things can't be denied. Your village explains the things we do with religion, but the Sovereign, as you've recently discovered, aren't exactly real. At least, not as your people think of them."

This is so weird. I might be sick.

"Are you feeling okay, Harper? You look a little pale."

"I don't . . . None of this makes any sense."

Dr. Tori nods empathetically. "I know. It's quite a lot to process. Right now, I want to focus on your medical needs and make sure you're healthy enough to move out of your hospital room. Then, we'll prepare for your orientation, where I'll answer all your questions. How does your head feel?"

I forgot my head had even been hurting.

"It was hurting pretty bad when I first woke up, but I don't notice it as much now."

"Good, that's very good news. Now, if I release you from your restraints, will you promise to stay in bed and let me help you get up safely? It's a good idea to start sitting up and walking around soon to help your recovery. Staying in bed for too long won't benefit you."

I nod my assent. I'm still insanely confused, but I'm starting to believe that Dr. Tori is helping me. I'll give her a chance, and if she doesn't answer my questions, I'll find a way out later.

She unstraps my ankles first. Sitting at the end of my bed, she touches the soles of my feet.

"Can you feel that," she asks.

I nod. "It tickles."

"Good, that's just what we want." She smiles.

Elysium

She continues to poke and prod at my feet and legs for a few more minutes. She seems pleased when my toes curl or I jerk my feet away.

"Sensation and reflexes seem to be intact," Dr. Tori says to no one in particular. Greg scribbles furiously on the clipboard she handed him a few minutes ago.

Next, she unstraps my wrists. Taking my hand, she gently helps me sit up. She continues holding onto me, watching me carefully.

"How's your head now?"

"I was a little dizzy for a second, but I'm okay now."

"Great! Now, look at me. I need you to follow my finger with your eyes, but keep your head still. Good. I'm going to shine a light in your eyes. Just keep looking at this finger." She wags her left index finger to indicate which one she's talking about.

She gets out a long, thin piece of metal. It makes a clicking noise, and the end lights up as bright as the sun. I blink against it involuntarily.

"I know it's bright, and you're not used to this thing."

"How do you do that without a candle?"

"It's called a flashlight, but I can teach you about that later. For now, keep watching my finger." She waggles her index finger again, and I give it my careful attention. She moves it from one place to the next and, though I'm watching her finger, I can tell she's staring intently at my eyes. I wonder what that light even does. What does it help her see?

"Everything looks good there, too," Dr. Tori says, and Greg scribbles some more. "Now, I'm going to listen to your heart and lungs."

I expect her to put her ear up to my chest to listen

like Sophie does when we're sick, but instead she takes a strange-looking necklace off her shoulders. She puts two ends in her ears and places the other end—an ice-cold metal medallion—against my chest. She directs me when to breathe and when to hold my breath. I do as she says, but I simply cannot figure out how any of this works.

"Well, Harper, everything looks good so far. I don't want to rush you, so for now, we'll stick to sitting up in bed. I'll have you taking walks before you know it, but I want to make sure you remain stable for a little while first. Do you think you could handle some visitors?"

I feel my face scrunch up again. "Visitors?"

Dr. Tori smiles her cheerful smile and pulls a small rectangle out of the pocket of her white coat. She taps her thumbs to it repeatedly. Then, she drops it back into her pocket and seems to be waiting for something. After a few moments of silence, there's movement in the hall. I turn and see two white-clad figures walking toward my room, escorted by another adult in a long white coat. The glass slides open again, and the figures race into my room, plop down on either side of my bed, and hug me tight from both sides.

"Ava! Matthew! I'm so glad you're okay!"

REUNITED

They squeeze me so hard I can barely breathe, but I don't even care. My face and shoulders are wet with tears. Who those tears belong to is hard to say—all of us probably. We hug and we cry for so long that I'm genuinely surprised to see Dr. Tori still standing in the room watching us when we finally release.

"We were afraid you wouldn't wake up," Ava cries.

"I thought you were both dead," I stammer through the sobs that rack my body.

Ava wraps her arms around my neck again. With no room to join in, Matthew takes my hand instead. I can't believe they're here and they're okay. Not just *alive*, but perfectly and completely fine, from the looks of things.

Dr. Tori clears her throat, and all three of us pause to look at her, Ava wrapped up in my messy tangle of curls with her tears still pouring down my neck.

"Are the two of you comfortable staying with Harper without a doctor or nurse to assist you?"

"We can manage, Dr. Tori," Matthew croaks, drying his eyes on his white sleeve.

Dr. Tori smiles that contagious smile again. "You

remember how to call for help if any of you isn't feeling well, right?"

Matthew reaches behind me and picks up a small rectangle that seems to be attached to my bed with wire. It has several small squares embedded into one side, and Matthew is pointing to the one that's labeled *CALL*.

"Excellent. I'll give you three some time to catch up. I know your company will be good for Harper. She'll have so much less to worry about if she knows you're both near. Use the call button if you need help. I'll be back in an hour or so to check on Harper's progress."

The glass wall slides open again, and Dr. Tori leaves the room. I watch her walk down the bright hallway and turn a corner before I open my mouth to speak.

"What happened to you guys? What is this place?"

Matthew takes a deep breath, a thoughtful and serious expression on his face. Finally, he speaks. "When we ran from the Sovereign that night, my little sister started to cry. I set her down behind a house to make sure she wasn't hurt. That's when I saw you and Ava being attacked. I sent her to hide with some boys from school and came back for you, but they were too strong for me. They stabbed me with something that knocked me out."

He shrugs his shoulders and shakes his head, as if trying to access memories that just won't come. "The next thing I knew, I was waking up here, in a room just like this."

I turn to Ava, who has fresh tears in her eyes. She nods in agreement. "That's about all I remember, too. What happened to you after they took us?"

"I thought you were both dead. I watched you go limp and get dragged away into the dark. I thought about running away on my own, but I knew I had to get to the Orphan Home in case anyone else made it there safely. The whole town was overflowing with Sovereign. I had to crawl on my belly to get from the equipment barns to the tree line. I had to hide in a pile of dead bodies to keep from getting caught."

An unexpected sob wells up in my throat, but I don't let it overtake me. "When I finally got to the Orphan Home, everything was knocked over, and there were drag marks on the floor. I couldn't find anybody at all, so I ran into the forest."

"You made it all the way out of town on your own?" Ava's eyes are wide as saucers.

I nod before continuing. "I ran through the woods. I used some of my old hiding places, like that hollow log. . . . Anyway, I thought I got away. I made it all the way to the Stronghold. I blocked off the entrance and hid in the chest. I thought if I could just make it until morning, they wouldn't be able to get to me. I was pretty sure they'd only come in the dark. But I was so tired. I fell right asleep, and when I woke up, there was someone in the Stronghold with me. I tried to fight him off, but he pinned me down. He stabbed me with the same thing that knocked you both out. That's the last thing I remember before today."

"That was Corporal Collins who got you," Matthew says. He beams with pride when he adds, "They said you fought him harder than anyone expected—broke his nose. He even had to get a bunch of stitches, and his face was all bruised and swollen. He wasn't very happy to get beaten up by a thirteen-year-old girl."

Ava cackles, the kind of laugh she gets when she can't

control herself anymore. It's so familiar; it feels like home.

Home . . . What's happening there? Why are we even here at all? Dr. Tori said that they're the Sovereign, but they're just regular people. So if they weren't real after all, why would they want to take any of us?

"What about Mama and Papa?" I ask. "I thought they must have been killed along with everyone else, but if you're both alive . . ."

"Dr. Tori says everyone at home is safe," Ava replies. "They made them go to sleep, too, so they could get us out without hurting anyone. They figured there would be a fight over taking us, and they knew they could keep everyone safe if they just knocked us all out."

"But is there proof? How do we know they're all okay?"

"They promised to show us at orientation," Matthew says. "They wanted to make sure you were well first. They wouldn't tell us much of anything until you were awake and could hear it all, too."

"You've been asleep such a long time," Ava interjects.

Worried, I demand to know. "How long?"

Matthew looks uncomfortable, as if he's afraid I'll be angry with his answer. "Six days. We really weren't sure if you'd ever wake up, but Dr. Tori said you'd be okay, that your body just needed a lot of rest. So far, everything she's told us has been true."

"Six days. Wow. . . . Wait, what about everyone else? Who did they take?"

"All the Orphans. We're all here, Harper." Ava grins meekly.

"All of us. What do they plan to do with us?"

Matthew shrugs. "Orientation."

"Got it. They really won't tell us anything yet, will they?"

"No, not much anyway. We've been allowed to walk around and visit each other in the hospital wing. This hallway is what they call the ICU—intensive care unit. They kept you here because you needed so much extra attention. It's mostly empty. The rest of us weren't hurt like you were, so we've been in the other halls. Dr. Tori said we'll have orientation once you're well enough to walk around. Hopefully in a day or two."

"But we're so glad you're okay!" Ava exclaims. "Nothing else matters as much as that."

I sigh deeply. Nothing else, as long as Mama and Papa are really okay. I don't want to bring the mood down too much, though. They're right—we're back together again. This is a time to be happy. I can worry about Mama and Papa later.

"What are you wearing anyway?" I laugh as I inspect their bizarre all-white pajamas. "Ava, you're wearing pants!"

Ava blushes and giggles. "All the women wear pants here. I haven't seen anyone in a dress at all! They call these our 'hospital pajamas.' All the patients have to wear them. Greg said they're easy to clean, and they're meant to be comfortable for anyone who has to stay in bed a long time. But they're soft and snuggly and way better than that itchy burlap. And the best part is no corsets!"

I can't help but laugh. Only a short time ago, I was excited to try my first corset, but there's no denying how stifling they are. I'll always be more comfortable without one.

"What do you think you're wearing under all those

blankets anyway?" Matthew teases.

I pull down my covers to reveal my own set of soft white hospital pajamas. It really hadn't occurred to me to worry about my clothes.

"But where are the clothes we were wearing?"

"You mean our nightgowns?" Ava asks. "I wouldn't worry too much about that. It doesn't sound like yours could've been in very good shape anyway by the time you were finished with Corporal Collins. I'm sure they threw it out. But they said we'll get new clothes after orientation. We'll get to choose our own, but I don't think they'll be like the clothes at home."

"That might take some getting used to," I reply.

"Look around you," Matthew says. "I have a feeling there will be a lot to get used to."

MEMORIES

It was a groan that should be heard for miles. Never had John woken with such a splitting headache. He stretched his stiff muscles, mumbling to himself about livestock and firewood. When he finally opened his eyes, Maggie's beautiful brown face stared down at him full of concern.

"What happened? Am I sick?" John asked her, attempting to sit up with great effort.

"You'll be fine," replied an aged voice.

He squinted around to find its owner. The most senior healer, Sophie, handed him a steaming mug.

"Drink that. It'll help with the headache. You'll need to get yourself hydrated again, too. And I wouldn't try to walk around any time soon. You must've gotten a massive dose. You've been out for hours longer than most everyone else."

Confusion spread across John's bearded face. "A massive dose of what?"

"We were drugged somehow, put to sleep," Maggie said. "The whole village."

"I'm not sure what it was or how it happened," Sophie added. "Just that people gradually started coming around in the early hours this morning, and no one seems to remember much of anything about last night."

John blinked in disbelief, then put a hand on either cheek and rubbed vigorously at his beard with his palms. "There isn't even anyone around," *he started to say.* "The girls . . . Are they okay?"

Tears filled Maggie's dark eyes as she replied, "We haven't found them yet. Several people are missing. We don't officially know who all of them are, but we know not everyone has made it home."

John suddenly tried to stand. He wavered briefly as vertigo threatened to overtake him, but he managed to stay upright through determination alone. Only once the dizziness ebbed did he realize he was standing out in the field nearest his home. He hadn't even realized he was outside. As he took a long, hard look around, he noticed his rifle on the ground.

"What were we doing out here?" *he asked Maggie, alarmed.*

She shook her head, the creases in her forehead deepening. "We're not sure. No one we've spoken to remembers anything."

John held his head in his hands for a moment. "Anyone injured?"

"No major injuries to speak of," *Sophie replied.* "My healers and apprentices have treated a few minor scrapes and sprains. Nothing life-threatening. Not even so much as a broken bone."

"Must've been fighting something, though," *John said thoughtfully, almost to himself.*

"Did anyone else have weapons?" *he asked louder.*

Maggie nodded vehemently. "Everyone. Men, women, children—from hunting rifles to kitchen knives and scissors. Everyone we've seen had something to defend themselves with."

"What could have been attacking us that left no sign or injuries?"

"And that could've drugged us on a large scale," *Sophie*

added quietly.

John looked her dead in the eyes, more gravely than ever before. "You don't think—"

"The Sovereign," Maggie added in a hushed tone.

Sophie only nodded, a frown filling her face.

John held Sophie's gaze for a moment before he lowered his eyes to the ground. "I just don't understand what's happening."

"No one does, John, but we'll get through this," Maggie reassured him.

"We have to find the girls," John insisted.

Sophie's demeanor shifted significantly. With a hand on John's shoulder, she almost cooed at him. "I'm sure they're safe. Many of the children were asleep in hiding places. They're surely doing the same."

"We're going to call a meeting to form search parties," Maggie said. "We'll be sure to check all their usual hiding places. Do you know of any I might be forgetting?"

John stared at the freshly tilled field beneath his feet. He held up one hand and started ticking off his fingers. "The old Orphan Home, of course. The schoolhouse. The storerooms. The horse barns. Up any tree. Could they be knocked out in a tree somewhere? Wouldn't they fall?"

"I'm sure if they'd fallen out of a tree, someone would've found them by now. Harper's a smart one. She would've come up with something safer than that," Sophie comforted.

In the distance, a deep chime sounded, interrupting John's thoughts.

"There's the bell," Maggie said. "Do you feel well enough to walk?"

John nodded. The need to find his daughters had set off an adrenaline rush. He felt strong, purposeful, and determined as he accompanied his wife and their doctor through the village to the town meeting hall.

As the trio trudged through town, they saw throngs of confused people, some still struggling to walk unassisted. More than once, they passed by someone vomiting off to the side of the packed dirt road. Sophie stopped to assist those in need of medical attention, eventually ushering John and Maggie ahead without her. Sophie's apprentices were scattered throughout, checking on everyone they saw.

John and Maggie were among the last townspeople to enter the meeting hall. As an Elder, Maggie held a powerful and important role. Noting that the other Elders' spouses had joined them on the floor of the large room, John remained by his wife's side.

The room was a cavernous place inside a large brick building. The ceilings stood at least twenty-five feet above the old wooden floor. Faded markings, whose meanings were unknown, could still be seen here and there on the flooring. On either side of the substantial chamber stood rows upon rows of benches that rose like stairs across the entire length of the wall. They were full of drowsy-eyed villagers, waiting for guidance from their leaders.

The Elders and their partners circled up with their backs facing outward and spoke softly to each other before addressing the crowd. They needed to find out what each of their counterparts remembered before they could speak to the people. They went around the circle, each speaking in turn, sharing the last thing they remembered.

"I remember the Festival and then going to the barn dance."

Nods and murmurs of agreement spread through the small circle.

"I remember dancing and watching the children—all the girls huddled in one corner to giggle over the boys."

"Could there have been something in the food or the drinks?"

"What about the families who chose not to attend? Were any of them unconscious?"

More nods. *"Yes, our neighbors stayed home to keep their newborn baby on his schedule. The wife and child were found huddled in a closet at home, and the husband was out in the field with his rifle."*

"Does anyone remember leaving the barn dance?"

The group grew quiet as each one racked their brains for memories.

"I think I recall walking home in the moonlight. Everything seemed normal."

"Yes, I remember! I tripped, and you caught me!"

"Yes, a moonlit walk home. I remember calling the children to leave, and we all walked home together. They kept chattering about the dance and the games at the Festival."

"That's right. Everything was fine at the end of the dance."

Maggie finally spoke. *"We walked back along the path just ahead of Harper and Matthew. Ava kept looking back and snickering at them."*

John nodded in agreement. *"I remember shushing her. I didn't want Harper to be embarrassed by her sister, but she didn't even seem to notice we were there."*

"Smitten," replied another woman with a light chuckle. *"The barn dance never changes, does it?"*

Deep in thought, John continued talking without acknowledging the comment. *"I waited on the porch for the two of them, while Maggie took Ava inside to dress for bed. Matthew kissed Harper on the cheek, and I pretended not to see. Then she went inside, and I watched him walk back home. Everything was quiet, except—"*

"Except for the insects," someone interjected. *"There weren't*

any. No sounds at all apart from us."

John nods again. *"That's what I remember, too. The quiet was unnatural. I don't know what happened next."*

"Does anyone know?"

Heads shook all around the circle, looks of bewilderment on faces old and young.

"I guess we know where to start." Maggie cleared her voice, and the Council and their spouses parted to face the crowd in both directions.

The townspeople, noticing this abrupt action, quieted themselves. Their rapt attention landed on Maggie, the de facto speaker and leader of the Council of Elders. She raised her hands before she spoke.

"It is clear that there is some type of crisis happening among us. The events of last night remain a mystery that we must uncover. The Council plans to take a thorough headcount and to send out search parties for those missing. Before we take action, however, we must know what is remembered among our people. The Council has concluded that all was well at the barn dance until an eerie silence was noted afterwards—no insects buzzing or animals rustling. Who among you recalls this silence? Please raise your hands high."

A smattering of people raised their hands here and there throughout the assembly. Maggie waited and watched more hands raise as the people processed their gradually returning memories.

"And who among you holds memory of the events that came next?"

This time, there were no hands. Another eerie silence filled the room, as they all looked around at one another.

Sophie stood at the front of the benches and offered a suggestion. *"Perhaps these memories will be recovered with time. The brain needs to allow bits of information to trickle back slowly, especially as toxins leave the body over the next several days. Memory loss is a common side effect to drugs like these, after all."*

Maggie nodded, looking at the other leaders for their approval. Only John looked frustrated. "Thank you, Sophie. We will allow for more time for memories of these events to surface. Should anything come to mind, you are to notify an Elder without hesitation. Even the smallest detail may be of the utmost importance. Sophie, what advice would you give us in our recovery?"

"Continue drinking teas and lots of water for the next week. You may tire easily or feel nauseous. All of that is normal. Rest if you grow weary and keep drinking—at least twice as much as usual."

"Perfect advice. We will need volunteers to carry in additional water from the pumps around the clock, as well as to help the healers gather additional herbs. Their stores are no doubt under considerable strain after this morning. We will also need volunteers to search for the missing. But first, we will form lines, and each family will check in with their designated Elder for a headcount. We have already collected this year's census documents. Once each Elder's headcount is complete, the Council will convene to create a list of the missing."

RECOVERY

For the next couple of days, Ava and Matthew visit my room regularly. We talk and laugh and make wild guesses about Elysium and the Sovereign. Sometimes, we cry for the new families we've already lost. We can only hope they're really okay. The only way to find out is for me to get well enough for orientation.

Several types of healers visit me each day, too. Back home, we have a few healers, and they have apprentices, but there's really only one kind. They all take care of every kind of injury and illness. Here, different healers have different jobs. I have a physical therapist, who makes me exercise and helps me get strong again; an occupational therapist, who helps make sure I'm able to do all my everyday things; a neurologist, who seems mostly concerned about my brain; and Dr. Tori, who really just seems to be in charge. Then there's Greg and Tina, who are in and out of my room all day long, bringing me food and water, helping me clean up and use the bathroom, changing my clothes—they basically do everything for me that the doctors don't take care of themselves.

Today, my physical therapist wants me to get out of

bed and try walking. I can barely contain my excitement. I've been trapped in this bed far too long, but Dr. Dalal tells me I've regained enough strength to give it a try. When he enters my room this morning, I practically leap out of the bed at him. He lifts up both his hands and pats them down into the air—a gesture meant to tell me to stay in bed. Suddenly grumpy, I lie back against my pillows, crossing my arms in front of my chest.

What are we waiting for? I need to get out of here!

"I know, I know. You've been ready to get out of that bed for days," Dr. Dalal tries to reassure me. "We just have to take things slowly to be safe. If you fall and hit your head again, you'll be in here for even longer—days, if not weeks."

I scrunch up my nose in disgusted frustration, but I have to admit he's right. I guess slow is better than not at all. I take a few deep breaths to center myself like my therapist, Julia, has been teaching me. She says I've been through serious trauma, and I need to give my mind time to heal just like my body. She's the healer I like the most. The others are things our healers at home could do, but there isn't anyone there that helps us with our minds.

One more deep breath. "Okay, Dr. Dalal, you're right. I'm ready."

He smiles a broad grin across his surprisingly smooth dark face. I've never seen a man without a beard before. His face always surprises me. *How does he keep the hair from growing?* His skin isn't as dark as Maggie's, but it's darker than Ava's or Matthew's—sort of like mine. I wonder if we could be related somehow. Maybe we have some ancestors in common.

"Now, take my hand, and we'll get you sitting up on the edge of the bed."

I follow his directions, but I must still be trying to go too fast.

"Nice and slow, Harper, nice and slow. We don't want you getting dizzy."

More deep breaths, and I slow myself down. Finally I'm sitting straight up under my own power, and Dr. Dalal helps me turn and scooch carefully toward the edge of the bed, swinging my legs over the side.

"Good. How does that feel? Any pain or dizziness?"

I shake my head. I feel totally normal. Everyone here is so cautious, and I think it might drive me insane.

"Good, good. . . . Now let's gently slide out of the bed until your feet touch the floor."

Dr. Dalal holds both my wrists firmly, and I hold his. He guides me and helps me keep my balance as I sidle out of the bed. The tiled floor is cold and smooth under my bare feet.

"Great, now keep holding on and gradually start putting your weight on your feet. I'll help you stand, but don't let go until we're sure you're steady."

I nod, suddenly feeling the importance of following Dr. Dalal's instructions. My feet spread ever so slightly as I put more and more weight onto them. They feel surprisingly sore. I pull myself up slowly until I'm fully standing. When I start to wobble, I let go of Dr. Dalal's hands and grasp onto his shoulders. He lets his arms drop, and I wonder why he's not trying harder to keep me steady.

"There you go! You've got it." He smiles warmly, creases forming at the corners of his muddy eyes. "How

Elysium

does everything feel?"

"My feet hurt, and my legs are a little sore."

"Dizzy at all?"

"Nope."

"You seem to be balancing well. Do you feel a little steadier now?"

I nod. "I thought I would fall at first, but it's getting better."

"Good. Don't worry too much about the soreness. Your legs and feet haven't held your body weight in a while. You'll get used to things. Are you ready to take some steps?"

"I think so." I'm way more scared than I expected to be. A few minutes ago, I was ready to take off running. Now, I'm not so sure I can even take two steps.

Dr. Dalal takes a small step backward, and I have no choice but to follow if I want something to hold onto. I shuffle my right foot forward, feeling it slide across the hard floor. He takes another step back, and I feel my left foot shift forward. My toes catch on the ridge between the tiles, causing me to lose my balance.

"It's important to pick up your feet," Dr. Dalal reminds me.

Fighting the urge to roll my eyes, I make a concentrated effort to lift my right foot for the next step. It gets a little easier each time, but it's definitely harder than I expected. I guess Dr. Dalal was right—getting out of bed and running the halls wouldn't have gone so well.

We take several more steps, Dr. Dalal leading me slowly around the room in my white pajamas. He must think I'm doing well because he reaches up, loosens my grip on his shoulders, and instructs me to try on my own. Holding the glass wall for support, I take one step, then another.

"Lift those feet," Dr. Dalal warns.

Obediently, I lift my feet a little higher so I won't trip. I take a few more steps, still holding on, and then I let go of the wall.

"Try to make it back to the bed on your own," Dr. Dalal instructs, "but remember, I'm right here if you need to hold onto something."

He stands right next to me for my solo trip across the room, not holding on but making sure his arm is within reach if I need help. My stubbornness takes hold, and I silently refuse to hold onto him. The sooner I'm able to do this on my own, the sooner I can get some answers. Though I'm painfully slow, I make it to my destination, collapsing onto the bed in exhaustion.

"Wonderful! We'll start going for several short walks every day to build up your stamina until you're able to do it on your own. You're making such good progress that I don't think it'll take too long at all." Dr. Dalal seems pleased, and I feel my face glow with pride. It seems stupid that taking ten steps alone should be an accomplishment, but then again, it felt like an awful lot of work.

In a few hours, Dr. Dalal is back with Greg, whose hair flows long around his shoulders today. The doctor watches as Greg helps me out of bed, letting me hold onto his shoulders for support. Greg takes my hands off his shoulders immediately. He places his left arm under my right with his other arm on top. I like this approach; it gives me just enough support to balance, but not so much that I'm not holding my own weight. He leads me across the room, where the wall slides open, and we go out into the hall. Dr. Dalal never moves from his chair. He simply turns and observes us as we walk.

"How are you feeling today, Harper?" Greg asks.

"Good," I reply.

"Excited to be out of bed?"

We both laugh. "Of course I am! It's harder than I thought, though. I was hoping we'd do orientation today."

Greg looks at me out of the corner of his eye. "Just have to build up your strength a little first. Knowing you, you'll be running by tomorrow."

"I don't know about that. Greg, how old are you?"

"Twenty-four," he answers. "I've been doing this job since I was about your age."

"I don't want to be rude, but . . . Well, back home, only women have long hair. Why's your hair so long?"

He chuckles and says, "We don't have those kinds of rules here. Men and women can dress and act however they want—long hair, short hair, pants, dresses, whatever. Everything is okay for everyone here."

I think about that for a few minutes. I wonder how I would choose to look if I could choose anything at all. I never even thought of pants or short hair as an option since I'd never seen it before. I guess now that I'm here, I'll get to decide what I actually like.

"Okay now, Harper, let's turn around and go back. See if you can do it without holding on this time."

His words interrupt my thoughts, and I realize that we're in a completely different part of the hospital. There are bigger rooms with no beds. Many of them have large machines or rows of counters.

"What's this part of the hospital for?"

"This part of the hospital is used for different kinds of tests. That room there," he points to our left, "is the lab. They check blood samples from people and a lot of other things there. There's a lot of machines that do different things."

"And what about that room?"

"Up ahead is radiology. There's all kinds of different machines that actually take pictures of the inside of your body."

"How can you get pictures of the *inside* of someone's body?"

Greg smiles. "It's a little complicated, but I promise that it works. I'll ask Dr. Tori to show you the X-rays we took of you when they first brought you in."

"Fascinating."

Greg explains a lot of the different rooms and machines as we pass by them. The conversation keeps my mind off the walking so well that we're back in the ICU before I know it. Dr. Dalal closes a device in his lap—a computer, they've told me. It holds more information than a book and runs off something called electricity. I guess that's how they get so much light underground, too, but it doesn't make sense to me so far. Greg says I'll learn all about it before long, and it won't seem so weird to me anymore.

"It looks like everything went well," Dr. Dalal says when we return to the room. "Any pain, dizziness, weakness?"

"No," I answer. "Actually, I feel really good—not even tired this time."

"That's excellent news!" he declares. "We'll have a

couple more walks today and tomorrow, too. If you keep progressing this quickly, we may be looking at orientation the day after that."

I whoop with joy, and the two men chuckle.

"Don't go getting too excited, Harper," Greg warns jovially. "You're not ready to jump up and down just yet."

I grin from ear to ear as I sit on the bed, picking up a book from my side table.

"Greg, do you think you could get me a book about electricity? And computers?"

"I'll see what I can find in the library," he says, leaving the room with Dr. Dalal.

6

ORIENTATION

For the past two days, I've gone for walk after walk, first with Greg or Tina, and then with Matthew and Ava. They've shown me all around the hospital wing. Since they're not allowed to leave the hospital yet, they don't know much about the rest of Elysium. I'm looking forward to exploring it later.

Between walks, I've been reading the books Greg brought me. Electricity seems like magic to me. It's fascinating the way human beings can harness energy and use it to power all kinds of amazing things, like light bulbs. At home, we only have candles and lanterns. One of the books even had pictures of generators, which look exactly like the enormous machines Ava and I passed on our way to spy on Maggie's surprise meeting that stopped the Sending for good. Our little town must have had electricity a long, *long* time ago, but no one knows how it works anymore. Those generators are a mystery to even the oldest residents alive today.

I can barely even wrap my mind around computers. Ava and Matthew are just as amazed by these discoveries as I am. Matthew is extremely interested in computers. Somehow, they just seem to make sense to him, way more than either me or Ava. I can't wait to see his face the first time he gets to use a real one.

All these things have kept me occupied so far, but nothing can hold my attention today. It's finally orientation! Dr. Tori came to tell me last night after dinner. I thumb through one of my books without really paying attention to it.

The door to my room slides open, and Tina enters with new clothes. She picks up the rectangle attached to my bed—a "remote control"—and presses the button to close the shades on the glass walls that surround me so I can change in privacy.

"Good morning, Harper. You must be excited to go to orientation. I usually have to wake you up in the morning."

"I can't wait!" I practically shout at her, swinging my legs wildly over the side of my bed.

Tina blinks rapidly, wiggling a finger around in one ear while she feigns temporary deafness. She winks at me and lays her armful of clothes in one of the chairs.

"I just have to take your vitals first, and then you can choose some fresh clothes. Uncross your ankles, please."

She puts a little gray gadget on the end of one of my fingers, then slides a blue cuff of fabric up the other arm. She presses a button, and the cuff begins to contract around my arm with an uncomfortable squeeze. I've learned the right words and grown accustomed to the sensation over the past weeks, but I still don't love this process.

While Tina takes my blood pressure, I eye the stack of clothes. These are no white hospital pajamas. All kinds of colors are present in the pile—red, yellow, purple, green, blue, even gray and black. I'm practically drooling.

"Tina?"

She looks up at me with her kind green eyes.

"I thought we didn't get to choose our own clothes until after orientation, but those aren't hospital pajamas."

She smiles. "Well, you get to wear regular clothes for orientation, but there aren't a lot of choices there. You'll have more options to choose from and figure out what you *really* like a little later."

The blood pressure cuff keeps squeezing my arm. When it finally stops, I clap my hands together excitedly while Tina writes in my chart.

"Oh my gosh, Tina, hurry up!" I whine. I've never felt like a bigger baby, but I don't care. I'm sick of these stupid pajamas.

She looks at me over the top of her clipboard, a sneaky grin forming on her pale face. She keeps writing and writing and writing until I grab the clipboard and discover her pen wasn't even touching the paper.

"You're so mean!" I squeal, while she laughs at me.

"Okay, okay. Calm down."

She moves to the chair piled with clothes and pulls out one item at a time. She holds each thing up to her own body so I can see what it looks like. I choose a long-sleeved yellow top and a pair of wide light blue pants—jeans.

I've never worn pants before except for my hospital pajamas. I pull them on, and Tina shows me that I need to button the top before I pull up the zipper. It feels so awkward that it takes me a few tries to get it right. She also teaches me how to fasten a bra, which is kind of like a corset except you can actually breathe. Once I get my clothes on, she hands me a strange-looking pair of shoes called sneakers.

"Are they supposed to help you be sneaky or something?"

Tina laughs. "I guess they're probably sneakier than boots, but I don't really know why they call them that. Some people call them tennis shoes, after a sport they used to play up on the surface. Either way, they'll be the most comfortable shoes you've ever worn."

I pull them on and tie the laces. It almost feels like I'm wearing nothing at all.

"Wow!"

"Comfortable, right?"

"I can't even believe how good they feel! My old boots were always pinching my toes, and they were hard under my feet. These are squishy and soft like pillows."

"Memory foam," Tina says knowingly. I must give her an odd look because she adds, "It's the stuff inside that makes them so comfy."

Once I'm completely dressed, Tina spends some time taming my wild hair.

"I usually wear braids. My hair is hard to deal with, but my mama's hair was just like it, so she knew what to do." I swallow back tears before they make it to my eyes.

"I have a lot of little cousins with hair like yours. Don't worry: I know what to do. We don't even have to do braids. We could just let it be natural."

"Natural?"

"You know, big and curly. Or we could twist it. I brought some things that will help."

She reaches down to the floor and pulls up a bag full of bottles and jars I didn't notice before.

39

"A lot of people who live here look like you. They've found lots of things they can help keep their hair looking how they want it. Do you want to try some?"

"Sure," I reply uncertainly. I've only ever worn my hair in braids or a bun like Mama. Girls weren't allowed to do anything else.

Tina wets down my hair with water, then pulls out a jar and smooths something sweet-smelling all through my hair. She twists pieces of hair together patiently. It takes a while, but when she's finished, she pulls out a mirror.

"What do you think?"

I can't even speak. It completely takes my breath away. I don't look like a little girl anymore, or even like a settler. I look Elysian. My black hair falls in beautiful twisted strands all over my head. It gives me a bit of height, too, rising higher above my scalp than any other style I've had.

"It's gorgeous," I breathe.

"I'm so glad you like it. Maybe I can teach you some different things to do with it once you're out of the hospital."

"I'd really like that. Thanks, Tina." I fall into her, hugging her tightly. This must be what it feels like to have an older sister.

"You're welcome," she says, hugging me back.

When she pulls away, there are tears in her eyes. She wipes them casually on the back of her hand and stands, sniffing slightly. "Come on. It's time for orientation."

She leads me down the long hallways, taking turn after turn until I'm completely lost. She unlocks a set of double doors by holding a small card up to a black panel on the wall. Beyond those doors, all the rooms have desks and chairs and shelves lined with books. All the desks have computers. Some of the rooms appear to be occupied by doctors in white coats.

"These are the offices where the doctors work when they're not with patients," Tina whispers. "They don't like to be disturbed, so we should talk quietly."

Finally, we reach a room with a sign outside that reads *CONFERENCE ROOM*. She opens the door, revealing a room with a long table surrounded by seven of the ten Orphans who were taken—all except the babies and toddlers. They all sit in strange, albeit comfortable-looking, chairs with wheels on the bottom instead of regular legs. They swivel around in their seats, and they all rush into me, nearly knocking me to the ground.

From the opposite end of the room, Dr. Tori looks on serenely while I'm mobbed by younger children. After a few minutes, she clears her throat and stands.

"Children, I know you're all excited to see Harper doing so well, but it's best if you give her some space now."

With disappointed moans and groans, they all return to their seats. Matthew gets up and moves over one chair to make a space for me between him and Ava. They each hold one of my hands, anxious to get some answers at last. When everyone is seated, Dr. Tori begins.

"Welcome to orientation, our way of welcoming you to our city and teaching you about what to expect here."

My hand shoots into the air, almost of its own accord. Dr. Tori nods at me kindly, then gestures for me to put my hand down.

"You'll have a chance to ask as many questions as you

like, but if you'll let me explain first, you might find that I'll answer many of them before you need to ask."

My hand finds its way back into Ava's. My cheeks are hot with embarrassment, but I pretend everything is fine.

"Now, I know you've all noticed that we have many things here that you didn't have at home. Our technology is much more advanced, allowing us to have light underground and power machines without animals or fire. One of the new things you'll see today is this." Dr. Tori points to a large white square that takes up the majority of the wall behind her.

"This screen allows us to display still pictures, moving pictures, and even written words. Many of the things I'm going to explain to you will appear here while I talk. I don't want you to be alarmed when you see it."

She presses a button on a remote control, and the screen is illuminated by a bright white light. The lights above our heads begin to dim until the screen becomes the predominant focal point of the room. A picture of a group of adults in white doctors' coats, along with a few teenagers and smaller children, appears on the screen.

"As you know, you are in an underground city called Elysium. These," she gestures to the people on the screen, "were Elysium's founders. They were a group of scientists and their families who escaped the Global Devastation by living in the underground bunker that eventually became our city."

A new picture appears. People with the biggest guns I've ever seen kill each other. More pictures appear, one after the other, all of violence and destruction. Then, a picture of an enormous explosion in the distance with a black cloud shaped very much like a mushroom.

Dr. Tori explains. "Earth was once populated by billions and billions of people—more people than you can probably even imagine. Unfortunately, these people had trouble agreeing on things, and they failed to care for one another. Instead, there were wars and death and violence. Over three hundred years ago, the Global Devastation began. It did not last as long as other wars had. People chose to end it swiftly with the use of nuclear weapons, causing huge explosions that devastated the earth and wiped out most of its population.

"The first Elysians" —the photo of the scientists pops up on the screen again—"were a group of scientists who sealed themselves away in an attempt to survive the nuclear war. They devoted their time to researching ways to heal the earth from the destruction. Part of their research involved studying human genetics."

"What are genetics?" someone blurts out.

Dr. Tori smiles. "Genetics are a bit hard to explain, but they're the tiniest parts of you—so small that you can't even see them. Those tiny parts are called 'genes,' and—"

"You mean like our pants?" Ava interjects.

"No, that's jeans spelled with a J. These are genes with a G. These kinds of genes are so tiny you can't see them. They're the parts of you that decide all kinds of things about how your body will be—how tall you are, what color your hair is, or your skin or eyes. We get them from our parents—half from our mothers and half from our fathers. That's why most people you know look like one or both of their parents. And even though most of you won't remember your parents, you probably look very much like them."

All around the room, eyes fill with tears. Hands squeeze each other for comfort. Dr. Tori hugs those who look most upset.

"I know it's hard. Being orphaned is a terrible thing, and I'm so sorry for what all of you have been through . . . But I need to finish telling you about genes. It's an important part of the reason you're here."

"Dr. Tori," I say, waving my hand in the air, "if genes are too small to see them, then how did the scientists study them?"

"An excellent question, Harper. They used a machine called a microscope that allows you to see very tiny things. In fact, things that small are called microscopic because you need a microscope to see them. We have several microscopes in Elysium, and you will all have a chance to see and use them at some point in your studies.

"Now, the most important thing for our Elysian founders was the theory that exposure to nuclear radiation might change people's genes in harmful ways. They stayed locked in their bunker for several years until they thought the danger to themselves had passed, but they were constantly studying their own genetic codes to ensure no harmful changes had occurred. When they finally ventured out onto the surface, they discovered a small settlement not too far away."

A picture of an older woman with long, wavy gray hair appears on the wall behind Dr. Tori. She's standing somewhere vaguely familiar.

"That's the northwestern part of our town—the older houses that border the woods!" Matthew shouts out, pointing.

"That's right, Matthew," agrees Dr. Tori. "This woman,

whose name has been lost over time, was the first leader of your little village. She rescued two hundred people from the Global Devastation and began a small farming community, believing they were the only survivors in the entire world. She was a wise woman and a strong leader who protected her people from hardships and danger.

"When the Elysian scientists discovered her town, they approached her with an offer of peace. The timing was fortuitous—your community's crops had just suffered from a devastating disease that wiped out their entire harvest. There was not enough food left to keep all the people alive. But our city, with its many resources and scientific advancements, was already able to grow enough food to spare. They struck a deal: Elysium would provide the community with enough food to ensure their survival, and your community would assist us with our research. Together, we worked to ensure the survival of the human race.

"As we began our research efforts, our scientists made a startling discovery. There was a genetic mutation among the people who lived on the surface. This mutation led to illness and death, causing many in your village to be orphaned. The existence of this mutation has somehow even led to new forms of contagious virus that could wipe out our entire population. To ensure the survival of both communities, the decision was made to cut off physical contact between our two peoples. We could not afford to have the surface illnesses spread through our city.

"Though your community was more self-sufficient than before, they were unable to properly care for those orphaned by the mutations and viruses. You see, without specific medical care and intervention, most Orphans from your community die by the age of sixteen. I know that you all recently found new families, and we would never have desired to take you from them if you could have survived there. The only way to save your lives was to bring you here."

Shocked gasps and expressions of wide-eyed terror fill the room.

"You mean we're gonna die," a small voice calls out.

Dr. Tori smiles reassuringly and hugs the little one who asked. "Of course not. You're here now, and we'll keep you safe and sound. But I want you to understand that we brought you here to keep you alive. Everything will be okay as long as you stay here and receive regular treatments."

Matthew pipes up. "If there was an agreement between the two towns, then why don't we know anything about you? What happened to the agreement?"

Dr. Tori sighs, clearly burdened by the information she holds. "Unfortunately, the lack of contact between our two peoples resulted in a great deal of lost information in your community. Superstition prevailed, and people began to mythicize the true history of our connection. The legend of the Sovereign was born. Our people could only safely visit yours once every ten years, at which time we would collect all the Orphans to provide them with treatments. We come at night to have less direct contact, in an attempt to avoid illness. Since your people never saw us, they stopped believing we were human and made up their own stories to explain the Sending. What is, in reality, a life-saving scientific mission became a religious sacrifice to save the rest of your people. Granted, we do continue to study your genetic codes, and we believe we are finally quite close to finding a cure."

This time, Ava speaks. "But you've already had more than three hundred years. Why didn't you find a cure already?"

"Another excellent question. You see, genetic mutations don't just change once and then stay that way forever. They keep changing and mutating. Until just recently, we didn't have the technology to get ahead of those mutations. Every time we thought we had a cure, we would find that a new mutation had occurred, and the cure was no longer effective. In the past ten years, our scientists have developed new methods and tests that we believe may actually allow us to cure the mutations and illnesses before the next set of mutations take hold.

"Now, of course, the choice is yours. We have brought you here against your will and separated you from your families. You can choose to go back to them and live a fulfilling, albeit significantly shortened, life with them. Or you can stay here, receive your treatments, and help us cure the mutation that holds you here. If we cure it in your lifetime, you will be able to return to any life you choose."

Folding her hands in front of her, Dr. Tori looks around at us expectantly.

"What about our families?" I ask. "Where are they? Are they safe?"

"Your families are alive and well. Everything is as it was, minus ten Orphans."

"You said you would have proof?"

Dr. Tori smiles her contagious smile. "Of course."

She clicks another button, and a new picture appears

on the screen, only this time, it moves. We see our families there, living and working just as they always have. Everyone appears to be in good health and even better spirits. John and Maggie sit on their porch together. Matthew's parents play with his younger siblings in the yard. We see people planting this year's crops. Tears of joy spring to my eyes.

"And they know we're okay? That staying here is the only way for us to survive?"

Dr. Tori nods. "They do. They fought because they wanted to keep you, but once everything was explained to them, they realized they had no choice. They want you to live, even if it means you can't grow up in their homes."

"And . . . and now that they know about you, are we able to talk to them?"

"I'm afraid not—not until we cure the illnesses. It isn't safe for you to leave here, and our people can't risk exposure more than once every ten years. I would love to let you go for visits, but it endangers everyone. We can't even risk writing letters due to contamination risks. We are able to collect occasional surveillance with our drones, though—machines that take pictures from the air. We will be able to provide you with pictures, at least, to help you know that your families are well. Do you think you can be okay with that?"

We all look around at one another. Finally, everyone is looking at Matthew. He's the oldest, after all. He nods solemnly.

"I want to see my family, but I don't want to put anyone in danger. Staying here is the right thing to do."

SEARCH PARTY

Of the nearly six hundred villagers in the small settlement, some thirty-seven were reported missing. Maggie managed to maintain an aura of calm, but John was an entirely different story. He was nearly beside himself when the Elders reconvened and it was discovered that all ten adopted Orphans were reported missing. Elder Samson, the oldest man on the Council, responded in kind, but for separate reasons.

"It's clear what's happened," Samson snapped at the group. "They've been taken by force because you" —he jabbed his finger at each of them accusingly—"stopped the Sending! Who knows what punishment the Sovereign will have in store for us?"

Elder Rebecca Johnson gave him a stern look and, clearing her throat, responded in an exaggeratedly sweet voice, as if speaking to a toddler throwing a tantrum. "Samson, there is certainly nothing about this situation that is clear. It's entirely possible that those children, having grown up together so closely, had a secret hiding place they went to together. They may not be awake, or if they are, they may be too afraid to come out."

Nodding his head in agreement, Elder Marcus added, "We

must approach the situation logically, with a clear head. Shouting and making accusations doesn't help us. Besides, there are twenty-seven other residents missing who must be accounted for. Did the Sovereign also take them?"

Samson crossed his arms, looking positively venomous, but made no further retort. Elder Isaac Prewitt, the only other Elder who had fought vehemently against preventing the sacrifice of innocent Orphans, shot him a meaningful look.

"Now that that's settled," Maggie chimed in, "it's time we set our search parties to work locating those who are missing or potentially injured. We'll need a horse and wagon with each team to carry back the injured for medical attention."

"Why don't we send a healer's apprentice with each team?" Rebecca suggested.

Maggie nodded. "Yes, we'll do that. Excellent idea, Rebecca."

Within the hour, nine teams of ten people each, plus one healer's apprentice, set out to search assigned sectors of the town, fields, and nearby woods. John and Maggie joined the team assigned to search the southwest corner of the town, where the abandoned Orphan Home stood. It seemed likely to both of them that Harper and Ava would have returned to familiar ground to hide. Both girls knew every nook and cranny in the Orphan Home and everywhere nearby. If there was a hiding place there, that's where the girls would be found.

When the search party arrived at the Orphan Home, they found the front door standing wide open. John entered first, taking a protective stance in front of Maggie. The sitting room stood bare, just as the rest of the rooms in the enormous house that had been stripped of their furnishings for use in other parts of the town. The lack of furnishings was not a surprise, but what was alarming were the signs of struggle. Small muddy footprints were scattered all over the room, and drag marks disturbed the dust that had collected on the formerly gleaming hardwood floors.

"I don't know if you should come in, Mags," John called out behind him while keeping his eyes on the room.

"Why? What's in there? Is anyone hurt?" she called back.

"No one hurt. Looks empty. But there were definitely children here, and it looks like they were dragged out."

"Dragged out?" she repeated. She appeared in the doorway, wide-eyed and slack-jawed. She surveyed the room herself and gasped in horror.

"Could Samson have been right? Could the Sovereign be real after all?" she asked her husband desperately.

John shook his head. "Let's hope not. Now that you've seen it, you may as well help me search."

A search of the home turned up empty. More footprints, more disturbances in the dust, more drag marks. The few remaining furnishings and crates had been knocked over, leaving items strewn haphazardly across floors. It became clearer with each room that someone had been here and tried to fight off some kind of attack. By the time they finished, the usually stoic Maggie was in tears. She grasped John's arm tightly.

"John, what have we done? Our girls . . . we put everyone in terrible danger!"

"You don't know that, Mags," John cooed softly.

Calls from outside echoed through the room.

"They must've found something," John said. He and Maggie rushed out to find the source of the shouting.

Hidden in the stack of firewood behind the supply shed was a young girl, who sat crying in her sleeping mother's lap. She was not an Orphan, but she was unharmed, and her mother was breathing steadily. A volunteer lifted the child into her arms and took her back to the wagon to see whether she needed medical care. Two men lifted the mother as gently as possible and laid her in the back of the wagon. They would have the healers check her over and then return her to her bed while someone looked after her little one.

John congregated with some of the other men to debrief about their search of the Orphan Home and its large surrounding area. "Anyone else found?" he asked gruffly.

Heads shook grimly all around. "Let's hope they're having more luck in the other sectors," Elder Johnson's husband offered.

Josiah, a freckled young newlywed with sandy hair and a long nose, nodded his shaggy head. "We found Caroline's daughters hiding in the treehouse next door. They were awake, but afraid to come out. Surely, there are more kids with secret hiding places, and we just have to find them."

"Treehouse!" John whispered to himself with marked realization. He rushed over to the wagon where Maggie was assisting with the crying toddler.

"Maggie!" he shouted through labored breaths. Her head snapped up, alarmed eyes searching for the source of his voice. A question spread across her face.

"A treehouse! Didn't they have a treehouse in the forest?"

Maggie's eyes went wide, and she nodded emphatically. "They called it the Stronghold."

"Do you know where it is? Could they be hiding there?"

"I'd bet my life on it."

THE FIFTH FLOOR

Making the decision to stay in Elysium was oddly empowering. As Orphans, our entire lives were decided for us. We didn't have choices or the opportunity to ask questions. Who would have thought we would have that opportunity with the Sovereign? We mostly thought we'd be dead.

Now, we have so many opportunities we never anticipated. Our whole lives revolved around this supernatural, spiritual purpose to be the salvation of our community. Little did we know, we might actually be the salvation of the entire human race if our genes are the key to finally cracking this mutation. *Who knows? Maybe one of us will be the one who cracks it!* Living in Elysium, we'll have the chance to become scientists, doctors, nurses, or basically anything else we could dream of. Not like home, where you have to learn how to do whatever your parents do and where women just take care of babies, houses, and husbands.

The younger children are being placed with new families, but Ava, Matthew, and I, as the only ones over eleven, were given a choice about what we want to do. We can choose to live with another new family or we can live in dormitories supervised by rotating adults, much like the Caretakers in the Orphan Home. It should be a difficult decision, but I'm not so sure any of us wants to replace our families. We only lived with them for a little while, but they were *ours*.

The three of us sit around the long conference room table while Dr. Tori introduces the younger children to their new families. Ava looks back and forth between me and Matthew. She looks about to cry. I catch her eye and sigh heavily.

"I know it's hard, Ava, but it won't do any good to cry," I say.

She stifles a sob. "I know. It's just . . . I don't want a new family, but . . . will we still be sisters?"

I smile sadly at her. "Of course we will. It doesn't matter who we live with. We've always been sisters, and we always will be."

"Can we still share a room?"

"We can ask. Matthew, what do you think?"

"I agree with you both. I don't want a new family. I'll miss being a big brother, but I can help look out for the others."

"You've been a brother to the littles all along," I say.

"So I guess we'll be staying in the dorms then," Matthew announces. "I wonder what it'll be like."

I feel my mouth turn down into a frown. "Probably like the Orphan Home, I'd guess. We'll have bedrooms to stay in, and we'll eat together for meals and spend time together outside chores and classes. Can't be that different, can it?"

"I s'pose not," he answers thoughtfully.

"It's weird, though," Ava posits, "being an Orphan

Elysium

again."

Dr. Tori re-enters the room. She has this uncanny ability to appear exactly when she's needed. It's almost like she already knows what's happening. She sits down with the three of us and gently prods.

"Do you have a decision about what you'd like to do? Remember, you don't all have to make the same choice."

Her eyes sweep from face to face, as if discerning what we're about to say.

"We'd like to stay in the dorms," I declare, a finality in my voice that even I didn't expect.

"All of you?"

Matthew and Ava nod their assent.

"Harper and I want to share a room. Can we do that?" Ava asks.

"Of course you can," Dr. Tori smiles. "Most of our boarding students have roommates, in fact. Matthew, what would you think about having one?"

Matthew frowns, his trademark concentration overwhelming his usually handsome features. Clearly deep in thought, his face betrays his emotions. He looks as though a spoonful of something bitter has been shoveled into his mouth. He clearly finds the idea distasteful.

"Should I take that as a no?" Dr. Tori asks with a chuckle. Reading people is a special gift of hers.

"I'd rather not," he says with a sour look. "There's enough new things to get to know around here without trying to live with someone I've never met."

"I understand," Dr. Tori replies. "I had a feeling you would choose the dormitories, so I went ahead and made arrangements. Follow me. I'll show you your rooms."

We let Dr. Tori guide us through unfamiliar halls to find our new lodgings. She leads us out of the conference room in the opposite direction from where we came. At the end of the hallway lies a bank of strange silver double doors all in rows next to one another. The walls on either side of us have inlaid buttons—an up arrow and a down arrow.

Dr. Tori presses the down arrow, and one set of doors to our left slides open from the middle, disappearing into the wall on either side. She places one hand against the wall where one door vanished, as if to stop it from closing on us, and motions for us to enter a tiny box of a room. Curiosity has always been a bit of a hindrance to me. Where Ava and Matthew walk right in, I stop and examine things first.

There is a large crack between the floor and the strange metal box before me. It's clearly not part of the actual structure. Peering down into the crack, I get the sense that there's nothing down there at all—just a deep, dark chasm.

Gulping, I ask, "Are you sure it's safe? There's nothing down there."

Dr. Tori's grinning lips part to speak, but Matthew beats her to it. "It's called an elevator, Harp. It takes us up and down between floors instead of stairs. There's a lot of floors here. Using the stairs all the time would get exhausting."

I glare at him. "How would you know what it's called?"

With a sheepish shrug, he replies, "I read about it. I've read all about Elysium already. I wouldn't be in here if I didn't know it was safe."

"Yeah, well, you've been awake a lot longer than I have,

haven't you?" I say it playfully, but I'm a little annoyed. All those feelings of inadequacy I used to get when he'd feed me answers in the Orphan Home schoolroom are trying to break through. At least now I know he's not being pompous or showing off. He's genuinely trying to help, but it bruises my ego anyway.

It's not Matthew's issue, I keep reminding myself. *It's mine. Why do I always have to be the smartest person in the room? Why can't I just let someone else be right sometimes?*

Negative self-talk rushes through my head—that's what my therapist calls it when I think mean things about myself. I move forward, cautiously stepping over the crack in the floor. I stand in my usual spot between Ava and Matthew and turn to face the doors like they do. They each take one of my hands, Ava to receive comfort and Matthew to give it. He looks down at me, worry etched across his face. I can tell he thinks I'm angry with him, but I get angrier with myself these days. I try to smile up at him reassuringly, though I know my eyes just look sad and pathetic. I take a deep breath and remind myself that I'm still smart and capable even when someone else knows something I don't.

Dr. Tori follows me into the elevator and presses a button to close the doors. The shiny metal wall to the right of the doors is lined with numbered buttons. She presses the five, and it lights up with an orange glow. The floor beneath us lurches. Suddenly we're all holding onto each other much tighter. A bit of smugness still living in me is amused and even pleased that Mr. Know-It-All beside me looks just as terrified as I feel. I try to squash it down to keep it from showing.

The movement of the elevator stops with a sudden

jolt. We all three look at each other, wide-eyed. *Is it over?* we ask each other silently. The doors slide open to reveal a completely different place. *That magic box really did take us somewhere new!*

The hospital was white and sterile with sharp smells and official-looking plaques and paintings on the walls. This place is something else altogether. Wall-to-wall rugs cover the floor, thick and plush in mottled gray tones. Instead of a narrow hall like the one we just came from, the elevator here opens into a beautiful sitting room full of overstuffed armchairs and sofas. A large black screen hangs from one wall, reminiscent of the screen that displayed Dr. Tori's moving pictures during orientation. All the furniture is centered around it. A warm fire crackles pleasantly below it. *How can they have a fire underground?*

Dr. Tori waits and lets us take it all in. This process seems to be quite ordinary to her. How many times has she done this? She could be older than she looks. Maybe she's helped a lot of other Orphans get acclimated.

"Dr. Tori?" I ask.

She smiles. "You're wondering about the fire?"

I nod. Two weeks ago, I would've thought she was something of a mind reader, but now I realize she must get this question every time she has new Orphans.

"It's not real. It produces warmth and makes the sound of a fireplace, but there's no actual fire in there. Just an illusion—much safer for life underground."

What a wonder! They can create so many things that I've never even dreamed of. *A fake fire! Who even knew such a thing was possible? What else will we find here?*

"You've gotten accustomed to much in the past few

weeks, but there will still be many things to marvel over and pique your curiosity. You'll feel as though you're learning constantly in the months to come. Let's not spend too long looking around here. You have your bedrooms to see!" Dr. Tori begins walking as she finishes her last sentence, and we follow dutifully.

"This is the fifth floor. This is where all the classes are housed, as well as the dormitories and the dining hall for dormitory students. Classes for younger students are off that way." She waves behind her in the opposite direction. Glancing back, I see that the floor extends in the opposite direction, though not nearly as far before the hallway forks into a T.

We walk down a wide carpeted hallway with numbered doors on either side. "These are some of the dorm rooms. Most of our students choose to live here while they study around the age of thirteen or fourteen. Rooms are interspersed throughout the floor."

We take a few turns here and there before the hall widens into a large open room lined with tables. Some are long with benches, while others are smaller circles or squares with wooden chairs. Delicious aromas fill my nostrils. I breathe in the scents of food, some new and some old but all making my stomach grumble.

"This is the cafeteria where you'll take your meals. You are free to eat here with other students or to take meals back to your rooms. We do encourage students, especially those new to Elysium, to eat at least one meal a day in the dining hall to build relationships and begin acclimating to the culture of our city, but it's not required. You'll notice the kitchen on this side of the room."

Dr. Tori gestures to her right, where a long row of shiny metal carts sits. Windows lie at an angle over large metal containers covered with matching lids. Stacks of plates rest at the end of each long cart. If this is where they serve the meals, there must be hundreds of different foods available each day. Behind these counters, doorways into large kitchens are visible. People clad in long aprons and hats bustle around, clattering and clanging pots and pans, dishes and utensils as they work. Suddenly I can't wait for lunch.

"Lunch begins in about an hour," Dr. Tori announces, clearly noticing our longing expressions, "and will last for two hours. We'd better finish our tour and get you to your rooms, so you have enough time to get settled before you eat."

She hurries back into the hall and leads us through more twists and turns. I make mental notes of our route, so I can lead us back to lunch without getting lost. My sense of direction never failed me in the woods; why would it fail me down here? Except that there isn't any sunlight, and everything looks the same. Sighing, I try to remember room numbers instead.

"I like to keep our newcomers relatively central to everything they'll need on a daily basis. Your room will be in this hall, so you're near both the dining hall and the classrooms. Makes it harder to get lost," Dr. Tori adds with a wink.

"We'll quickly visit the school, and then I'll bring you back to see your rooms. This way."

She takes a right at the end of the hall, and we follow behind. There's another bank of elevators here. I'm sure we're not back where we started. There must be elevators all over this place.

"These elevators will be more convenient for you," Dr. Tori explains. "Most students use these since they're closer to everything else. The next floor down is where you'll find the library and recreation rooms. There are various sports and games, a track for walking or running, exercise equipment, and even a swimming pool."

Ava's forehead wrinkles. "A swimming pool?"

"It's like a lake or a pond, but it's indoors. The water is clean and warm, and no plants, fish, or animals live in it. It's exclusively for swimming."

We stare at each other with our wide eyes again. I have a feeling we'll be doing this a lot.

"Now if you follow me this way, the school is on the other side of the elevators." She leads us into another sitting room, but this one also has wide tables and a few desks, presumably for studying.

"If you'll notice the four hallways," continues Dr. Tori, "you'll see that they each focus on a different area of study. The first is biological sciences, the second is technological sciences, the third is education, and the fourth is safety and security. You'll each take general courses in each discipline for a few months to ensure you're up to speed. Before long, you'll undergo a series of skills, aptitude, and interest inventories—tests—to determine which academy you're best suited for."

Seeing a concerned look spreading across Ava's face, Dr. Tori quickly adds, "I know you're all fond of other activities, as well. These academies are for professional study to prepare you for a job that contributes to the mission of Elysium. These careers help ensure our survival and further our research toward a cure for the illnesses that ravage the outside world. Rest assured, you'll still be able to do everything you loved on the surface, including artwork and even climbing trees."

"You have trees down here?" I practically shout the question in utter disbelief.

"Yes, we do. The first floors of Elysium are dedicated to agricultural development. Shafts in the top floor let in sunlight that allows us to cultivate every species of plant from the surface, including a wide variety of trees. We mostly grow those that produce fruit, but we have a few others as well. We also grow crops and have several gardens."

"Animals, too?" Ava asks.

"Animals, too," Dr. Tori answers with a nod. "The second floor is where our animals live. They do have artificial light, but we ensure they have plenty of space to move and exercise. There are special shafts dug into the second floor to release gasses and odors to the surface, and we're able to take their droppings up onto the greenhouse floor for fertilizer. We also compost food and human waste for the same purpose."

"What about birds?" Ava asks, a note of desperation in her voice.

"Yes, I should've thought to mention them! There are birds on the first floor. The orchards serve as an aviary of sorts. We have birds and insects to help keep the natural ecosystem in place. Everything grows better that way, and we don't have to pollinate every plant by hand."

Ava looks more relieved than I think I've ever seen her.

"Where are all the other students," Matthew inquires.

"They're all in classes right now," Dr. Tori answers. "That's why the hallways are so deserted. Don't worry.

It'll be busy at lunch. You'll be surprised at just how many students we have here. It's a much larger place than your village. Come on, let's get you back to your rooms to rest a bit."

When we re-enter the hallway near the second set of elevators, Dr. Tori shows us to two doors on opposite sides of the hall. Each door is labeled with a small golden plaque—582 for us and 583 for Matthew. Dr. Tori swipes a card in front of the door handles, and they open immediately. Then, she hands us each our own card.

"These will unlock your doors for you. Keep them somewhere safe, and be sure not to lose them. Your doors will always lock behind you, so you won't be able to get in without your keycard. We can always make you a new one, of course, if yours is truly lost, but we would rather save those resources. Please be careful."

We all three nod in agreement as we enter our respective rooms. Ours has two small bedrooms with the largest, most comfortable-looking beds I've ever seen, a small desk, and a large closet full of clothes. The main room has a kitchenette, a small dining table with room for four, a couch, an oversized armchair, and a small black screen on the wall.

Our very own bathroom stands off the kitchenette, and let me say that I am in love with indoor bathrooms! Not having to go out into the cold to do my business is one of the best things ever. And hot water whenever you want without heating it over the fire for a half hour first? Forget about it!

Ava squeals with delight from one of the bedrooms.

"Look at all the choices!"

I peek through the door and find her standing inside

her very own closet. Sure enough, one room has a closet full of clothes in her size and the other in mine. Each one also contains a small chest of drawers full of socks, pants, and undergarments. Dr. Tori steps in from the hall and nods her approval.

"I see you've found your closets. We brought in a wide variety of different things in your sizes, but of course, I'm sure you won't like them all. The storerooms on floor eleven have items you can choose from when you have a better idea of what you want to keep. You can return anything you don't enjoy."

She stands in the door a bit longer, observing. Then, she announces her departure. "Well, I'd better be getting back to my other patients. I hope you enjoy your rooms. Lunch starts in half an hour. If you get there early, you won't have to wait in line as long. There are maps and other information for each of you on your desks. If you get lost, ask anyone you see for help. Someone will check in on you soon to let you know more about school. For now, feel free to explore and see what you can find to do in Elysium. I doubt you'll get bored easily."

Ava, Matthew, and I congregate in the hallway to watch her walk away. As soon as she's gone, we're jumping up and down, shrieking with excitement. We all pile into Matthew's room to take a look around. We spend our next thirty minutes examining the map of Elysium and deciding what to explore first.

TESTS

For the next three days, Ava, Matthew, and I explore floor after floor of the underground city while most other people are at school or work. Everything here is manmade. Elysium is more of an enormous, labyrinthine underground building than an actual city, though it does seem several thousand people must live here.

I can't help but wonder how they managed to build all this. Was it this big from the start or have they continued to build as their population grew? It's such a relief to live in a place where I can ask questions and actually find straightforward answers.

On the evening of the third day, we take our dinners into Matthew's room and sit at his little four-person table. We haven't eaten in the dining hall yet. There's just an overwhelming number of people in there each time. We have gotten a little more adventurous with the food we choose, though. We eat in awkward silence, knowing that tomorrow is our first day of Elysian school and each of us is too afraid to say what we're feeling. I look from Ava to Matthew and back again. Neither of them makes eye contact with me, choosing to look at their plates instead.

When everyone is finished eating, Matthew stacks all our dishes and trays together and walks them back down to the kitchen alone, as has become his custom these past few days. Ava glances up at me nervously.

"What do you think it will be like?" she whispers, as if she'll be punished if someone overhears her talking about it.

I shake my head. "I don't know. Maybe not too different from the schoolhouse?" I suggest hopefully.

"But there's so many kids and so many hallways," she protests.

I nod, and we go back to sitting in silence on Matthew's couch, deep in thought. Ava pulls her legs up to her chest and lays her forehead against her knees so that almost none of her is actually visible. She used to sit like this in the Orphan Home when she'd been scolded. I know she must be feeling a lot of terrible things. So am I.

The door opens, and Matthew appears. He pulls up one of the chairs from his dining table and sits near me, but not next to me. Things have been a little awkward between us lately, maybe because Ava's always around. Things have been bizarre since the barn dance. At that time, we had thought we knew what to expect from life. Things would be safe and calm, and we would court under Mama and Papa's supervision and the watchful eyes of Matthew's parents, Mr. and Mrs. Aaron.

Now our lives are uncertain. I don't know what to expect about anything. I still care about Matthew, and I can tell he cares about me, but surely there are more important things than courting at the moment. After the dance, he kissed me on the cheek. I thought in that moment that I was falling for him, but now I get annoyed with him about little things. He's always trying to reassure me and do things for me, and I just want to be free and take care of myself. It's complicated all of a sudden. I know he senses it, too. That's why he doesn't sit too close to me or try to hold my hand.

Finally, Matthew breaks the silence. "So . . . school tomorrow."

It feels like it ought to be a question, but he doesn't say it like one. Ava peeks sheepishly out from between her knees, but says nothing.

"School tomorrow," I agree with a sigh.

"It'll definitely be different," he replies.

Ava whimpers without showing her face. I shoot him a glare, and he puts his hands up in surrender. *Sorry*, he mouths, then looks away.

"Julia volunteered to meet us here and walk us down so we know where to go and what to do. She said we can wear anything we want, and she'll be here at seven-fifty in the morning. She even showed us how to set an alarm clock that rings to wake us up at the right time. I can teach you if you want," I offer.

"That would be great," Matthew replies, but I can see a hint of something on his face that tells me he probably already figured it out on his own.

Patronizing.

He follows as I sit on the edge of his bed and pick up his alarm clock. I show him which buttons to press and how to set the time to where he wants it. Then, I show him how to make sure it's turned on and how to turn it off when it rings in the morning.

Why don't I just ask him if he already knows how to do

this? It would be simpler, but it feels good to be useful. I'm so anxious that I feel like my bones might vibrate right out of my body if I sit still for too long.

I set the alarm clock down and lay my hands on my knees for lack of anything better to do with them. Matthew covers one of my hands with his. It's warm and comforting. I look up and find myself staring right into his gray eyes.

"It'll all be okay," he says. "You'll be the smartest one in the room, like always."

I blush and turn away, tears stinging my eyes. I know I've been annoyed with him lately, but I'm relieved to hear he still thinks I'm smart. This place has left me feeling totally inept. There's so much I don't understand. I'm not sure I'll ever catch up to Elysium's kids, and I won't even be a kid much longer.

Though I don't look him in the eye again, I squeeze his hand and flash a small smile. "Thanks, Matthew. Really. . . . Well, Ava and I had better get some rest. Tomorrow will be here before we know it."

Ava squeaks from her place on the sofa, but she gets up and moves toward the door. She looks green, like she might throw up at any moment. When we get back to our room, we dress for bed in total silence. Ava doesn't look like she can handle any conversation, so I give her a huge hug instead. When I pull away, there are tears in her eyes.

"I miss Mama and Papa," she says.

"Me, too."

I give her one more hug and climb into bed, and the next thing I know, she's there beside me. We used to do this in the Orphan Home during thunderstorms when we were little. We both felt safer this way. I suppose we still do.

Cuddled up beside me, Ava is snoring lightly within half an hour. I, on the other hand, toss and turn through a long, sleepless night full of nerves and angst. We've done this once before—this starting over—when we left the Orphan Home, but at least we knew the village and its customs already. This time is different; we don't know anyone or how anything works.

What if they don't really want us here? What if everyone hates us because we weren't born here? Our mere existence above-ground surely puts their very lives at risk. Why would they want to take us in? Tomorrow's going to be the worst day ever. We'll be lucky if they don't kick us out and send us back to die of a terrible disease out in the open air.

When the alarm finally goes off, I could swear I've only been asleep for an hour. Exhausted and nauseous, I roll over and pull the blankets over my head, but Ava won't stand for it. She yanks them away from my face.

"Harper, you have to get up now."

"I'm so tired."

"Didn't you sleep last night?" she asks.

I shake my head. "No, I barely slept at all. Ava, I don't want to start school. What if they hate us?"

Ava lies back down and wraps her skinny arms around me from behind. "I'm nervous, too, but they wouldn't have brought us here if they didn't want us."

I roll over so we're nose to nose. "What if it's just the scientists who want us? What if everyone else wants us to go back home?"

"Harper, come on. They've been taking Orphans for over three hundred years. If everyone hated it, they would've stopped a long time ago."

My eyes sting, but I swallow hard and nod.

"Are you ready to get up now?" Ava asks me.

I nod again and shimmy my way out of the bed. Ava has already retrieved my carefully selected outfit from my closet and laid it across the back of the desk chair. After removing my nightgown, I pull on a pair of wide-legged gray pants and a red short-sleeved sweater that hugs my body in ways we weren't allowed to show off back home. The neck is still high; some of the clothing in the storehouse is too low-cut for me. Maybe someday I'll take that risk, but I've never seen that much of any woman before. For right now, it's just too much.

Ava sticks to a long dress, but with a much louder pattern than we had available to us above-ground. It's a bright turquoise color covered in dark green palm leaves and bright pink birds called flamingos. When she chose the dress, we went to the library and looked it up. She was so fascinated with this bird she'd never seen before. She had marveled at the sheer size of it. I wonder if any still exist after the wars. The book we read said they only live in tropical places, so I doubt we'll ever know.

I watch as she ties her golden hair up into a tight bun at the base of her head—a sign of womanhood in our village. It's still not quite long enough, so I help her pin some loose strands back.

"Want me to do a bun for you?" she offers. "Or the braids you liked to wear before?"

"No, I think I'd like to do something more"—I search for the word Tina used when I was in the hospital—"modern."

Ava raises an eyebrow, and I can tell she's skeptical. She

doesn't say anything, though. She simply watches my reflection in the mirror as I get to work, doing exactly what Tina taught me. First, I spray my hair with water and massage the roots to make sure everything is damp and even. Then I use a pick to untangle everything. Once I'm tangle-free, I use a special brush to fluff everything up. Now my black hair is big, standing up away from my scalp in all directions. I use my hands to shape it into a nice round shape and then lightly spray the ends again to shrink up any curls that stick out too far.

Ava's mouth turns down at the ends while her eyebrows raise, and she nods in approval. "I didn't know you knew how to do that!"

"Tina taught me in the hospital," I reply. "She called it an afro."

"It's gorgeous! I wonder what they would've thought if you'd worn it that way back home."

"Probably that I was insane. Can you picture Mama in an afro?"

What starts as a giggle ends in an uncontrollable laughing fit. I keep snorting, and Ava's face turns red as she struggles to catch her breath. A knock on the door stifles our hysterics.

"We're late!" Ava exclaims, wide-eyed.

"I'll get the door. You keep getting ready. You took too long watching me do my hair!"

I open the door to find Matthew standing with his hands in the pockets of his jeans, rocking back and forth on the heels of his sneakers. His well-fitting T-shirt, combined with his cardigan, looks so handsome on him that I can't help but smile. His return grin is the picture of relief. He's clearly been feeling the tension between us, too.

"Are you guys ready? Julia will be here in five minutes," he says.

"Just finishing up!" Ava calls from the bathroom.

"I have a few more things to do, too," I tell him.

He cocks his head and examines me closely. It's as if he hasn't actually looked at me yet today. He's probably too anxious, but now a real smile starts to creep in.

"What's left to do?" he asks. "You look great—like, really great. I love your hair like that! You really look like you belong here."

My heart quickens, but not because of nerves. Maybe today will turn out to be okay after all.

"Just a few finishing touches." I wink at him.

I rejoin Ava in the bathroom as she's putting on her deodorant with a sour look on her face. She has strong feelings about this particular practice. We didn't have deodorant in the village, and she finds it distasteful to slather something on her underarms. I personally enjoy how much better everyone smells here. I shrug at her with a mischievous look as I open a little bag full of makeup Tina gave me as a gift before I was discharged.

"What's that?" Ava inquires, forever curious.

"Makeup," I smirk at her.

"What does that mean?"

"Just watch."

I don't bother spreading it all over my face. Tina showed me lots of pictures of different looks in the hospital, and I just plain don't like how it makes people look like someone completely different. That's not what I want. I still want to be me but just a little more fun.

Ava observes in awe as I swipe a perfect shade of red

across my lips to match my top. Next, I sweep golden eyeshadow across my lids and finish off with a little mascara to make my lashes look longer. I stand back from the mirror and take a good look at the finished product. I still look like me, but somehow even better.

"Wow!" Ava gasps, letting her mouth drop open. "Matthew's gonna love it."

Another knock at the door tells us it must be time to go to school. My therapist, Julia, stands in the doorway with three school bags in her arms. In the community schoolhouse, we carried satchels with our lunches, but we had individual slates and chalk that stayed in the classroom. There wasn't much to carry back and forth. Here, the expectations are different. We don't need to take our lunches with us because all the food is made in the dining hall kitchens. Instead we'll get technology and books that we'll bring home with us each night for studying and homework. Homework wasn't much of a thing above-ground, so this will be a big change for us. The bags serve as a reminder of one more thing to be anxious about.

"Good morning!" Julia's cheer is almost contagious enough to dissolve the ball of hot lava forming in my stomach. Almost, but not quite. "You all look so great! Are you ready for your first day of Elysian school?"

We exchange nervous looks as we fidget in front of her, suddenly too anxious to speak.

"It's a lot, I know. It's completely fine to be nervous or anxious or scared. Just remember to use your strategies—deep breathing, grounding, whatever you and your therapist have decided works best for you. I promise everyone will be friendly and kind. Some of the

Orphans who arrived in the last Sending are about your age now. I'm sure they'll be excited to meet you."

"I hope so," Ava speaks first.

"Me, too," I say, taking one of those deep breaths Julia mentioned.

She gives us a hopeful, understanding smile before she starts handing out bags. "I brought you each a backpack to carry your things. You'll get everything you need in your classes."

Matthew takes a deep breath and releases it slowly and loudly. "Okay, let's get to it."

Ava and I nod back. He takes my hand and squeezes it briefly before letting go. I wish he'd hold on longer, but instead I focus on Ava. My little sister needs more support than I do today, and I'll be brave for her.

"Let's go," I tell her, smiling with confidence I don't really feel.

Julia leads us down the hallways of dorm rooms, bringing us into the main school lobby. It's bustling with teenagers who scurry about or stand in groups talking loudly with their friends. One boy with skin a shade darker than mine and some kind of short braids in his hair is clearly showing off for his friends. They circle around him as he dances in the middle, then drops to the ground and spins on his back. The growing crowd laughs and cheers loudly.

Maggie's the only person I've ever seen who had skin like mine. I've been so busy trying not to look at anyone when we've been in crowds that I hadn't noticed how many people here look like me. Scanning the room, I see that close to half of the other kids have complexions just like mine or darker. Dark curly hair abounds in all kinds of styles I've never been exposed to.

What kind of place is this?

I'm not the only one who notices. Ava tugs on my elbow until I finally look away from the dancing boy. "There are so many people here who look like you!"

Matthew nods along quizzically. "And look—there are a lot of other kinds of dark-skinned people, too."

"Like Dr. Dalal," I breathe.

"And other people, too. Look, some of them have lighter skin than you, but their eyes are different shapes. . . . This is amazing!" Matthew exclaims. "I've never seen so many different kinds of people!"

I can't answer. I'm so busy trying to take it all in that I don't even notice the small group of kids approaching. My racing thoughts are interrupted by a girl's voice practically shouting, "Are you the new Orphans from above ground?"

I startle and turn to my right to face four kids about our age—three boys and one girl. One of the boys has darker skin even than Maggie, and the girl has features similar to Dr. Dalal with tan skin and brown eyes, straight black hair, and a nose much narrower than mine. For the first time, I wonder why both she and I look so different from the fair-skinned people in my village.

The expression on the girl's face starts to shift, and I realize I've been staring at her. Somehow, my mouth still can't form any actual words. I stutter a little, but then Julia comes to my rescue.

"Yes, these are our new *students*, Jing," she replies, placing particular emphasis on the word students. "This first day can be especially overwhelming for newcomers, so please try to be understanding. They've only ever known their own little community. This can be a lot."

Jing nods her agreement, but then goes right back to shouting in my face. The three boys with her all make faces. She talks a million miles an hour. "We're all from up there, too, but we were little kids for our Sending. We don't remember very much. What's it like up there? We want to know everything. What's the Orphan Home like? Who took care—"

Julia cuts her off. "Jing," she begins sternly, "you have to give people a chance to think. And breathe. I'm sure they can answer your questions—*slowly*—in a week or so. Just please give them some time to adjust."

Jing takes a breath, apparently preparing herself to ask another barrage of questions, but Julia silences her with a wave of her hand. "Guys, I think you've met Jing."

The three boys snicker and elbow each other. Jing crosses her arms and pouts.

"And this is Grey, Jordan, and Amari." Each of the boys raises a hand as his name is said. Amari is the boy who looks like me. "Like Jing already told you, they were Orphans in the last Sending ten years ago, but they were very young. Your advisor here at school will be Mr. Weiss, who came here from your community as a teenager himself. He'll be very helpful to you. We'll let this crowd clear out before we go to meet him."

As if on cue, a chime sounds throughout the room, and students scatter in every direction. Grey and Jordan wave their goodbyes. Amari holds out his fist. I exchange looks with Ava and Matthew. We have no idea what he wants. He laughs, then reaches out and takes my hand. He forms my hand into a fist and bumps his into mine. Then, he holds it out to Ava and Matthew, who follow suit.

"We'll meet you back here after your tests, okay?" he asks.

Jing, who hasn't made a move yet, says, "Have you eaten in the dining hall yet? They have so much great food. You'll love everything, but the Chinese food is my favorite, for obvious reasons."

She keeps chattering as Amari physically spins her around and pushes her to move toward her first class. He rolls his eyes and looks over his shoulder at us.

"Would you believe Jing means peace and quiet?" He snickers as they walk away.

"Figures," Matthew mutters sarcastically.

"What's obvious about Chinese food?" Ava queries.

I shake my head. I have no idea what most of that interaction meant. Julia doesn't seem concerned, so I decide to brush it off.

"Come on. Let's go meet Mr. Weiss," Julia says as she starts down the education hallway. We walk in her wake through what is now a silent, empty corridor and stop in front of the second door on the right. The first two rooms on either side are labeled as offices with staff members' names on them. Julia knocks on the door that says *ROBERT WEISS*, to which a deep voice answers, "Come in!"

She cracks the door open and ushers us in one at a time. The room is so small that the three of us barely fit together. I'm not sure how Julia's going to get in here.

"All right, good luck, you three," she says with her usual chipper demeanor, gently closing the door in front of her own face. I guess she didn't plan to find space in here for herself, not that there's any to find.

Mr. Weiss gestures for us to sit in the three chairs opposite the small desk he's sitting behind, stacked with messy piles of books and papers. He's clearly not very organized. He smiles up at us through thick tawny whiskers that he strokes with long, pale fingers. His nails have been chewed to the nub, but he looks extremely put together otherwise. I wonder what causes this obviously intelligent man so much stress that he can't leave his nails alone.

"Harper, you're staring." Ava sounds appalled as she pulls me into the chair next to hers. *Sorry*, she mouths to Mr. Weiss, her cheeks turning bright red.

Mr. Weiss remains unbothered. "Harper, you're clearly a very observant young lady."

My cheeks feel warm, and I'm hopeful that my unique complexion—well, maybe not as unique here—makes it harder to see when I'm blushing. Mr. Weiss's good-natured chuckle reverberates through the tiny room. He holds up his hands in front of him, nails facing us.

"It's a bad habit I've had ever since the Orphan Home. No matter how long you're in Elysium, some habits are hard to break. I don't bite them until they bleed anymore, though, so I've made some progress."

"How old were you when you came here, sir?" Matthew inquires.

"Nine," Mr. Weiss replies, "and there's no need to call me sir. Mr. is pretty formal for Elysium. Titles like that are only used for teachers and doctors around here. What else would you like to know about me?"

Ava chimes in. "What was it like for you when you first got here? What was the Sending like? We didn't even have one. What about—"

Mr. Weiss raises his hands again, this time palms out, cutting her short. "I thought you might ask them one at a time," he replies with another lighthearted chuckle. "The Sending was probably a lot like how it's been described to you. We had the Festival and recited all our sacred texts and songs. Then the Caretakers took the smaller children home while the townspeople celebrated. I was old enough to stay and watch the festivities, but we didn't get to participate. We had to sit piously on the stage. After a few hours, the Caretakers came back to the square in a wagon full of sleepy little kids. There weren't very many older ones for my Sending. There had been a bad sickness during year seven that orphaned many babies.

"Anyway, they drove us all out into the fields. You've probably never been there since you didn't have a Sending of your own, but there was a clearing far out into the fields. We had to go through these high walls and sit on this giant stone altar. It was really boring, but then there was this loud humming sound, and we were all blinded by a blue light. The next thing I knew, we were waking up in the Elysian hospital. They took us to orientation, and we were all placed with families. No one was old enough to stay in the dorms my year."

"How long ago was that?" I barely recognize my own voice.

"Forty years ago. There have been a lot of Sendings since then. I'm always the advisor to our newcomers since I know what a jarring experience this can be. I also run a support group for former Orphans with some of the older folks who came even before I did."

Matthew looks incredulous. "How many older people

are there here?"

Mr. Weiss nods knowingly. "Not many people aboveground live too much past fifty, but that's not the case here. We have the technology and medicine to keep people alive into their eighties if they choose. There are people here who came to Elysium in Sendings seventy years ago."

"Seventy years," I whisper.

"I know it seems impossible, but in Elysium it's completely normal." He shrugs as if it's no big deal, but there's something in his eyes. *Discomfort? Guilt?* The look I thought I saw is gone in an instant. I probably just imagined it.

"I know it's strange to be here, especially at your age," Mr. Weiss continues. "You've lived a certain way for so long. And let's face it: The way you came here must have been traumatic. So much different from what any of the rest of us experienced."

Our mumbled agreement fills the room while we memorize our shoes and the pattern on the worn carpet, refusing to meet Mr. Weiss's eyes. We've all talked about that night with our therapists—it's the whole reason we even have therapists—but we've never brought it up with anyone else, including each other. I have a lot more to remember than Matthew and Ava. They were caught so early. All these weeks later, I still have nightmares about it. I wish I could just forget. I wish Mr. Weiss had never brought it up.

An uncomfortable silence fills the previously cozy room. Mr. Weiss clears his throat softly. I look up at him then, tears stinging my eyes. His face is the picture of regret. He, too, wishes he had never brought it up.

"I'm so sorry. I shouldn't have said that. I don't know what I was thinking."

Matthew steels himself, sitting up straight and tall. Whatever he's about to say, I can tell it takes a lot for him to do it. He's getting his body into its bravest stance.

"No," he says quietly, "don't be sorry, Mr. Weiss. We're supposed to start talking about it, normalizing it. It's just hard still."

Mr. Weiss nods thoughtfully, right hand back in his beard. Just as he's about to speak, Ava interrupts him.

"It was really scary. We thought there were actual monsters trying to kill us. I try not to think about it most of the time, but Harper was awake a lot longer than we were. She was the last one they caught."

Mr. Weiss looks from Ava to me, and suddenly my shoes seem ever so fascinating. "I'm sure it was terrifying not knowing what was going on. But"—he claps his hands together—"that's not what we're here to talk about, is it?"

I snap back up and meet his gaze, holding my breath. He's smiling like nothing happened. He raises an eyebrow and tilts his head slightly, as if to ask if this feels better. I release a tremendous amount of air from my lungs and offer him a tiny but relieved grin. With a nearly imperceptible nod, he turns his attention to my two companions.

"School in Elysium works a little differently than it does in the Orphan Home or in the schoolhouse. There, you had only one teacher who taught you multiple subjects and who focused heavily on religion. Here, you'll have different teachers for most subjects, though some of us teach more than one. We also don't teach any religious content. In fact, Elysium is a purely atheistic community."

"Atheist . . . does that mean without God?" I offer, remembering my Latin lessons from the Orphan Home.

Mr. Weiss nods. "It does. You must be great with languages," he beams. "Our society doesn't hold to any religious beliefs or worship any gods. Instead, we value science and the exploration of the real world around us. We endeavor to discover how things work and what things are beneficial to our people. It's really as simple as that.

"Because of our strong belief in scientific discovery, you will, of course, take science classes and learn the history of the world and of Elysium in greater detail. You'll learn about our system of government and why it works. You'll also take math and English classes.

"You'll be placed into those core classes starting tomorrow. Today, you'll take some tests to find out how much you already know, so I can be sure to start you at the right level. You'll also take interest and skill inventories to figure out which academy will suit you the best."

"Dr. Tori told us about those," Ava interrupts.

"I'm glad it's not a surprise! Some kids really hate taking tests. Our goal in the academies is to prepare you for a suitable and enjoyable career placement. We try to provide you with all the knowledge you'll need to enter a full-time career after your seventeenth birthday. You'll get to learn even more on the job after that, but I don't want you to think you'll just be sitting at desks listening and taking notes all day, every day. That's more of an above-ground way of learning. Here, you'll learn things and then put them into practice. We do a lot of hands-on activities and projects. Our brains learn better from doing than from listening, and sitting still all day is hard, even for adults. So, what do you think?"

It all sounds kind of amazing. Completely different from anything we've ever done before, but amazing.

"I don't know. It seems a little . . . odd." Good old Matthew, set in his ways. He has such a hard time with change.

I make a face at him, and Ava sticks her tongue out. Soon Matthew's laughing with us and agreeing to give it a try. Mr. Weiss rises to his feet. He's much taller than I expected and towers over us in our seats.

"Let's get started," he declares. "Lots to get done today."

He gestures toward the door, which he can't possibly get to while we're all still sitting here in his cramped little office. The three of us stand and try to move toward the door at once, awkwardly bumping into each other. A flurry of apologies and giggles follows until Matthew ushers us to the other side of the door. He pulls the door open, sandwiching himself between it and the wall to let the rest of us pass through first. He exits behind Ava and me with Mr. Weiss bringing up the rear.

Moving to one side of the hall, the three of us allow Mr. Weiss to take the lead. We follow him past rows of closed doors on either side. Long windows line the hallway between each set of doors. Each room is full of kids working in groups. Some build things, some work with complex arrangements of glass containers filled with colorful liquids, and some do physical activities while others appear to take notes. This is nothing like either of the other schools I've been to. It looks like a lot more fun.

Finally, we reach the hallway's end, where we could turn left or right. The last window on the left is dark. Mr. Weiss swipes a card against the reader above the door handle. The sensor flashes green, and the lights turn on automatically when he opens the door. The room is large and empty, filled only with rows of black-topped tables that house two chairs each. The walls are blank and boring beige, unlike the other rooms we passed that were filled with colorful posters and writing.

Mr. Weiss seats us each at our own table, far apart from each other. Then, he hands us each a large, thin black rectangle resembling the screens we've seen elsewhere in Elysium. He holds his own up in front to give us a demonstration. When he taps the screen with his finger, it lights up.

"These devices," he explains, "are like small computers. I know you haven't worked with computers much yet, and that's okay. You'll have a class to teach you all that later. For now, all you need to know is that each device will allow you to take the tests needed to place you in the right program. You move things around with your fingers, like this."

He places one fingertip on the screen and slides it around. Miraculously, the object he touches follows his finger, as if it were actually real. He makes a series of taps on his screen, and all of ours light up with the same objects. I giggle with delight when the objects on my screen follow my finger wherever I move it.

"This is a game you can play to practice," Mr. Weiss explains. "First, you'll sort all the objects on the screen by color, then by shape, then by size. It'll get you used to how this works."

After the sorting game, he taps his screen again, and a new game pops up. This time, we have to catch falling objects but only one specific type at a time. After that, we play a game where we move a small rectangle around the bottom of the screen to bounce a ball off it. The goal is to keep the ball from dropping. Finally, Mr. Weiss hands us each a small, thin device that looks a little like a long piece of chalk with a definite point at the end.

"This is called a stylus. You can use it just like your finger to drag or move things, but you can also write with it. You can write just exactly as you would with chalk on a slate, and the words will appear on the screen. Let's try."

Another series of taps brings up a white screen full of lines, not dissimilar to the lined green slates we used when we were just learning how to write years ago, except the lines are much closer together. Words appear at the top of my screen in perfect print like the antique books in Master Cowan's Orphan Home library.

Write what you see here.

"Go ahead and try it. Copy down the words," Mr. Weiss instructs.

When I finish my last word and add the period at the end, a big yellow star flashes across the screen. New words appear at the top, and I copy those, too. For each set of words I copy correctly, I get another star. When I write the wrong words, just to see what will happen, a too-round red face appears, its mouth turned downward. I let out an involuntary laugh, quickly slapping my hand over my mouth to stifle it. I don't want to get into trouble on my very first day.

"Looks like you're already testing the system." Mr. Weiss grins at me. "We like that kind of curiosity around here."

I feel the tension drain out of my body as a sigh of relief escapes my lips. I can barely believe he didn't scold me. I think I'm going to like this kind of school.

Once Mr. Weiss is satisfied that we understand how our tablets work, we move on to the actual tests. After what feels like hours and hours, we get to take a lunch break. Unfortunately, Mr. Weiss says we can't be around the other students until all our tests are complete, so someone brings lunch to us. He doesn't want any of them giving us answers or giving us ideas that might skew our results. We eat in the classroom together at one table. We're allowed to talk, just not about what we've done on our tests so far.

After lunch, we move to a much bigger room called a gym. It looks an awful lot like our town meeting hall, except it's filled with unusual equipment that I can only imagine is used for torturing Elysium's enemies. Unlucky for us, these machines are actually used to test our bodies.

Mr. Weiss and two other teachers guide us to locker rooms, where we change into T-shirts and shorts that will be more comfortable for the physical activities we apparently have to do next. We spend the afternoon working on strength, speed, balance, coordination, and even things like fitting large, oddly shaped blocks together into a giant cube and estimating how far away small and large objects are from us. They test how well we can see and hear and how fast we can think under pressure. They test basically everything that's possible to test, plus a lot of things that don't seem possible at all.

By the time they tell us we're done, we're all dripping with sweat. I collapse onto the floor just in time for another chime to sound through the cavernous room, as if from nowhere.

"That's it for today," Mr. Weiss calls out. "It looks like we might just have everything we need. You should be able to start some of your regular classes tomorrow. I'll walk you back out in a few minutes."

10

STRONGHOLD

When the wagon left to return the still-sleeping mother and her young child to the healers' care, John and Maggie departed on their own trek through the woods. Another search party probed this area for the lost and wounded, but the dedicated couple had a unique destination in mind—Harper and Ava's not-so-secret secret treehouse hideout deep in the forest. Though Maggie had never been invited to the Stronghold herself, she, like any mother worth her salt, knew where it was.

"When did you come out here with the girls?" John asked, brushing aside the flexible budding branches of the saplings tangled in his path.

"Well," Maggie replied, beginning to lose her breath on this long hike, "I never came out here with them exactly."

"You followed them." He eyed her suspiciously with one eyebrow raised, turning his face ever so slightly in her direction.

"Of course!" She giggled like a schoolgirl at his teasing. "I wouldn't let my children play somewhere I couldn't find them in an emergency or where I wasn't sure they were safe."

John shrugged carelessly. "You know, I've been out here to inspect their handiwork a time or two myself."

"Oh, have you?"

"Of course. I wouldn't let my children play somewhere I wasn't sure was safe! I watched over them the whole time they were building a few summers back. They did a mighty fine job."

Maggie winked at him. "You taught them well."

"How do you mean?"

"Well, you let them build that storage shed with you. Where did you think they got the materials and tools from?"

At that, he chuckled, his face turning a delightful shade of pink beneath his dark beard. "I did notice the extra supplies were going missing. That's how I found the treehouse in the first place."

"They weren't even ours yet, but I was already checking."

"They really always were ours, though, Mags, if you think about it."

She nodded silently, the oncoming tears causing her voice to catch in her throat. Stifling a sob, she continued on. For several minutes, neither said a single word, each lost in thoughts of their beautiful daughters, so different yet so alike—Ava, with her ivory skin and blonde hair growing ever so quickly toward her shoulders, and Harper, with her dark braids and light brown complexion, halfway between Maggie's and John's. They've never looked like sisters, but they always have been anyway.

Her boot catching on a fallen branch, Maggie clutched John's arm to steady herself. She felt his large strong hands grip her, keeping her from falling. When she looked up, she nearly cried out. Coming into view up ahead was Harper and Ava's treehouse, the Stronghold. John moved to sprint toward it, but Maggie grasped his arm tighter.

"Wait, John," she whispered. Something wasn't right. She just couldn't quite place it.

He stared at her, concern furrowing his brow.

What? John mouthed the word silently. Maggie only shook her head. Then, it struck her. She pointed up at one of the open-air windows. There hung a small snippet of thick black rope. It looked like it had snapped, the end frayed. Nothing like that existed in the community. Where could it have come from?

The creases across John's brow deepened as he surveyed the Stronghold for other clues. There was nothing else, but that rope clearly didn't belong.

"We'll be cautious," he warned his wife, "but we have to go in. I have my knife. I'll go first."

She clung to his arm with both hands now. "Do you think they're really in there?"

"Only one way to find out."

John unlatched the leather pouch that held his hunting knife at his belt and took off stealthily toward the Stronghold. Maggie, unarmed, followed at a safe distance. What were they thinking not bringing the rifles? They should've expected unknown dangers to be lurking nearby.

She stood at the bottom of the makeshift ladder nailed to the ancient tree's trunk and watched her husband's ascent. When he reached the top, he motioned for Maggie to stay where she was, then entered silently through the open trap door. After a few short moments, his face appeared at the top of the ladder.

"Come on up," he told her gravely.

Maggie, struggling with her heavy skirts as she climbed the child-sized ladder, called out, "What have you found?"

His somber reply came back sounding hollow. "They're not here. But it looks like someone was, and it didn't go so well. Come and see for yourself."

He was waiting just inside the gaping maw in the treehouse floor that the girls had used for a door. Offering his hand, he helped her climb into the house and get to her feet. She surveyed the tiny room in silence. The discarded furniture their daughters had assembled looked like it had been tossed around the small house. Things were overturned and broken. The small chest where they had kept their secrets was emptied of its treasures. Dried flowers, drawings, and beautiful stones were scattered across the room. The chest itself was knocked onto its side. A small branch lay near the center of the room.

Inside the window, a multi-pronged metal hook resembling a claw was embedded into the wooden frame of the window—a thick, black snake of a rope attached that had, in fact, snapped under some large force. Where would rope like that even come from? It didn't feel like any natural fiber either John or Maggie recognized.

"Looks like another struggle, just like the Orphan Home," she said, almost to herself.

"Except," John replied with resignation, pointing to a spattering of red on the wooden floor.

Eyes widening in alarm, Maggie practically shouted at him, "Whose blood is that?"

FRIENDS

Once we finally picked ourselves up off the floor, the adults escorted us back to the locker rooms to shower and dress. Now I stand fully under the warm water, watching it pour down my body and into the large drain on the tiled floor. It's amazing how quickly the idea of a shower became normal to me. No more once-a-week baths in front of the fire.

Ava's loud singing from the shower stall next to mine pulls me away from the old Orphan Home and back into the present. After turning off the shower, I flip my head upside down and gently squeeze as much water as I can from my thick hair. I emerge wrapped in a towel just as Ava's water turns off with a loud squeak of the knob.

"You done already, Harp?"

"Just trying to get away from your singing," I tease.

A sopping washcloth sails over the stall door and smacks me in the cheek before plopping onto the floor with a splat.

"What the—" I splutter as laughter erupts from the stall. "Gross! You are *so dead*."

"Guess I won't have to go back to school then," she retorts as she peeks out through a crack in the door.

When I start to roll my eyes, Ava pushes the door open and tries to rush past, but I saw it coming. She's been trying to distract me with eye-rolling comments for years. I pick up her nasty washcloth and lob it at her, hitting her square in her bare back just above her towel. When she tries to slide around the corner to the dressing area with her wet feet, she slips. Her feet fly out from under her, and she lands hard on her hip.

"Ava! Are you okay?"

She doesn't answer at first—just sits there facing the other direction. When I reach her, her eyes look watery, and I can tell she's holding back tears.

"I'm so sorry! I didn't mean to hurt you. Can you get up?"

Ava takes my hand and stands up. She closes her eyes, takes a deep breath in, and releases it in one big sigh.

"*You* didn't hurt me, Harper. I started it. Besides, I shouldn't have been running in here."

I wrap her into a big sisterly hug. "How's your leg?"

Ava pulls away and lifts the edge of her towel to reveal a big red spot on the side of her leg.

"Could be worse," she shrugs, "but it's definitely gonna bruise."

I try to help her walk back to our clothes, but she brushes me away.

"Come on, I can walk. I swear. You're not the only one around here who's tough."

"But I *am* the only one who broke a soldier's nose." I wink.

Ava raises one eyebrow. "Oh, you're proud of that now, huh? Beat up one grown man, and all of a sudden you're some kind of badass."

I gasp and cover my mouth with one hand. I don't think I've ever heard Ava swear. Pretending she doesn't notice, she saunters away, though with noticeably more care than before. Trailing behind, I blink away the shock, remembering that I turned into a little bit of a show-off around the time I turned twelve, too. Her birthday's right around the corner. It wouldn't have been a big deal in the Orphan Home, but it would've been to Mama and Papa. I wonder what they would have done for her.

No wonder Ava's started cussing all of a sudden. She must feel like she's missing out on so much by being here. It's one thing to want to keep Mama and Papa safe, but it doesn't take away the sting of your first birthday without them, especially when it was supposed to be your first birthday *with* them.

"Are you okay?" Ava asks. "You look like you're about to cry."

"Of course," I say, trying to convince myself more than her. "But I'm crazy tired from that workout. I can't wait to lie down."

"No kidding! I'm glad they gave us different clothes to wear, but a little warning would've been nice."

"Ugh . . . I know. And then I had to wash all my makeup off, and my hair is a mess."

"Well, at least we get to go home and rest for a while. It's not like you're gonna see anyone."

"Except Matthew," she adds, pursing her lips and making kissy noises.

I push her shoulder and roll my eyes. "Like he even cares about my hair."

Matthew and Mr. Weiss are waiting for us in the hall when we finally come out. Mr. Weiss shows us how to get back to the main school lobby, and we assure him that we know our way from there. As we near the end of the hallway, we start to hear voices.

Ava cocks her head and scrunches up her face. "I thought everyone else was supposed to be gone by now."

I shrug, trying to play it off, but my hands instinctively move to my unstyled hair. I comb my fingers through it, attempting to work out any obvious tangles.

"Maybe it's the custodians cleaning up," Matthew suggests, but when the corridor ends, I plainly see four kids sitting around a table talking.

The group is suddenly quiet as two sets of eyes raise to take us in. The others turn to look behind them, and we can plainly see it's the kids from this morning. The dark-skinned boy gets up and starts toward us. The other three follow, and I'm struck with guilt that I don't remember any of their names.

"Hey, guys," he says. "How was test day?"

"Long," Ava says.

"Exhausting," adds Matthew.

"They made you do the fitness tests, too, huh?" says a blond boy with chin-length hair.

I nod with wide eyes, hoping I look even the least bit natural.

"Man, that sucks," the blond kid replies.

We all three squint quizzically at each other.

"Sucks?" Ava asks.

The girl with the almond-shaped eyes laughs. "Yeah, like it's terrible. You guys don't say 'sucks' aboveground?"

"No," I reply. "I don't think I've ever heard that before."

The girl laughs again. "That's okay. Like I said this

morning, we came from up there, but we don't really know that much about what it's like. We don't really remember anything. Can we ask—"

A dark-haired boy with pale skin elbows her in the ribs. "Jing, stop it! We're here to be their friends, not to ask them a million questions."

Jing rubs her side. "Geez, Grey, I was just trying to be *friendly*. You don't have to manhandle me."

"Sorry about her," Grey says, tilting the top of his head in Jing's direction. "Jing just *loves* to talk."

"That's okay," Matthew grins. "Takes some of the pressure off. So you're Grey?"

"Yeah," he gestures around the group, naming each of his friends in turn. "You've met Jing already, and this is Jordan and Amari. Jordan and I are brothers. I was three, and he was only one at our Sending."

"So, yeah. They're thirteen and eleven now," says Amari. "I'm fifteen, and Jing is fourteen."

"I'm just relieved to have other girls around," Jing adds.

"I saw tons of other girls here this morning," Ava replies.

"Yeah, but none of them are from the surface. They don't know what it's like to be Sent."

"Neither do you," Jordan smirks.

Jing sticks out her tongue.

"Anyway, we don't want to bother you guys or anything. We just thought you might want to do something fun after the day you've had," Amari offers.

"Like what?" I ask.

I briefly meet his chestnut eyes, and I feel myself flush. I immediately look away. When he speaks again, I can hear the smile in his voice.

"Maybe we could go swimming?" he offers.

"There's an awesome hot tub, too. It's great for sore muscles," Jing adds.

"That sounds amazing!" Matthew says.

Ava nods along. "But what's a hot tub?"

Jing starts to answer, but Grey interrupts her. "You'll see when we get there. It's pretty self-explanatory."

"Do you guys have swimsuits yet?" Jing asks me and Ava.

We must look confused because she answers her own question. "I bet you do. Dr. Tori wouldn't let you go off alone if you didn't already have everything you need. Take me to your room, and I'll find your suits for you. They sent you to the storerooms to get clothes, right? Of course they did—look at both of you! I don't know much about the surface, but I know they don't dress like us. It's practically pioneer times up there."

Our group moves toward the dormitory hallways. Jing never stops talking. When we reach our rooms, Matthew points one thumb at her over his shoulder and asks Amari, "Is she always like this?"

Amari raises an eyebrow comically in an expression that tells us everything we need to know. Jing never even notices.

Have fun, Matthew mouths at us as he opens his door for the three other boys.

I widen my eyes so far they feel like they'll pop out, and I raise my hands above my head, miming a hostage situation.

Help me, I mouth back.

When Matthew's door closes, uproarious laughter erupts from behind it. I turn to find Ava walking limply into our room, followed by Jing, who has yet to stop talking.

"Okay, where do you keep your things?" Jing asks without bothering to wait for anyone to show her. She pokes through closets before opening drawers and digging through undergarments, nightgowns, socks, and T-shirts until she pulls out what looks like a brightly colored bra and underwear set for each of us.

Beaming, she holds them up to show us, one in each hand. "See? I knew they got swimsuits for you guys! What's the matter?"

"We're supposed to swim in those?" Ava says.

"In front of the *boys*?" I add.

"Well, what did you used to swim in?" Jing asks.

"We didn't ever really swim back home. There wasn't enough water for swimming anywhere," I answer.

Jing looks positively flabbergasted. "You didn't swim? Not even in a pool?"

"I told you there wasn't enough water nearby. Dr. Tori told us you have a swimming pool down here, but we've never even seen one before."

"Oh, wow!" Jing says. "It's wild the things that seem normal when you've had them as long as you can remember!"

"Yeah, like showers," Ava chimes in.

"Wait, you didn't have *showers* above-ground?"

"You really don't remember anything, do you?" I ask.

Jing shakes her head, her expression turning a little sad. "Sometimes, I wish I did. I mean, I love my family and everything, but I'll always know they're not my real parents, you know? They took me in for this big Elysian science experiment, you know, for the good of the world and all that. But I'll never know if they really *love* me."

I put one hand on Jing's back. "That sucks."

"You used it right!" Jing exclaims, all traces of unhappiness leaving her body instantaneously. "Anyway, we better get moving if we want to relax before dinner. Go try on your swimsuits."

"I don't know about this," Ava remarks. She holds her swimsuit at arm's length between her thumb and forefinger, wrinkling her nose like it's something rotten. "It seems somehow—"

"Indecent," I finish for her. "We've gotten used to wearing pants and everything, even showing our collarbones, but—"

"Oh, come on!" Jing chides. "It's totally normal here, I swear. It's what everyone wears to swim. Except the boys. They wear shorts."

"Shorts? *Just* shorts?" I ask indignantly.

Jing furrows her brow and nods. "Yes," she answers hesitantly.

"No . . . no shirts?" Ava inquires.

"*No*," Jing's eyes flick back and forth between us. It's like we're in some kind of standoff.

Finally, I shrug and head for my bedroom. "Well, this is going to be awkward."

A few minutes later, I reappear in the doorway wearing a pale yellow bikini. I can't help but laugh when Jing lets out a low whistle. I take a look in the mirror, and I have to agree with her. No one's ever seen my belly button outside of bath night, but I look good.

"Your turn, Ava," I tell her.

When she emerges in her hot pink bathing suit, she looks anything but confident.

"OMG, you look so good!" Jing practically shouts at her.

Ava peeks shyly in the mirror. With a pained expression, she wraps her arms around herself as if she's freezing. Jing must not be as oblivious as she seemed at first because she chimes in with the perfect solution.

"You can wear a T-shirt over it if you want, even in the pool. Lots of girls do that."

"Really?"

"Sure! No big deal. I promise."

Jing tosses her an oversized tee. Ava's relief is palpable as she pulls it over her head.

"What about you, Jing? Do we need to go back to your room so you can change?"

"Nah," Jing replies. "We planned to ask you swimming and put on our suits before we came back for you. See?"

She pulls up her shirt to reveal her own black bikini top and a bejeweled belly button.

"What's that?" I ask pointedly.

"What? Oh, this?" she says, lightly fiddling with the gemstone. "It's a belly button ring. You guys really are old-fashioned up there, huh?"

"I've definitely never seen one of those before, so yeah, I guess we are. Or were," Ava replies.

"Lots of people get piercings here. You've seen people wearing earrings, right?"

Ava and I nod together.

"Well, it's the same thing, but they can do it to just about any body part you want."

"What do you mean? How does it stay on a belly button?"

Realization spreads across Jing's face. "Oh, you've

never seen *piercings* before. Okay, so they take a hollow needle, and they poke it through your skin to make a hole. Then they put the jewelry through it and let it heal. You have to keep it really clean for a while to keep it from getting infected. After a while, it heals up, and you can wear all different kinds of jewelry in it. They do it on ears and belly buttons, but also lips and noses. Those are the most common anyway. My parents didn't want me to get one, but once you turn fourteen, especially if you live in the dorms, you get to make your own decisions about your body. I got mine on my birthday."

"Wow."

It's so beautiful that I can't help but look at it closer. My face is inches from Jing's bare stomach.

"Does it hurt?"

"It hurt for a second when they put the needle through and sometimes when I cleaned it after, but not very much. It never hurts now."

"It's really pretty," Ava says.

"Thanks!" Jing beams.

There's a knock on the door, and Matthew's voice echoes through the wood.

"Are you guys ready to go yet?"

I stand up and look to Jing for help. "Should I put something on over this for the walk down there?"

"Nah, don't worry about it," she replies as she strips off her own clothes. "And don't worry about shoes, either. We can just walk there barefoot. There's towels already down there that we can use, as long as we return them."

Jing turns the doorknob to reveal four shirtless boys standing in the hallway, impatient yet jovial. I feel suddenly exposed, too naked to be around all these other people. Matthew grins sheepishly, then looks away respectfully, but the other boys don't seem to have a problem looking. I blush.

Guilt spreads through me like wildfire at the attention. Matthew and I haven't talked about where we stand since we got here. Back home, we would have been courting very seriously after the night we had at the barn dance. We held hands, and he kissed my cheek. That means something up there, but here? I'm not so sure where any of that leaves us. I've assumed that we're together, but I don't really know.

Am I supposed to be committed to Matthew? Is marriage something we should even be thinking about?

Everything is so different now. I'm not sure what the expectations are for this new life, and I don't even have a mother to ask.

I've been so lost in thought that I haven't paid any attention to where we are or what's going on around me. Only the ding of the elevator arriving alerts me to real life. The doors slide open, and the seven of us squeeze in.

"You okay?" Jing whispers in my ear.

I nod stoically and whisper back, "I'll tell you later."

It's weird how Jing seems like such a loudmouth, but I still feel like I can trust her. She may talk a lot, but she definitely pays attention. I can already tell she cares about people.

The trip to the sixth floor is short and sweet. We've been down here to explore once already during school hours, so we wouldn't have to run into any other kids. There was a lot to see, but we didn't really know what to do with any of it. Nothing down here was familiar.

Nothing felt like home.

Today, it feels like a new world of possibilities. Our new friends lead us through a maze of varied activity rooms until we reach a set of double glass doors. The sign reads, SWIMMING POOL. NO GLASS. NO LIFEGUARD ON DUTY. SWIM AT YOUR OWN RISK.

Yeah, that's not terrifying or anything.

Ava, Matthew, and I trail behind the others uncertainly as they lead the way. I glance at Ava, who keeps her voice low. "Are you sure this is safe?"

Matthew shrugs and keeps walking. He doesn't look as sure as he did the first time we stepped onto that elevator, but then again, those doors weren't plastered in warnings.

"I hope so," I reply.

The air in the cavernous room is warm, muggy, and thick with a strong chemical smell that reminds me of waking up in the hospital. The stone floor is cool and damp beneath my feet, and every sound echoes fiercely. A large pale-blue rectangle shimmers in the center, inlaid in the floor and dotted with other kids our age here and there. It's not crowded by any means.

"How tired are you?" Amari asks us.

The three of us exchange looks, certainly exhausted but afraid to bog down our new friends' cheery moods.

Grey nods knowingly and beckons us toward the far end of the room. "Come on, then. Hot tub first."

When we get closer, I can see there's a smaller pool of water inlaid in the floor. Jing places herself between Ava and me and hooks each of her arms through one of ours, guiding us to the water. She places one foot into the hot tub, where it lands on a wide step that goes all the way around.

"Come on," Jing giggles, "but go slow at first. It's *hot*."

"Captain Obvious over here," giggles Jordan to Ava, who grimaces in return.

Jing holds up her middle finger for Jordan to see. "They've never been in a hot tub before, genius."

Jordan blushes and looks away, but not before showing Jing his own middle finger. Ava, undoubtedly seeing a bit of herself in Jordan, leans toward him and asks kindly, "Is that why Grey said it was self-explanatory before?"

Jordan looks up at her and nods. "It's just a really big tub of hot water."

He shrugs and grins at her apparent fascination. Leaving Jing standing with one foot in the water, Ava leans down to inspect it. She dips one finger in gingerly, gasping.

"Wow, it really *is* hot! You have to feel this, Harper!"

Rather than bend fully over in front of all these boys my first time in a bikini, I slowly slide my right foot in. My eyes go wide.

"Geez, it almost burns!"

I pull my foot back out, and the skin is a little pink. Everyone laughs, including Matthew.

I cross my arms in front of my chest and glare at him. "All right, tough guy," I say pointedly, "let's see you try it."

His smile slips, but he nods resolutely.

"No big deal," he says, feigning casual confidence.

He doesn't dip in a finger or a toe. He doesn't even slowly lower one foot in. Instead, he walks all the way down the steps and sits, wincing faintly as the water rises above his shorts. The other boys hoot and holler, clapping, stomping, and even dancing at Matthew's apparent victory—right up until he leaps back out, redder than a summer tomato. He hunches over and puts his hands on his knees, panting like a dog.

Now, all of us are making noise. This must be the hardest I've ever laughed. My stomach hurts, and tears stream from my eyes. Even the boys are cracking up. Amari pokes Matthew in the ribs until he joins in the laughter. The other kids in the big pool are staring, trying to figure out what's causing all the commotion.

"Shh!" Ava reprimands us through her giggles. "People are looking!"

"Let 'em look," says Amari. "Pretty soon, everyone'll know 'how much fun you guys are!"

When we've mostly caught our breath, Jing tugs on my arm. "Okay, for real this time, go slow. You'll get used to it a little at a time, and then it'll help relax your muscles after that crazy fitness testing today."

This time around, we *all* go slow, especially Matthew. One step at a time, we gradually submerge ourselves in the steaming water. Then, Grey turns around and presses a large button in the floor a few feet from the edge of the hot tub. Suddenly, the whole pool fills with bubbles.

"If you position yourself right in front of the jets, where the water's coming out hard," Grey instructs, "it'll massage your back."

"Ooh, it feels really good," Ava practically sings.

Jing squirms around and gets settled in before she starts talking again, "Okay, now that everyone is comfy—"

"Jing!" Amari shoots her a warning look.

She puts her hands up. "I'm not asking anything invasive."

"She's okay, Amari," I say, "really."

He looks skeptical, but keeps quiet.

"I was just going to ask if there's anything you want to know about Elysium," Jing continues. "I don't know a lot about the surface, but I know it's really different from this place."

"No kidding!" Matthew says.

"I have a really random question, actually," I say, turning to face her.

She nods and gives me her full attention.

"When we met you this morning, you were talking about the cafeteria and all the great food, and you said—"

"The Chinese food's my favorite?" she asks.

"Yeah, but you said it was obvious. What's obvious about that?"

"Do you know what Chinese means?" she asks, looking amused.

All three of us new kids shake our heads.

"You've probably noticed that there are all kinds of different-looking people down here. All different colors and hair and everything?"

We nod along silently.

"The different kinds of people originally came from different places. My ancestors came from a country called China, so we're called Chinese."

"So Chinese food comes from China?" I ask.

"Yep! It's not really my favorite, though, unless I'm missing my mom's cooking. It's just a stupid joke I make when I'm nervous. That's when I talk the most, too."

"Hadn't noticed." I giggle, and she splashes me with hot water. "That must be why Amari felt the need to tell me that Jing means peace and quiet this morning."

Now it's Amari's turn to get splashed. "It means calm and serene, know-it-all!"

"You're not exactly either of those things, either," Amari smirks.

"It also means quiet," she whispers to me, "but I'm not about to let him know that."

Louder, she tells the entire group, "It's kind of an annoying name, though, honestly, and not just because it doesn't fully embody my spirit. I get that my parents wanted to give me a traditional Chinese name, but . . . couldn't they have picked one that everyone can spell? Nobody even speaks Mandarin for real anymore!"

"Why? How do people spell it?" Ava asks. "It seems easy enough to me: C-H-E-E-N-G, right?"

Jing shakes her head, and I chime in.

"Or I-N-G?"

She sighs heavily. "This is the exact problem I always have. It's actually spelled J-I-N-G. In Mandarin, my parents' language from China, they don't even use the same letters as English, but the J sounds like a CH to most English speakers. And I'm an English speaker! But I know it would hurt my mom's feelings if I changed it."

"That's . . . unexpected," Matthew says.

"I know," Jing replies. "All the English letters make a different sound than you'd expect when you put them into Mandarin words. My parents have been telling me my whole life that I should be frustrated with all the English speakers who don't bother to learn how to pronounce words in other languages, but a lot of times I just get frustrated with the name itself. I mean, we live in what's probably the last city on the planet, and English is our common language. You'd think they could've picked something you could spell in English."

"I think it's a really pretty name," I answer. "I mean, I get that it's probably really frustrating that no one ever spells it right, but I think I understand why they would pick something that's not English. I only know what we learned in orientation, but basically the whole world was destroyed by war, right?"

Jing nods.

"If we're really the only ones left, then it's up to us to keep everyone's cultures alive, right?"

Matthew and Amari both smile proudly. And the guilt eats away a pit in my stomach again.

"You sound just like my mom," Jing moans.

"Ugh." I laugh. "Not your mom! But seriously, though, it makes sense that they'd name you in their language. What's it called again?"

"Mandarin."

"Right, it makes sense that they'd give you a Mandarin name. They want you to feel connected to where you came from."

"I'd like to learn Mandarin," says Ava.

"You would?"

"Yeah, it sounds like a really cool language."

"Actually, we could all learn Mandarin together," Grey announces. "They offer classes in every language that's represented here. We could take it together!"

"That sounds like a great idea!" Matthew says. "How many different cultures are there in Elysium anyway?"

"I don't even know for sure," Amari answers. "There's definitely white people like you, Black people like me and Harper."

Black people? Why do they call us that?

"And Chinese people like Jing, but there are also people from a lot of other places. There are lots of different Asian people—people from the continent Asia—like Indian, Japanese, Korean, Vietnamese. And then there's Indigenous people, who were here from the beginning before any of the rest of our ancestors came here."

"Where are Black people from?" I ask. "And why do they call us that?"

Amari takes a deep breath. "That's a long story. Black people come from some different places originally, like Jamaica or Haiti, but mostly from Africa."

"Africa? So why aren't we called African then?"

"Uh," Amari looks around for help, but only Jing returns his gaze, and she looks just as flustered. "Right, well, they'll teach you more about it in your history class, but, like literally thousands of years ago, a bunch of white dudes kidnapped a bunch of African people and sold them as slaves."

I gasp. "What? Why didn't we learn about this back home?"

Matthew's face is full of sorrow. "We were Orphans, remember? They only taught us the things we needed to know to get through the Sending. They might've taught it to the other kids at regular school. I don't think we were there long enough to know."

"I hope they did."

"Anyway," Amari continues, "a lot of really bad stuff happened. A lot of really bad stuff happened to everyone who wasn't white back then, actually."

"It was pretty messed up," Grey inserts.

"For sure," Amari agrees. "But the point is that most of that disappeared with the Global Devastation. The people who had the problems all killed each other, but Elysium's founders had totally different priorities. That's why they named it Elysium—it's paradise, Heaven, a utopia. Everyone is equal here, and all cultures are equally important. Only the best of humanity survived, and we're lucky we were chosen to be here."

Our whole group goes silent for a few minutes. We all stare into space digesting what we've just heard. It sounds like Earth was a really messed-up place before the war. I'm almost glad they all died, but that makes me feel like a terrible person.

Before long, we're talking and laughing again. The pool feels ice-cold after the hot tub, but only for a couple minutes. Our new friends teach us a little bit about swimming, since we've never been near enough water to learn, but mostly we just splash and float and relax. Eventually, we go to the dining hall for dinner, and Jing introduces me to Chinese food. She tells me which things are most like what her mom makes at home. I can't even believe how delicious it all is!

After dinner, we say our goodbyes. Grey, Amari, and Jing all have a lot of homework to get done before school tomorrow, and Grey doesn't want to leave Jordan on his own. When we get back to our rooms, we crash hard. Ava and I lie down in bed and turn on the TV, but I fall asleep so fast that I don't remember a single thing we watched when I wake up the next morning.

12

BREAKDOWN

The next morning my body does not want to get out of bed. Even though I'm sore all over, I stretch and head to the shower. I still smell like whatever chemical they put in that pool, and my hair and skin feel dry and itchy. I catch a glimpse of my reflection on my way past the mirror and gasp, catching Ava's attention. A hoarse cackle interrupts her yawn when she spots my dark frizz sticking out every which way.

Can't believe I forgot to wear my bonnet to bed!

Ava and I dress and get ready in relative silence today. She must be just as exhausted as I am. When there's a knock at the door, I open it abruptly, expecting to see Matthew waiting impatiently. Instead, there's Jing with bright eyes, a huge smile, and a tall stack of something I can only assume is our breakfast.

"Take one before I drop them all!"

The round tower leans to one side and then the other. I pick one up and examine it. It's small with a hole in the middle. Almost the color of the inside of a loaf of bread, it's coated in something white and crusty that makes my fingers sticky.

"I can't hold them. You gotta take another one!" Jing

declares as she glides into the room, as if on wheels. It reminds me of racing with books on our heads when we were little. You had to be fast to win, but you also had to keep all the books steady. I grab another one in my other hand as Ava reaches out and relieves Jing of half of the remaining items.

"What are these anyway?" I inquire, sniffing one warily.

"Donuts! Try a bite!" Jing sinks her teeth into one and lets out a low, pleased hum, closing her eyes in ecstasy.

I'm still sniffing mine when Ava calls out, "Oh, my Sovereign, this is the best thing I've ever tasted! It's so sweet! You have to try it, Harper!"

I've never tasted anything like it. It's sweeter even than Mama's birthday cakes. Of course, honey wasn't something we had a lot of, so we sweetened things sparingly up there. To make something *this* sweet . . .

"Where do they keep all the bees?" I mumble through a full mouth.

"What bees?" Jing cocks her head like a puppy.

"For the honey," I supply.

"To make the donuts so sweet," Ava adds.

Jing giggles. "Oh, we don't use much honey around here. We grow sugar cane on the greenhouse floor. It's a plant that you get sugar from. I *do* like honey, though."

Ava and I share a look and shrug in unison.

"It's really good!" I say.

"And there are perks—like we can eat and walk, so we won't be late."

I check my watch. "We're ten minutes early."

Jing pushes us out the door. "Not if we're taking the long way."

Ava and I turn right and start down the hallway, eating

and chatting. Ava stops dead and makes a face.

"What's wrong?"

"Where's Jing?"

We both turn around to find her still standing right outside our door, smirking.

"What are you waiting for then? Come on!" Jing beckons us to follow and takes off in the opposite direction.

We share a bemused look before trotting off to catch up with her.

"What about Matthew?" I ask.

"What about him?" Jing answers playfully.

"Shouldn't we go get him?"

"Nah, I sent him off with the guys before I even knocked on your door. I thought us girls needed a little privacy."

"Oh . . . What for?" Ava asks.

Privacy is rarer than honey back home.

Jing peeks around the next corner, ensuring that we're alone before she replies. "Something was bothering Harper last night, and she wouldn't tell me with all the *boys* around."

She wrinkles up her nose at the word boys like she just walked into a fog of skunk spray. Ava turns to me, concerned.

"You were upset last night? I thought we were having fun." Worry fills her glassy eyes like tears.

"So what's up, Harp?" Jing asks gently.

I sigh. "It's not that big of a deal. It's just—well, me and Matthew were courting back home. We ended our first date right before the Sov . . . uh, soldiers came and took us. But now everything's so different."

Jing nods. Ava stares. I realize we've stopped walking and are standing inside a very private little alcove that you might not even notice unless you knew to look for it. I sit on the floor, and the other two follow suit.

"I don't know. Our whole life just got turned upside-down. I don't know if falling in love and getting married is all that important right now."

Jing's eyes grow wide and she mouths *Married?* across me to Ava, who nods solemnly.

"Courting made sense when we had families and school and everything was, well, settled. We knew what to expect from our lives for the first time ever, and it turned out to be wrong. Everything's so confusing now."

I sigh and shrug. "He hasn't held my hand or kissed my cheek or been even remotely romantic with me since we woke up here. And I've been getting so annoyed with him about these little things he's always done. They were annoying before we got together, and then it didn't bother me so much. It felt like he'd changed or something, but now it's all driving me nuts all over again."

"Like what?" Ava asks.

"Like how he knows something about everything or tries to jump in and do everything for me. I'm not helpless. I can do plenty of things on my own!"

"Of course you can, Harper," Jing says. "I don't know Matthew very well yet, but I don't get the impression that he's trying to look down on anyone."

"No, he's not," Ava agrees with her. "He just likes to be helpful. He knows all of this has been hard. I think it's just his way of being there for you."

"It's a little overbearing," I tell them.

The silence hangs in the air.

"Harper, I think you have to talk to Matthew," Ava advises.

"I know. I know I do. But it's hard. What if he gets mad that I've been annoyed with him? Or what if he stopped liking me after the barn dance, and I've just been too stupid to take the hint? What if I don't want to be with him anymore, and I don't know it until he tells me we should stay together?"

"That sounds really confusing. No wonder you've been upset," Jing finally says.

The moment the first tear lands on the back of my hand, two sets of warm arms wrap around me. Jing gently pulls my head onto her shoulder, and I cry there for a moment. Finally, I lift my head, sniffle, and wipe my nose on the inside of my shirt where no one will see it.

"I don't think I could handle either option. Either he stopped liking me a long time ago, or I break his heart because I'm not sure anymore. I hope he hates me. I deserve it."

"Stop that right now," Jing commands, holding her hand up. "You don't deserve that at all."

Ava nods so vigorously she looks like her eyes might pop out of her head. "Harper, you know Matthew has only ever tried to do what's right. He would never put any pressure on you. He only wants you to be happy."

"That just makes it so much worse," I moan, attempting to stifle a new sob.

"That's just the guilt talking," Jing says.

"It's totally the guilt," I reply, knowing the issue but not how to fix it. "The guilt is overwhelming!"

"I know," Ava says, standing up. "But you haven't done anything wrong."

"And we're here for you, no matter what happens," Jing says, squeezing me tighter.

"You guys are kind of the best," I say, wrapping my arms around them both.

"Oh, shoot! Now we really will be late," Ava laments.

"Nah, we'll just tell Mr. Weiss you guys got lost, and I came to find you and help you get to school. No big deal."

I still don't know how to feel about Matthew and Amari and dating and this whole big, new life, but I do know one thing now. Even though I don't have a Mama or a Papa anymore, I definitely still have a family. And it's growing.

13

A NEW MESSAGE

After finding the treehouse empty with blood on the floor, John and Maggie scoured the surrounding forest. Finding nothing, they returned to town as quickly as their tired legs would carry them, hoping against hope that their children were found and waiting for them there. As they approached the town meeting hall, they heard someone shouting. John quickly spotted Caleb, a nineteen-year-old young man, standing on top of the large brick building that housed the meeting hall.

Caleb continued shouting and gesturing frantically, but his words were unintelligible. John shook his head and raised his hands high into a shrug. He gestured for the boy to come down, while the boy, in turn, signaled for John and Maggie to come up onto the roof.

Exasperated and exhausted, John and Maggie exchanged looks. Maggie sighed. "I suppose we should go and see what he's shouting about."

The pair strode toward the ladder on the side of the meeting hall and willed their weary bodies toward the roof. Young Caleb's words were clearer now. He had found a message.

"What's this about, Caleb? Why are you up here in the first place?" John demanded, directly but not unkindly.

"I was coming back to the meeting hall, and I thought I was noticing a strange pattern in the town square, like someone had carved something into the ground. Just look." Caleb pointed to the square below.

In all the commotion, the people must have missed it. Everything had seemed out of place when they woke that morning. The strange ruts and grooves flowing throughout the square had barely even registered. In the ground, carved in large letters that could only be read from high above, was a message.

WE TOOK WHAT WAS OWED.
REPENT OR PAY THE PRICE.

A strong, independent woman like Maggie was not prone to fainting, but she felt her heart flutter and feared she might collapse. John, sensing her distress, wrapped his arms around her from behind.

"John, what have we done? First Sammy, and now Harper and Ava. We've lost our little girls!" She turned around and wept into his shoulder.

"Caleb, Maggie and I have been all over the woods. We're exhausted and obviously upset. You'll need to ring the bell to call everyone back. Get the rest of the Council up here. They need to see this," John commanded.

Caleb nodded and rushed to descend the ladder at the side of the building. Maggie dropped to her knees, and John lowered himself to sit with her. He held her close and stroked her dark curls while she sobbed against him.

Within minutes, the meeting bell rang, and people started appearing in the square and entering the meeting hall. One by one, the other elders materialized on the roof, scrutinizing the *message written in the square.*

Whispers spread among the small group, growing steadily louder as the group grew in size. Several of them visibly shrank back when they saw Elder Samson climbing the ladder to join them. When he finally appeared over the edge of the roof, he faced them with a perturbed look on his face.

"We've been out searching for missing folks all day. I've barely had any rest. Now the sun's about to set, and you're demanding I climb a building. What's all this nonsense about?" His voice was sour and demanding.

Elder Johnson spoke up first, her face a few shades paler than usual. "It seems the search parties have found everyone, except the ten Orphans. And now . . . well, there's a new message."

She gestured toward the square as Samson raised his bushy gray eyebrows. He swept around and gazed down at the ground a hundred feet below them. His form appeared to sink in on itself, and he looked defeated. All of a sudden, he turned on them, railing against the Council's decisions of the past few months.

"This! This is what we tried to warn you about! We told you the Sovereign were real. This was not some archaic ritual with no point or purpose!"

Elder Prewitt joined in next, ranting alongside his partner of thirty years.

"We knew no good would come of any of this! You"—he pointed an accusatory finger at Maggie—"You started all of this! With your hysterical ideas about the personhood of Orphans and giving justice to the children. You're the one to blame!"

John was on his feet now, standing nose to nose with the old man. "How dare you speak to my wife that way!"

"How dare I?" retorted Isaac. "How dare you defy the

authority of your Elders? Presuming you know better than we do."

Maggie continued to sit, weeping. In a small, resigned voice, she said, "They're right, John. This is my fault. I led the charge to give the Orphans homes and make them real people. I led the movement to stop the Sending. I'm responsible for everything that's happened."

The other Elders stood silent, horrified looks on all their faces as realization crept in. They had gone along with Maggie's plans. They had agreed with her, thought the Sending was a pointless sacrifice to imaginary gods that would accomplish nothing. They had, each one of them, conspired to change their community's laws. They had brought the people together and forced the rest of the Council's hand. They had thought they were saving innocent children, but now it was clear that they had doomed everyone else to certain punishment. Three hundred years ago, the Sovereign cut off the people's crops, and they nearly starved. Now, it would seem They had something even worse in mind. What could possibly be worse than slowly starving and watching your children die?

Elder Marcus attempted to swallow, though his throat was dry and tight. His voice came out in the faintest croak. "We'll have to tell the people."

The others nodded their agreement. Isaac and Samson looked quite pleased with themselves, but the remaining Elders looked as though they were about to receive a death sentence. And who could know? It wasn't outside the realm of possibility.

14

ASSIGNMENTS

By the time we get to school, the lobby has already emptied. Only a few kids are still in the hallways. Mr. Weiss stands in the middle of the lobby, looking stern. Beside him, Matthew makes a face that tells me everything I need to know. We're in for it, or maybe Jing is.

Jing pulls the most worried expression I think I've ever seen. She looks so sincere that I'd think she was telling the truth if I didn't know any better.

"Oh, Mr. Weiss," she cries, "Ava and Harper took a wrong turn on their way to school this morning. They ended up lost on the other end of the floor, by where the little kids go to school. When they weren't here, I went to their room to find them, but they were already gone. It took me ages to find where they'd ended up, and once I did, we were already late."

Jing's eyes glisten with tears. She is a much better actress than I'll ever be.

Mr. Weiss must be eating this up. Concern spreads across his face. "Well, I'm so glad you found them, Jing! You girls better remember to bring your floor map with you until you get the hang of things, okay?"

"Yes, Mr. Weiss," Ava and I say with deference.

"Jing, you'd better hurry to class."

She nods and starts to walk away, turning back to wink at me over her shoulder.

"Oh, and Jing?" Mr. Weiss calls after her. "You'd better stop by my office after school today to serve your detention for that little lie."

Jing deflates immediately. "Okay."

Shoulders sagging, she continues down the hall and turns a corner.

Mr. Weiss winks at me and Ava. "You get a pass for today since you're new, but make sure you're on time from now on, okay?"

"Yes, sir," I say.

"No need for sirs and ma'ams around here, Harper. Mr. Weiss is almost too formal for my taste. All right, I have the results from yesterday's tests, and I have to tell you that you are some of the most impressive Orphans we've ever seen. Most students who come from the Orphan Home have only religious knowledge of the mythological Sovereign, but you three are very well rounded, even advanced in some areas."

We beam at him but stay silent, waiting for more information.

"We'll need to place you in an accelerated history class to help you learn our history and the history of the world before Elysium. It will move at a very fast pace, hence *accelerated*, but I doubt that will be a problem for any of you. There are some sciences you'll need to catch up on as well, but your learning gaps are much smaller than what we normally see. Do you do a lot of reading?"

"I've read everything in the library about birds, Mr.

Weiss," Ava offers.

"I've read pretty much everything in the library," Matthew replies, "and I'm pretty sure Harper used to sneak books out into the woods all the time."

"How did you know that?" I demand.

"You *really* want to know how Matthew knows so much about you?" Ava teases.

Matthew blushes and looks away.

"Well, it served you all well. The trouble you'll find is that the people above-ground lost a lot of knowledge in the past decades. Without access to electricity and other technology, they had to move backward to more primitive ways of doing things. Plus, survival was their main objective, for obvious reasons, so a lot of science and history wasn't exactly relevant for them.

"It might seem difficult at first, but I think you'll all catch up with relative ease. It will be a lot of homework and studying, though, so be prepared. It looks like you'll be able to join math classes with your same-aged peers, and all of your reading and writing skills are well beyond the usual level, even for Elysian children.

"Let's talk about your pathways. You'll have some say in what fields you choose for your careers, of course, but students usually begin apprenticeships the fall after they turn twelve. If I'm not mistaken, that's not too far off for you, Ava. Normally our children have been thinking about their skills and interests for a long time, but the Orphans from the surface obviously haven't had that opportunity. You'll be missing some of the background knowledge you need to begin your apprenticeship on time unless you do some very fast catching up.

"Matthew and Harper, you'll find yourselves at even

more of a disadvantage since your peers have been apprenticing for nearly two years already. You'll need to take extra classes over the summer to get up to speed and then work very hard in the fall when you begin apprenticing. Do you think you're up for it?"

I swallow, but nod along nervously with the others. *I'm smart. I can handle this . . . right?*

"Since you've missed out on all the career education we do at younger ages, it will be difficult for you to make an informed decision about your futures here. Because of that, you will be placed into a pathway based on your aptitudes and the result of your skills and interest surveys, but you'll have choices about where you'd like to go within those pathways.

"For example, there's not just one career possible in biological sciences. It spans everything from agriculture to healthcare to veterinary medicine. Technology, education, safety and security—they all have a lot of different directions you can go within them. That being said, here are the pathways you're being assigned.

"Ava, you're being assigned to Biological Sciences. Since Elysian students usually start their pathway when they're eleven, you won't have as much catching up to do."

Ava grins, obviously pleased with her assignment.

Mr. Weiss continues. "Matthew, you'll be in Technological Sciences. You have a clear talent for understanding how things work."

Matthew nods. "I'd love to go into computers or engineering or maybe—"

Mr. Weiss smiles knowingly. "You'll have plenty of opportunities to explore your options so you can make an informed decision, Matthew. Not to worry! Now, Harper, for you there's been a special request."

"A request?" I ask.

"Yes, General Yarrow herself personally requested that you be placed in Safety and Security."

My brow furrows. "Who's General Yarrow?"

"Elysium's Secretary of Defense. She is the leader of our military and all our security operations. In fact, she's requested to speak with you face to face later today. I'm sure it sounds strange to you, but you should consider it a real honor. It's unheard of for a student to be specifically requested for any pathway, especially by a government leader."

I gulp. "So, this is a really big deal then?"

Mr. Weiss chuckles. "You could say that, yes. I think she's looking for more from you than a simple security guard. To be chosen like this signifies that you're of a higher caliber. She'll likely want you to specialize in a specific area—technology or medicine or something like that. Is there anything you think you'd like to specialize in?"

I shake my head, blinking furiously. "I wouldn't even begin to know what the options are. Like you said, we've barely ever had the opportunity to think about what we'd do with adult lives. There were only about two months when we even thought we'd have adult lives, you know, before we were taken."

"That's completely true and totally understandable. I assume General Yarrow will give you more details that can help you make your decision this afternoon. But until then, let's get started on some basics."

Mr. Weiss leads us back to the same empty classroom

where we took all our tests yesterday. Here, he begins teaching us the history and science we have to catch up on. When a disembodied bell rings, the door opens and Jing, Jordan, and Amari enter.

"You wanted to see us, Mr. Weiss?" Amari says.

"Yes, I'll need you to escort Ava, Matthew, and Harper to their next classes, please."

He hands each of us a packet of papers. On top of my packet is a schedule of classes, then a map of the school, and what looks like a bunch of information about my classes and the Safety and Security pathway. Jing takes me to the Algebra class that we share. When it's over, she walks me to an English class full of mostly older kids. She doesn't have this class with me, so she hurries off to wherever she needs to be next.

After English is lunch, followed by some kind of physical training class. This one's in the gym where we did all our physical testing yesterday. Looking around, I realize I don't recognize anyone. These kids are all older and, honestly, kind of huge. I know I'm fast and strong, but I do not have the kinds of muscles these kids all have.

What am I doing here?

When the bell rings, the instructor immediately blows a whistle and starts shouting.

"Today, we'll be working agility and climbing drills. We also have a new teammate joining us." He points his clipboard at me. "This is Harper. You may know her as the girl who broke Corporal Collins' nose."

The class erupts in cheers and laughter, but I swear I hear a comment or two about my size thrown in.

Yeah, I'm small. So what? I'll show these dummies a thing or two.

As it turns out, agility drills involve a lot of running while weaving, bobbing, jumping over, diving under, or otherwise avoiding obstacles. Sometimes, those obstacles are giant seventeen-year-old boys who are trying to tackle you. One of them moves to take me down, but I leap over him, grabbing onto the rope dangling from the ceiling just behind him. I easily make my way to the top, where I ring the bell to score a point for my team.

The shrill sound of a whistle rips through the air.

"Harper!" I hear the instructor shout. Still at the top of the rope, I turn to look at him. He waves me over with his clipboard, and I notice a terrifying woman in a uniform standing next to him. Putting the soles of my sneakers against the wall, I rappel down the rope. Seconds later, my feet are back on solid ground.

When I reach the two adults in the room, Coach blows his whistle yet again. "All right, everyone, back at it!"

The room erupts in fresh movement. Shouts, grunts, and the squeaking of shoes permeate the space.

"Yes, sir?" I ask. The woman standing next to Coach looks pleased, but somehow still terrifying.

"Harper, this is General Yarrow. She'd like to talk with you."

"Incredible display out there! Pleased to meet you, Harper." General Yarrow holds out her hand.

"Uh, yes ma'am. It's nice to meet you, too," I reply, pressing my sweaty palm to hers for an uncomfortable handshake.

"You can use my office, General," Coach says.

"Thank you." General Yarrow leaves the gym, leading me down the hall to a small office.

Like Mr. Weiss' office, it's somewhat cramped. A desk

stands in the middle with a large chair behind it and two smaller chairs in front. General Yarrow surprisingly sits in one of the smaller chairs, turning it to face the other. She gestures for me to sit.

"Now, Harper, you're likely already aware that I put in a special request to have you placed in the Safety and Security training program."

I nod, but she doesn't acknowledge it. She simply continues on.

"Your skills are very impressive, and I don't just mean the way you handled yourself when you believed your village was being attacked. Although, many of us were delighted with the way Corporal Collins looked on his return."

I can't help but grin alongside her.

"We've been watching your whole life. I'm sure it won't surprise you to hear that we surveil the entire surrounding region for threats of any kind, and that means that we keep an eye on your people as well. You've always been strong, fast, and decisive. You can make hard decisions based on logic, instead of always going whichever direction your emotions push you. On top of that, you're smart, and you're a leader. People trust you, look up to you. You could do a lot of very good things for Elysium and for your community back home."

"Okay," I say hesitantly.

"There are a lot of options within Safety and Security—Mr. Weiss no doubt gave you an informational packet this morning—but the one I really want you to consider is Black Ops. You can't repeat any of this to your friends, mind you. It's all highly classified. But another one of your skills is keeping secrets, isn't it?"

I nod, bewildered.

"What's Black Ops?"

"Black Ops is a special sector of our military. They run classified missions of the highest importance. Only our most skilled soldiers are ever approved. It was a Black Ops team that brought you here. Of course, you'd have to work your way up. There's no Black Ops apprenticeship, but I think you'd make an excellent operative."

"I'd have to work my way up." I think out loud. "So what does that mean? Where would I start?"

"Well, you'd start by taking classes, of course—history, government, technology, basic medical training. After what I saw a few minutes ago, I don't think physical training is going to be much of a problem. Your performance between now and the fall term will give us an idea of what kind of apprenticeship will be appropriate for you. You might start in basic security, policing the halls of the city. You could start in the surveillance offices, or maybe even with field work outdoors, securing our perimeter.

"The most important thing, besides maintaining high marks in your coursework, will be proving your loyalty and dedication to Elysium. Like I said, Black Ops work is highly sensitive and involves our most difficult assignments. Soldiers must not only be highly skilled in a variety of areas, but they must also be beyond trustworthy. Do you understand?"

"Yes, ma'am," I say.

"One more thing, Harper," she says. "A lot of these teachers around here are going to try to get you to talk to them informally. I don't recommend that. It's not how we do things in the military."

"Of course, ma'am," I say. "Uh, before we go, could I

ask you another question?"

General Yarrow nods.

"What kinds of assignments does Black Ops do?"

"That is classified."

"I understand. But then, how will I know if it's something I want to do?"

"I have a nose for these things, Harper. You just take your classes and pay attention to which things you like the most. Trust me, you want to do this."

General Yarrow stands and walks out of the room. She's halfway down the hall by the time I collect myself enough to follow.

"Keep up the good work, Harper," she calls without turning around, somehow sensing that I've left the office.

"I'll be watching. And remember"—General Yarrow taps the side of her nose and then points at me—"classified."

15

MISUNDERSTANDING

When I emerge from my therapy session in Julia's office, Jing is waiting for me in the hall. I slipped her a note at the end of the school day, asking her to meet me here alone at the end of my session, and here she is.

"I told Ava I wanted to do my homework during your session so we could all hang out together tonight." Jing shrugs. "What's up?"

"Ava's birthday is next week." I try to continue, but Jing interrupts me by shrieking and jumping up and down.

"Okay, okay, settle down," I urge, my eyes bulging with embarrassment. "I guess birthdays are pretty important here?"

Jing raises an eyebrow. "Are they not important where you're from?"

"No, they are. I mean, for the regular kids," before I quietly add, "just not for the Orphans."

"Oh," Jing says, suddenly pensive. "Oh."

I can tell she's realizing this would've been her, too. No birthdays, no special occasions, no real clothes. No name. She's never asked about our numbers, which is pretty surprising for someone who's so curious about our lives before. I don't exactly know how to respond to all that, so I decide to shake it off.

"Anyway," I say, changing the subject back to Ava, "it was going to be a really big deal at home—the first birthday we got to celebrate outside the Orphan Home—and I want to make it really special for Ava."

"Yeah, of course! We can do all kinds of amazing things for her. What are her favorite things?"

We talk all the way back to my room. By the time we get there, Jing and I have the most incredible surprise birthday party planned for Ava. She'll be beside herself if we manage to pull this off. She'll never even see it coming.

About an hour later, we meet the whole gang for dinner in the cafeteria. A lot of kids eat in their rooms or with their families in the evenings, so it's not very crowded. At a large round table for eight, I grab a seat next to Jing. I expect Ava to sit on my other side as usual, but I turn just in time to catch Amari sliding in next to me. Ava glares at him from a few feet away and sits next to Jing instead.

Matthew, settling into the chair on Amari's other side, has a strange expression on his face. Whatever's on his mind, he doesn't mention it. Instead, he asks, "So how'd it go with General . . . Arrow? I never got the chance to ask you this afternoon between pathway classes and your therapy session."

"General Yarrow," I correct him, glancing at Amari curiously out of the corner of my eye. "She definitely recruited me for Safety and Security, but I'm not allowed to say much about it. I told her I'm not sure I know enough about it to know if it's what I want to do, and get this—she said *she* knows it's what I want to do! Can you believe that?"

"Yeah," Amari says seriously. "I can. General Yarrow's a beast. She watches like a hawk, and she *knows* people. You can't pull one over on her. Ever."

"She can't possibly know me better than I know myself, can she?" I ask incredulously.

"You'd be surprised," Gray replies through a mouthful of bread.

"If General Yarrow says you want to do it—" Jordan starts.

"—then you want to do it," Jing finishes.

"Like, because I'll get in trouble if I don't do what she says?" I ask, fear creeping into me.

"No, nothing like that," Jing says.

"Well," Amari says, raising his eyebrows.

I round on him, silently pleading.

"I mean, she *is* the most powerful person in Elysium," he answers.

"I thought that was Dr. Tori," Matthew posits.

"Nah, Dr. Tori runs the research and the hospital," Gray says, "but General Yarrow's the real powerhouse."

"They work together really closely, though," Jing offers.

"But Dr. Tori's not *in charge*," Amari says. "Sure, General Yarrow makes a lot of decisions based off Dr. Tori's information, but she's still the one calling the shots, isn't she?"

Heads nod all around the table, as Matthew, Ava, and I quickly become even more astonished.

"You mean, she's like the leader of the Council?" Ava asks with wide eyes.

"Nah, we don't have a Council," Jordan replies.

"The military runs things around here," Amari explains. "It's how we've stayed safe enough to keep our technology going all this time. But honestly, I can't believe you met General Yarrow *in person*."

"I know! How've I not asked you about this yet?" Jing exclaims. I shoot her a look, and she shuts up fast, not wanting to spoil Ava's surprise.

"What's she like?" Jordan asks.

"She's"—I think for a second—"She's kind of intimidating at first, you know, with the uniform and medals and all that—"

"Plus the whole president of Elysium thing," Amari chides snarkily.

Ignoring him, I continue. "But when it's just the two of you, she's actually kind of funny."

This time, it's the Elysians who look astonished. Jaws drop all around.

"She's *funny*?" Gray asks.

I raise my eyebrows and nod in amusement.

"I didn't even know she was famous!" I snort. "She was making jokes about me beating up Corporal Collins."

The entire table roars until everyone in the dining hall is staring. Once Gray catches his breath, he says, "She must really like you."

Everyone is still laughing when Amari casually puts an arm around me. I freeze, eyes wide. I look at his hand draped over my right shoulder, then at him on my left, and back at his hand. *Why is he acting like this is perfectly normal?* No one else seems to notice except for Matthew, who's staring at us. Deciding not to make a big deal of it, I flick Amari's hand off my shoulder so his arm drops. He cocks his head at me in a silent question, and I feel my eyebrows draw together as I make my what-do-you-think-you're-doing face and shake my head.

The next thing I know, the entire table has gone silent. Everyone is watching me and Matthew stare at Amari, who is growing steadily more uncomfortable by the moment. He pulls his hands into his lap and caves in a little, his face now devoid of its previous smile.

"Amari, what are you doing?" Ava accuses.

"I was wondering the same thing," Matthew says, a little louder than necessary. His face is mottled and red. He looks like he's been trying to hold his breath for too long.

Amari doesn't answer. He stares at his plate but lets his eyes flick up toward Grey, pleading for help.

"I saw what you just did to her!" Matthew declares angrily.

"We all saw it, Matthew," Gray says calmly. "I don't mean any disrespect, but I don't understand why you're so upset."

"Why wouldn't we be upset?" Ava shouts. "Amari, how could you?"

Then Jing speaks up, slowly, gently. "Ava, stop. That's not helpful. We're not on the surface right now. The rules are different here."

Ava's mouth snaps shut.

"I swear, I didn't mean anything bad," Amari says to me. "I thought we liked each other, that's all. That's how we let someone know we're interested down here. I didn't even think about it being different on the surface."

I gulp, barely even knowing what to say. "It's not just that. It's . . . well . . ."

Jing takes over for me, somehow sounding almost as

uncomfortable as I do. "Harper and Matthew were kind of . . . together . . . before they came here."

Amari groans. "I feel like such an asshole. I had no idea!" He slides his chair backward so he can see me and Matthew at the same time. "I'm really sorry, you guys. I really didn't know you were a couple. I swear, I never would've made a move if I'd known. Please believe me."

Matthew shakes his head and gets up from the table. "Unbelievable." He storms out of the room. Amari starts to follow, but I stop him.

"Just let him go," I say. "He'll get over it. He just needs a little time. I'm sorry if I gave you the wrong idea."

Amari sighs. "No, it's not your fault. I was being a jerk. I really didn't know you guys were dating, I swear."

"I can't blame you for that. We definitely don't act like we're together. He and I have some things to work out. Just let me talk to him first, okay?"

Amari nods and returns to his chair. I think it's safe to say our dinner is ruined. I clear my dishes and head back to the dorm to have the dreaded talk with Matthew.

16

PENITENCE

"We'll have silence!" Elder Marcus demanded of the crowd.

Chaos had erupted in the large meeting hall as soon as the people heard about the dismal new message carved into the square. People were screaming, threatening the Elders and one another, and generally losing their minds.

Normally, Maggie's voice would be the one to get the crowd back in line, but she hadn't spoken a word since the rooftop meeting. It took some time and several attempts, but Marcus was able to quiet them.

"Now then, we must identify our next steps and take immediate action if we are to avoid the Sovereign's wrath," Marcus informed the assembly.

Isaac stepped forward to make a suggestion. "First and foremost, we must remove the Elders who stopped the Sending from the Council. They should be replaced by those who are more faithful."

Shouts of agreement echoed through the chamber. The remaining Elders' faces were downcast and pale. Although no one was calling for the death penalty at present, they could only imagine how much worse things were about to get.

"A vote!" Isaac shouted, and nearly every hand in the room

was raised in favor.

Immediately, nominations for replacements came flooding in. All five replacements chosen were men, older and deeply devoted to the ideals and values of Sovereign worship. It seemed clear that the community no longer trusted the judgment of strong women. The new Elders joined the floor, but those who were just voted out had not been allowed to leave.

"There is a question of punishment," Samson declared. "Is removal from the Council enough to soften the Sovereign's wrath?"

All around the room, heads shook from side to side. Of course, the people would demand blood. They wouldn't get away so easily. The crowd shouted suggestions, and the new Elders seemed to drink them in. One new Elder, Josiah, spoke out.

"Death removes the opportunity for repentance. The Sovereign have demanded that we show sorrow over our actions, and who better to express true sorrow than those who instigated our current circumstances? No, they should not be put to death. They should, instead, show suffering through life."

John breathed a sigh of relief, but Maggie knew there would be more.

"What do you propose to do with us, Elder Josiah?" Maggie inquired, keeping her eyes glued to the floor.

"An excellent question, my dear Margaret," Josiah replied. "I do believe we have received many fine suggestions already. You have already been stripped of your power and position. I propose that you should be moved into different housing, rather than remaining in your large Council homes. You should live a simple and modest life to show your penitence. You will don the burlap attire of Orphans to show that you no longer consider

yourselves worthy of the community's respect, and you shall live out your lives separately from us. There should, of course, be additional punishment. Perhaps the loss of a finger would do? It would serve as a lifelong reminder of your arrogance and wrongdoing."

Applause erupted among the townspeople. Maggie, never once raising her eyes from the floor, simply nodded in resignation. Tears wet her ashen cheeks before the mob swept her away. Her fingers made a valiant attempt to keep her husband's grasp, but they could not hold one another tightly enough. People grappled with her as she fought against them and strained to find her husband's face. He was nowhere to be seen. The physical pressure against her body was intense. No amount of struggle would save her. Instead, she gave in and let herself be carried out into the square.

There, someone had brought a large stump onto the stage that had been used to honor the Orphans and their families just twenty-four hours ago. They laid Maggie's left hand upon the stump, a large man holding her wrist so she could not move it. Elder Isaac appeared beside her with a large cleaver. Now, Maggie could see John's face in the crowd. He was shouting and pushing, trying to get to her, but there wouldn't be enough time. As the cleaver came down on her index finger, Maggie's scream echoed throughout the village. The last thing she saw was the tears soaking John's graying beard. He had finally made it to her, moments too late.

When Maggie regained consciousness, Sophie was beside her, tending to her missing finger. Other healers were working on the other four disgraced Elders to ensure proper healing and avoid infection. But why was everyone still here in the square? They had received their punishments. What else was there to watch?

A shriek tore through the air, and Maggie became aware of a loud snapping sound nearby. Peering around, she discovered Anna Aaron, Matthew's adoptive mother, being flogged on the stage by Elder Samson. With each crack of the whip, poor Mrs. Aaron cried out anew. The back of her dress was ripped, and angry red welts showed through the fabric. When blood began to dot her bodice, Samson stopped, and another adoptive couple was forced onto the stage. They were each given lashes until blood was drawn—the husband always first so he would be too weak to protect his wife. The crowd cheered in sickening fashion. The people who only yesterday revered and honored these families now celebrated brutal violence against them.

Sophie clicked her tongue in apparent disgust. Maggie looked at her with a question in her eyes. Surely disagreement wouldn't be safe for Sophie.

"I cannot abide violence," she muttered under her breath, watching Maggie's face for a hint of reaction. Maggie only dared blink at her to show she had heard.

"Can't do anything about it but keep you all alive, though." She shook her head sadly, checking over her work before she got up and went to tend to Mr. and Mrs. Aaron's wounds.

When the floggings were over, Maggie could only hope that the people were finally sated. Elder Josiah now came onto the stage, wringing his hands with an approving look on his face.

"This day, you have witnessed the punishment of those who caused harm to our community. It is with great sorrow that we have enacted this punishment, but what other choice do we have? The blasphemers who ended the Sending and took in the Holy Orphans as real children will be separated from our community from this day forward. They will be rehoused and wear special dress to indicate their low status. They will be shunned. You are not to speak to them or help them in any way.

They will receive the last rations and be as the least among us."
Cheering.

Those people were our friends, *Maggie thought*. What's become of them?

Maggie felt that she would be sick, but only partly from the blood loss. John sat with her, cooing over her and stroking her hair. Try as he might, he could bring his wife little comfort. The new Council had made one thing quite clear to everyone in the village: Those who defied the Sovereign or questioned the traditions of the Elders would be punished severely. There would be no escape.

17

MATTHEW

I stand outside Matthew's door awkwardly for several minutes before I work up the courage to knock.

"Hey," I say when he comes to the door.

"Hey," Matthew replies.

"I'm sorry about what happened back there. I swear I didn't do anything to encourage him," I blurt out. "Amari feels really bad."

"He should feel bad. You don't just put your arm around a girl you hardly know without permission!" He's clearly still fuming.

I shrug, helpless. "That's how they do things here."

"Well, it's not how we do things."

We make eye contact, and I see a lot more than anger there. "Matthew," I say softly, putting a hand on his arm.

He wipes away a tear, hurt and confusion spreading across his handsome features. "He really didn't know?"

I shake my head. "Did you tell him?"

"No, but . . ."

"We don't exactly act like a couple. You haven't even said two words to me about courting since we got here. I have no idea how you've been feeling or thinking about me. How could anyone else possibly know?"

"I guess we have some things we need to talk about," Matthew says.

"Yeah, I guess we do."

He moves out of the way and gestures for me to come in. We sit in awkward silence for the next few agonizing minutes. I have no idea how Matthew spends this time, since I just stare at my knees. Finally, he clears his throat, and I feel his weight shift across the couch cushions. In my peripheral vision, I can see that he's turned his whole body toward me.

"I don't want to put any pressure on you," he starts.

"I was afraid maybe you didn't like me anymore."

"I've always liked you," he says with far more certainty than I've felt in the past weeks. "I think I always will."

"How can you possibly know that?" I turn and look him in the eye.

Matthew shrugs and looks embarrassed. "I just do. You've always been a constant in my life. You've always been so certain about everything—"

"I've hardly ever been certain of anything in my life!"

That look of hurt is back. "Not even me?"

There are my knees again. Swathed in denim. Safe to look at. No tears forming in the corners of their eyes.

"I thought I was," I say softly. Another minute of silence passes—the longest minute in my life.

"But not anymore," Matthew says, and it's not a question. "Is it because you like Amari now?"

I sigh, exasperated. "Of course not! I don't even *know* Amari."

"But you'd like to."

I nod. "Sure, I'd like to. I'd like to know lots of people.

That doesn't mean I'm in love with them or something."

"I guess," he says, sounding dejected. "Do you still like me?"

"Of course I do. But Matthew, this place is so different. It's this whole new beginning, and we don't really even know anything about it. Does it really make sense to try to be together right now when we don't even know the rules?"

His eyes are wide. I'm not even sure when I started looking at them again. "So you don't want to be together anymore?"

"Were we really even together in the first place? We went to the barn dance together, you held my hand and kissed me on the cheek, and then we were basically kidnapped."

"I thought we were," he says quietly.

"Yeah, back home we would've been. We would've been courting, and maybe we'd have gotten married in a couple of years. But everything is different now. I mean, I was in a *coma*."

Matthew nods. The wheels are turning in his head. "You're right. I know you are. Everything has changed so much, but *we* haven't."

"I have."

"You have?" he asks, puzzled.

"Well, yeah," I reply, gesturing to my hair and clothes.

Matthew shakes his head. "You've changed the way you look, but you're not really any different on the inside."

"No, I'm different inside, too. Because of you, I didn't just try to save myself that night. I could've run straight into the woods and found a hiding place, but instead I went back to the Orphan Home to see if anyone had made it. I wanted to make you proud. For once, I wanted to make the selfless choice. I wanted to be able to live with myself if I was going to live."

A sad smile creeps across Matthew's face. "I don't really think that's too different for you."

"Look, I don't want to court someone else. I'm just not sure I want to court at all right now. I want to get used to this place and figure out how everything works. I want to get caught up in school and to make real decisions. I want to figure out how to have a life here, and I don't think either of us can do that if we're trying to figure out a courtship at the same time."

This time, it's Matthew who sighs. "Yeah, you're probably right. I wish you weren't, though."

"Yeah," I say, "me, too."

"Can you do something for me, though?"

"Anything," I reply.

"Can you just let me know before you court someone else?"

"Matthew—"

"Please?"

"Of course, but I'm not doing this so I can court someone else. I'm really not."

"I know, but I think that opportunity might present itself sooner than you think."

"And who says I'll even be interested when it does?" I ask. "I have a whole life to figure out."

When he doesn't answer, I feel the urge to fill the silence. "I care about you a lot. I'm not saying we'll never be together. I just need to pause things for a little bit while I try to understand who I am in this new life. I think it would be a good idea for you to do the same thing."

"It probably would," he says. "So . . . you're not going to start courting Amari?"

"No, Matthew, I'm not. I swear that's not what this is about. I've been confused ever since we got here, and I think you have, too. Otherwise, you wouldn't have kept your distance so much. Besides, with how bad Amari feels about everything, I don't think he'd be interested in me anymore anyway. You need to give him a chance to apologize."

"Yeah." Matthew's expression softens a little. "You know, I think he actually might be a pretty good guy, based on how he reacted."

"Good because you need more friends in this place than just me and Ava!"

"And you're right, you know. I did keep my distance. After everything that happened, I wasn't really sure how this would work any more than you were. It just doesn't feel very good to break things off."

"No, it really doesn't. But we're still friends, right?"

"Yeah, we're still friends. Always."

"And you'll tell me before you court someone new, too?"

Matthew practically guffaws.

"Matthew," I say, dead serious. He turns and looks at me, and his expression changes.

"I'm not gonna court someone new, but if I was . . . yeah, I'd tell you first. It's all gonna be okay, Harper. It'll work out."

Matthew puts one arm around me, and I lean into him. I think he must be crying, too, because my forehead feels a little wet.

18

JING

"So you broke up with him?" Jing asks, practically unintelligible with a French toast stick stuffed so far into her mouth.

I nod and burst into tears again. Ava hands me a donut, which I depression-eat it in about one bite. They were asleep when I finally wandered back over here late last night after crying on Matthew's shoulder for hours. Ava and Jing were both in my bed waiting for me. Not wanting to squeeze into the limited space available, I took Ava's empty bed and still woke up this morning with one of them on each side of me.

I had to slide down to the end of the bed and out the bottom of the covers before I crept into the shower. When I got out, I found them waiting for me with every sugary breakfast treat known to man. Misery food. We've been stuffing our faces ever since while I recount my breakup story. I only hope Matthew's new friends are as good at commiserating as mine are. I'm sure he needs support this morning even more than I do.

Ava considers her next words carefully before speaking. "How did he take it?"

"Better than I thought he would. We cried together for

a long time after we decided, but he totally understood. Everything is weird for him, too. He asked me to let him know if I decide to start courting someone else."

"He's worried about Amari," Jing says bluntly. Ava nods.

Tears flood my eyes. "I asked him to do the same thing."

"Who are *you* worried about?" Ava asks.

Jings crinkles her nose in apparent disgust. "*I* don't want to date Matthew!"

I chuck a donut hole at her, hitting her right between her eyebrows. "I don't think he wants to date you, either! But we're both going to be meeting a lot of new people, and even though I don't think it's a good idea to be together right now, I'm not ready to see him with someone else."

"It's probably not smart to be courting anyone until we get used to how this place works," Ava says.

"Exactly," I nod, "but I think it'll hurt if he starts courting someone else no matter when it happens."

"He feels the same about you." Ava squeezes my hand.

"I think you're both being really smart about all of it," Jing says, "but can you please stop talking about courting like a dork and say *dating* instead?"

I don't even try to stop my eyes from rolling. "Fine," I say with as much drama as possible.

"Okay, I know you needed time to talk, but we better hurry up. We're gonna be late for school," Ava nudges.

"Ugh, school!" I groan. "Do we *have* to go?"

"Uh, yeah," Jing chides. "It's only Thursday. I don't know how things work on the surface, but here, we go to school five days a week. You've still got two days left."

I mope and whine, but allow myself to be guided out the door. Unfortunately, Matthew's door opens the same time ours does. There he is, standing in the doorway, a startled deer hoping if it holds still enough I won't be able to see it.

"Hey, what are you doing? We're gonna be late." A voice trickles out from behind him and into the hall. Amari's face suddenly appears over Matthew's right shoulder.

"Oh," he trails off, refusing to meet my eyes.

"Uh, hey, Amari," Jing says, her eyes flicking back and forth between the two of us from the hallway. "We were just leaving."

Jing reaches behind her and grabs my hand, pulling me away quickly. Ava brings up the rear, no doubt attempting to shield me from view.

"Well, that was awkward," I hear Amari's voice say. "I'm still really sorry."

I don't catch Matthew's response. Jing is pulling me so fast that we're already around the corner and halfway down the next hall.

"Geez, slow down! I don't think they could catch up to us now if they ran all the way to school."

Jing glances behind us before deciding it's safe to stop. Ava doubles over with her hands on her knees, trying to catch her breath after being dragged down two long hallways at top speed.

"Okay, I know I needed to catch my breath, but they might actually catch up if we don't keep going," Ava announces.

"How are you feeling?" Jing asks, starting back toward school at a much more manageable pace.

"Well, *Amari* wasn't the person I expected to see in Matthew's room, that's for sure."

"Yesterday was a total disaster, but he's actually a really nice guy," Jing offers. "He was probably checking to make sure Matthew was okay."

Ava eyes me warily.

"It's fine," I tell them both with a chuckle. "It's weird. It's awkward. But I'm fine. They're not fighting over me this morning, and that's a good thing. I hope this means they'll be able to be friends."

"Yes," Ava agrees with flair, "he needs friends his own age who are *boys*! He can't just hang out with the two of us for the rest of his life."

"Just like I need girls," Jing interjects.

"Wait," I say. "You've been here almost your whole life. You don't have any friends who are girls?"

Jing shrugs and looks uncomfortable. "Not really. I don't know if you noticed, but I like to talk. Like, *a lot*. Most of the other girls think I'm weird."

"Maybe they just haven't taken enough time to get to know you," Ava replies.

"You've only known me three days!"

"Yep," I say, "but in those three days, you've been there for me in a way that only Ava ever has. I think you just talk more when you're nervous."

"Those other girls *do* make me pretty anxious."

"What do you think it is about them?"

"I don't know," Jing says, shaking her head. "They're always talking about boys and clothes, and they gossip about each other. They're just so much more complicated than the boys."

"And by the boys, you mean Grey and Amari?" Ava asks.

"Because I haven't seen you spend time with anyone else yet this week."

"Hey, I have other friends!"

I cross my arms in front of my chest. "Yeah? Who?"

"You haven't met them yet," Jing pouts.

"Well, what are their names?" Ava teases.

"Fine, they're my cousins, and they only hang out with me because we're family." She puckers her lips like she just bit into a lemon.

"Well, we'll fix that," I announce. "Lots of other kids have talked to me this week. They've been really nice so far."

"I mean, you're right, though," Ava says. "Boys *are* easier to deal with. Girls are just so—"

"High maintenance," Jing supplies.

"Yes!" Ava and I exclaim together.

"Great minds."

"Great minds?" I ask.

"Oh, it's this old saying we have here: Great minds think alike. It just means we're all equally awesome."

"We are pretty awe-inspiring," Ava says, pretending to smooth her hair and show off how pretty she is.

"Seriously, though," Jing says, "I don't know if it's a good idea to let your other friends know that you like me. They'll just dump you."

"So what if they do?" I counter. "If they don't want to get to know you, then maybe I don't want to get to know them."

19

REHOUSED

Within twenty-four hours, John, Maggie, and the other shunned villagers had been moved from their large family homes into the northwest section of town, where the oldest homes stood. These houses predated the small settlement and were some of the only structures remaining from the times before the global disasters that devastated humanity. Of course, the new and remaining Elders assigned the disgraced families to the most dilapidated buildings—those that had not been lived in for decades.

John and Maggie surveyed a decaying one-bedroom bungalow with a wagon of only their most essential belongings nearby. Anything deemed nonessential or frivolous had been redistributed to other families. With a heavy sigh, John limped toward the small porch, his middle-aged body still sore from his lashing, and cautiously tested the rotting floorboards. They sagged beneath his weight, but they held.

The front door opened with a loud creak when he tried the ancient knob. Maggie let out an uncharacteristic shriek when a raccoon emerged and skittered between her feet. The events of the past few days had made her understandably jumpy. She clutched her hands to her chest and let out a sigh of relief that quickly turned into a sharp gasp as pain surged through her bandaged left hand. Sophie had packed the wound with a poultice to prevent infection, but it didn't prevent the constant ache or the agony of touching it without thinking.

"John?" she called out from her place beside the wagon. "How does it look inside?"

His muscled form appeared in the doorway. "It'll take some work, but I think we can have it back in shape before too long. The floor'll hold—that's the most important thing. It's dusty and musty and probably full of critters, but it's still better than camping. Come on in and see for yourself."

Cradling her aching hand, Maggie climbed gingerly up three front steps and onto the sagging porch. Her breath caught in her throat when she spied the state of the small house. She steadied herself on the doorframe, afraid to step inside. John was barely visible through the gloom, surveying a hole in the far corner of the modest sitting room's dirt-caked floorboards. A small sapling tree was growing up out of it, and a strong smell of animal droppings permeated the air.

They would make do—they always did—but this would be no easy task. Their girls were gone, everything they thought was true turned out to be a lie, and they were being reduced to poverty-stricken beggars. Not that begging would do much good. Nobody would possibly do anything to help them after those vile men had taken control of the Council yesterday.

They spent their day sweeping out the dirt and pulling weeds out of their floor, as carefully as possible so as not to upset their injuries. The Aaron family came around before too long to check on them. With their many children, they had been able to clear out their new home and get settled relatively quickly, so they volunteered to lend a helping hand to other displaced families.

"Thank you so much, Anna," Maggie said. "I know you're

all just as spent and sore as we are."

"Not quite," Anna said with a glance to the bandage where Maggie's missing finger once was.

"I suppose that's true," Maggie replied, gingerly touching the bandaged hand. "How are you holding up?"

"Missing Matthew fiercely. The girls have already been told how wicked our family is for trying to deprive him of his true spiritual purpose. They'll all be brainwashed before long, won't they?"

"If they're not already."

"What are we going to do about it, Maggie? It can't be true, can it? But that message!"

"That's been bothering me, too," Maggie nodded to her friend. "There must've been some truth to it. Maybe the Sovereign are real after all, and we defied them by refusing to give them the Orphans."

"But surely the Sovereign must be at least somewhat benevolent. They've been ensuring our harvests all these years, and they didn't make us starve when we didn't hand the children over. They just took them and left a warning. If they were cruel gods who delight in suffering, don't you suppose they'd have watched us all starve? Or at least been a little harsher with us?"

"Maybe," Maggie replied, rubbing the side of her face in thought.

"We can't just sit back and let them continue to mistreat people. We have to stick together," Anna said, clearly fired up. "Taking care of children doesn't make us monsters!"

"No, it doesn't, but I'd be cautious about how you talk just now. You can't be openly calling them children or trying to defy the new Elders. There's no telling what the next level of punishment will be for you then."

By suppertime, every family who had adopted an Orphan had come around to see John and Maggie. All shared views similar to Anna's. They pooled their meager resources and cooked a meal together over an open flame, seeing as how none of them had a working fireplace. Although they shared their outrage and were convinced that the Sovereign must be more benevolent than they'd been given credit for, John and Maggie managed to convince them that this was not a safe time to be openly defiant. All they could do was work together in their own little community to make sure each family was cared for.

That night, they all slept on floor pallets since they no longer owned beds or mattresses. They woke the next morning to the clanging of the meeting bell once more.

"John, wake up. They're ringing the bell again."

"So soon? What could it be now?"

"Nothing good."

The pair emerged from their two-room shack cautiously alongside their new neighbors, all of them peering around to gauge this morning's atmosphere. No one seemed to have a clue what this was all about. They made their way to the meeting hall together to discover a new horror awaiting them.

The Elders were standing upon the little stage in the square as the townspeople congregated before them. Beside it stood gallows erected overnight and a pit of burning coals. All the people murmured and trembled in fear, milling about the square while they waited. Finally, Master Cowan took the stage.

"As our community's foremost expert in religious matters, the Council has asked me to lead us in daily devotions to the Sovereign. Those who are unwilling to recommit themselves and participate in religious revival, shall face . . . uh, severe . . . consequences," the beak-nosed man stammered, clearly uncomfortable. "The Council has also determined that those

who had previously fallen from the faith should recommit themselves publicly by being branded so all may see that their devotion is true."

Several astonished gasps rang out, and people began to whisper fervently among themselves. So this was it. They were to be branded like cattle to show they belonged. Would any amount of punishment be enough?

Master Cowan, now labeled Father Cowan, much to his chagrin, led the community in prayers and songs. He had dug up an extraordinarily long-winded prayer of repentance from at least a hundred years ago, teaching the community their response portion as he went.

When the painfully long penitent prayer ended, Father Cowan's posture stiffened. He glanced around at the Elders seated behind him and was given a nod of encouragement. Resigning himself to the inevitable, he spoke again.

"Now the branding ceremony will commence. If the adoptive families would please come to the front."

Someone shouted from the crowd, "Children, too?"

"Children, too," came the response from Elder Prewitt. The crowd nearly came apart. Father Cowan bore the unfortunate responsibility of explaining to them.

"After reading our religious histories, the Council has determined that the Sovereign hold descendants equally responsible for the sins of their forebears. Therefore, if true penitence is to be had, the children must also suffer for the sins of their fathers and mothers." A tear glistened on his cheek.

One young mother cried out, "You can brand me, but you won't lay a hand on my baby! She's done nothing wrong!"

She handed the child to her older son, who took off at a dead sprint to hide. She and her husband fought off those who tried to pursue the boy, but they were soon overwhelmed by the Council's goons. Their hands tied behind their backs, they were dragged onto the gallows and made to wait while their children were retrieved.

Father Cowan prayed another prayer of repentance over the children, who were then branded, each on the inside of the right wrist. They screamed and wailed in pain with no mother to comfort them. She cried out for her children from the gallows, weeping and moaning until the deed was done and she hung limply at the end of the rope. Her husband soon followed, and the bodies were strung up in the square for all to see.

The healers and their apprentices sat nearby to apply a cooling salve to the children's brands. At least there was some mercy, albeit slight, until Elder Samson stood to address the crowd.

"May the Sovereign bless these, our first Orphans of the new Sending. The Orphan Home must be reopened and new Caretakers named to watch over them until the next Festival."

Father Cowan grimaced, but read off the names of the new Caretakers dutifully, likely out of fear that he could be next on the gallows. After the public hangings, all the adoptive families lined up to have their wrists branded, including the poor children. The infants were the worst; their screams could no doubt be heard for miles.

"And now the rest of our citizens will be branded to show their commitment to the Sovereign and their repentance for their own part in the sins committed over the past months. No person in our community—man, woman, or child—shall eat without presentation of a brand. No rations will be provided without such presentation, and all those who violate this law shall be punished accordingly."

Father Cowan caved in on himself as he gestured to the

gallows, a movement that was evidently commanded in the script from which he read. If the town was in an uproar over the injustice, they didn't show it. Instead, fear lined every face, and each person took a place in line to be branded.

20

SURPRISE

I never knew how difficult it is to steer a blindfolded person where you want them to go without bumping into things.

"Ouch!" Ava shouts. "Harper, stop doing that!"

"Here, let me take over," Jing says.

This is clearly not the first time she's done this. Maybe for her little cousins. Jing skillfully guides Ava around the corner to the bank of elevators.

"Oh . . . the elevator. Which floor are we visiting?" Ava asks when she hears the familiar ding.

"Oh, we're not taking you to another floor," Jing teases. "We just thought we'd let you ride the elevator up and down for a few hours. That's how we celebrate birthdays here."

Ava scrunches up her face and sticks out her tongue. Even though she's facing the wrong direction, she still makes her point, but we let her sweat it out. It wouldn't be much of a surprise if we told her where we're going.

When the doors slide open again, Jing expertly guides Ava into the most boring hallway I've ever seen. Not too far down, we enter a set of double doors and find ourselves in a small alcove with another set only a few feet away.

Without saying a word, Jing motions for me to shut the door behind me before she opens the next one. I raise one eyebrow at her before making sure the door closes and gently checking that it's latched. Jing nods at my silent thumbs up, opens the next door, and ushers Ava through.

Although I helped plan this party, I've never actually been in the aviary before. The room is vast, with high ceilings barely visible among all the trees that have been strung with brightly colored party decorations. A huge crowd of new friends, mostly eleven- and twelve-year-olds from Ava's classes, waits in suspended animation for the blindfold to be removed.

Ava, not having the first clue where she is, cocks her head. "What's that sound? Is that . . . birds?"

Jing puts one finger up to her lips, shushing the waiting crowd, while I carefully untie her blindfold. I pull it from her eyes, and everyone shouts at once.

"Surprise!"

Ava stands in stunned silence before turning to me and whispering, "What's happening?"

"It's your birthday party," I whisper back.

The Elysians, not registering Ava's confusion, rush around her, hugging her and wishing her a happy birthday. She stands in a sea of well-wishers, blinking in stunned silence, right up until Jing's dad appears. A shorter man with slightly darker skin than his daughter's and the same almond eyes, he's dressed in a uniform of all khaki and carries an enormous bright blue bird on one arm.

Ava's eyes grow wide, and she pushes her way through

the crowd to reach Mr. Zhou.

"Is that a hyacinth macaw?" she gapes at him.

"You really know your birds, young lady," Jing's father beams with pride. "This is the largest parrot in the world."

"But how did you get one in Elysium? I thought they only lived in Brazil!"

Mr. Zhou's smile broadens until it looks dangerously close to overwhelming his other features. "Ah, yes! That is true. But when war was on the verge of breaking out centuries ago, our founders spirited away as many species as they could find in hopes of repopulating Earth once it was safe to emerge. Luckily, the animals seem to be immune to the pestilence that plagues our world, but we've kept many that were too far from home to return to their natural habitats. Others have injuries or disabilities that would prevent them from being able to survive on their own."

"So they're like pets now?"

Mr. Zhou chuckles. "I suppose you could think of them like pets, but we don't let people keep them in their homes. We care for them here."

"You said they collected a lot of species. But how did they get them here all the way from Brazil?"

"Many of our animals' ancestors came from zoos."

Seeing the look on Ava's face, Mr. Zhou explains, "In the world that was, people brought animals from all kinds of distant places and kept them in places called zoos. There were large open-air cages that resembled the animals' natural habitats, and people came to see what different species looked like and how they lived. They learned a lot and saved many different kinds of animals from extinction."

"So when the war came, the scientists rescued animals from zoos so they wouldn't go extinct?" I ask.

"Exactly right," Jing's father declares. "Now, birthday girl, would you like to hold this not-so-little fellow?"

Ava's face lights up. Mr. Zhou demonstrates how to hold her arm out, straight in front of her with the elbow bent, to make a perch for the macaw. Then, he holds his arm up to hers and lures the enormous bird onto Ava's arm with the promise of a macadamia nut. When the macaw, named Hank, dismounts from Mr. Zhou's arm and lands on Ava's, she's immediately thrown off balance by the weight. Jing and I grab on to help steady her as she laughs with delight.

Mr. Zhou places a macadamia nut in Ava's hand. "Now hold your hand out to Hank. Keep your palm flat, so he doesn't accidentally nip your fingers. . . . There you go."

The bird stretches out his neck, snaps up the nut in its beak, and gobbles it down. Mr. Zhou holds out a bag of nuts for Ava to take more as she pleases. Before I know it, a line of younger kids has formed, each waiting for their own turn to feed Ava's new best friend.

After a while, Mr, Zhou takes Hank away and comes back with more birds for Ava to befriend. He teaches the children different calls to attract specific birds fluttering from tree to tree, and he occasionally brings out special treats for them.

All this excitement seems to be old news to Jing. She and I hang back and let the younger kids have the time of their lives.

"I can't believe your dad is an actual zoologist," I say.

"Technically, he's an ornithologist," she replies. "He

specializes in birds. It's just good luck that Ava happens to be nuts about them."

"She's gonna want to do her apprenticeship up here."

"I practically grew up in here," Jing tells me. "Birds aren't really that interesting to me, though. But I do love the ones that can talk."

"There are birds that can talk?" My jaw practically hits the ground. "I can't believe Ava never told me that."

"Oh, yeah. You used to spend a ton of time out in the woods, right?"

"Yeah, why?" I ask.

"Did you ever hear voices that shouldn't be there?"

"What, you mean, like ghosts? Yeah, actually. It was pretty creepy."

"It was probably crows."

"Crows?"

"Yep," Jing says, delighted to be teaching me something about my own world. "Crows can mimic human speech. So if they've been around enough humans talking in the woods, they can start to say words, and it's impossible to tell where it's coming from."

"Oh my gosh, that is so cool!"

"Yeah, and you should hear about—" Jing cuts herself short.

"What's wrong?"

Her eyes flick behind me urgently. I turn to see Amari approaching.

"I better go help my mom get the cake ready," Jing says. "She'll kill me if she has to take care of everything herself. See you!"

"Hey, Harper," Amari says, both hands in his pockets.

"Hey, Amari."

We haven't spoken since he tried to put his arm around me a week ago. It's been getting increasingly awkward since we all still hang out in the same group. I've been hiding behind Grey, pretending I don't see him while making the most random conversation with Jing and just generally trying to avoid him, even when we're within three feet of each other. I've had to get pretty creative.

"Look, I know things are weird between us now," he starts.

"Yep," I nod slowly, not meeting his eyes.

"I just wanted to say again that I'm sorry. Matthew's a really good guy. I'm glad I'm friends with him. And I'd like to be able to be friends with you, too, but I don't know how that's ever gonna happen if you keep avoiding me."

"I'm not avoiding you!" I say a little too loudly. My face feels suddenly hot.

Amari smirks. "You're blushing."

"What? No, I'm not!"

"The white folks on the surface can't tell when you're blushing, huh?" He grins. "Makes it that much more obvious that you are, in fact, avoiding me."

"Well, we're talking right now, aren't we?"

"Only because Jing agreed to keep you busy long enough that you wouldn't be able to run away."

I glare at Jing, who's pretending not to be watching us from across the room.

"Look," Amari continues, not noticing my silent exchange with Jing, "I just want you to know that you don't have to worry. I'm not gonna try anything else. I'm still really embarrassed, and I feel like a real jerk. I'd never hit on someone else's girl. You obviously weren't feeling the same way I was, so . . . I'm sorry."

"Thank you," I say. "I'm sorry I've been so awkward. I've never had anything like this happen before. I don't have a clue how to act now."

"I get that. What if we just start over and pretend it never happened? I don't like you like that now that I know. I'd really like for things to be normal between us again."

I let out a breath and relax a little bit. "That sounds great."

"Perfect," he says. "Let's go get some cake. It's time for Ava to blow out her candles."

21

FINAL EXAMS

Weeks later, Ava is still talking about her birthday party. She keeps spouting off random facts about different birds she got to see. I'm beyond thrilled that Jing and I were able to give her "the best birthday ever," but I'm about ready for her to shut up about birds already. I'd never say that, though, at least not to her face.

"And did you know that, once, the south Philippine dwarf kingfisher was so endangered that no one saw one for almost one hundred and fifty years? They thought it was extinct, but now Mr. Zhou has so many of them that his tropical aviary is bursting at the seams!"

I silence my inner thoughts before I say something I can't take back. This is her ten thousandth random bird fact since we left class for the afternoon. I know she loves her bird books, but we came to the library so we could study for finals.

"Shh!" The other kids in the library must be as irritated with her as I am.

"So I take it you'll be applying for an apprenticeship with Mr. Zhou for the fall?" I whisper with much more patience than I feel.

She shakes her head and furrows her brow. "No, why would you say that?"

Astonished, I reply, "It's the only thing you've talked about in over a month. You've loved birds more than anything for as long as I can remember. I'm pretty sure *bird* was your first word!"

"Well, yeah, I do love birds, but I don't want to work with them for a job. Mr. Zhou says I can volunteer at the aviary on the weekends, though."

All this time, I thought I knew everything about Ava.

"Well, what apprenticeship do you want to apply for then?" I ask.

"Medical research."

"Medical research? You've never said a single thing about medical research!"

"I didn't want to say anything until I was sure. I want to see how I do on my exams first. You have to have top scores to apply."

"You'll probably do better if you actually open a medical textbook," I tease, pushing her stack of bird books to the other side of the table.

"Yeah, okay," Ava grumbles.

"But seriously, why do you want to do medical research?"

"It's stupid," she says.

"More stupid than ten thousand things I never wanted to know about birds?" I ask.

I immediately slap my hand over my mouth, realizing I said it out loud. I'm about to apologize when she starts talking again, oblivious to the burn I just dealt.

"I want to find the cure. I want to be the one who fixes this, so we can be a family again."

I just stare at her, my eyes filling with tears. Finally, I put my hand on top of hers.

"I miss them, too."

Ava nods and wipes her eyes with the back of her hand.

"My stupid bird facts help me focus on the good things about being here."

I swear inwardly. *She heard me after all.*

"I'm sorry, Ava. I shouldn't have said that. I never thought about it like that—that it helps you feel better about being here."

"I know it's annoying," she says sadly.

"But maybe less now that I know why you're doing it. You know you can always talk to me about this stuff, right? We used to tell each other everything."

"I know. It's just . . . some of my feelings have been so . . . I don't know. Awful? It's different than when we were in the Orphan Home. We did everything together, but now everything is so much more separate. We still live together, but we have different classes and different friends, and pretty soon we'll have different apprenticeships. You'll always be my sister, but it feels like I have to start dealing with more stuff on my own."

"I guess that's true. We're not in the same room for school or sharing every little thing like we used to. Now that you mention it, I kind of miss you, too, not just Mama and Papa. I guess I would've been starting an apprenticeship back home anyway. It's just something we'll have to get used to."

"Love getting used to new things," Ava replies sarcastically. "I haven't had enough of that yet."

I giggle. "Just promise you'll tell me all the important things, like when you're feeling awful and need to use a weird coping skill."

I wink at her.

"Deal," she says with a laugh. "Now, if you'll excuse me, I really have to study. Finals start tomorrow, in case you didn't notice."

I give her shoulder a light shove and get back to studying for my Elysian Historical Foundations exam. The last six weeks have been a crash course in Elysium's founding principles. Mr. Weiss likened it to the citizenship test for the former United States, except I'll still be a citizen if I fail. I'll just have to take a remedial course next year and lose eligibility for the higher-level Safety and Security apprenticeships. You know, the ones I want the most.

The longer Ava and I study, the more the library fills up with anxious students prepping for their own tests. Jing and Grey join our table, followed by Jordan, who sits next to Ava in what looks like a very intentional attempt to be near her. Before long, Matthew and Amari appear, too, both of whom are just as obvious about leaving the seat next to me *empty*. Matthew doesn't look terribly pleased when a boy from my Fitness Training class takes the spot.

"Hey, Harper," he says too loudly.

The room erupts in a shower of shushes and angry glares. He's really reinforcing the stereotype that S&S meatheads have never been inside a library before. If it wasn't already hard to keep a straight face, Amari's bizarre attempts to distract us from Matthew's withering stares make it impossible.

"Hey, Rome," I whisper, trying not to laugh uncontrollably.

"What are you studying for?" Rome asks, a bit quieter

this time.

"Elysian Foundations," I reply, closing my book halfway to show him the cover. "You?"

"Military Formations and Strategy." He shakes his head. "This stuff sucks. I'm better at math."

"And how're you at math?" Matthew asks pointedly. Amari elbows him.

As one of the most confident people I've ever met, Rome doesn't pay any attention to it. "I took Calculus for fun last year," he shrugs.

Matthew does not look pleased, but it shuts him up.

Maybe helping Rome will distract me before I get us all kicked out. "What if you thought about it in mathematical terms?"

"What do you mean?" Rome asks.

"Well, formations and strategies must have some mathematical basis, right? Like, think about the geometry of the formations."

The wheels in Rome's head are turning as he considers this. To Rome's right, Matthew sighs.

"Or angles and distance involved. Do you play chess?"

I can tell from his tone that Matthew doesn't really want to help, but he can't stop himself. Is it that he needs to be helpful or that he needs to be smarter than Rome? Whatever it is, Rome's face lights up.

"Oh, that's a really good point, you guys. Thanks!"

Rome immediately buries his face in his book with renewed vigor and begins scribbling notes and diagrams in his multiple notebooks. Every few minutes, he makes a small noise that tells us he's still engaged and having a great time figuring out how math applies to all these concepts.

Amari engages Matthew in a moderately intense whisper fight. I can't hear a word they're saying, but everyone at the table knows what the argument is about. Everyone but Rome, that is. He's still engrossed in his notes.

Grey leans over and elbows Matthew hard in the side. "Will you two *shut up*? You're going to get us kicked out!"

Amari shoots back at him. "Well, if Matthew would just—"

"God, Matthew," Jing says with all the sass she can muster, "we know you aren't dating Harper anymore, but that doesn't mean no one else is allowed to be interested in her."

Matthew's face deepens a few shades, and Amari stares at Jing in horror. She slaps her hand over her mouth. Ava nudges me from the left and glances over my shoulder toward where Rome is sitting.

Oh no.

Rome is also turning a deep shade of vermillion. There's no way he didn't just hear Jing. He starts tossing his things back into his bag in a rush and stands way too quickly to be healthy.

"Rome, please don't—" I start, but he cuts me off.

"Sorry, just realized I'm late. See you tomorrow, Harper!" Rome waves over his shoulder as he sprints out of the library, leaving behind all the possessions spilling from his half-open bag.

"Thanks a lot, you guys!"

Matthew sinks into his chair, mumbling under his breath. I round on him.

"What was that, Matthew?"

He slams his book down on the table. "I said you're

not supposed to be dating someone new without *talking* to me about it anyway. What right do you have to be the one who's mad?"

"I'm not *dating* anyone!" I'm shouting now. People are looking, and I don't care. "He's my friend and my platoon leader. I have to see him every day and learn things from him, and now I look like a complete idiot with a secret crush on my commanding officer! Everyone's going to be talking about it, and I might even get an official reprimand!"

"Oh." Matthew sinks down lower.

"Oh? Is that all you have to say? You could have just ruined my chances at getting a good apprenticeship, which, in case you hadn't noticed, means you could've ruined my whole career trajectory in this place! You know what? I'm done here. I'm gonna go study at home. I don't need this from any of you."

"Harper, wait," Jing says, trying to catch up with me.

"I don't want to talk to you right now either, Jing," I say as I storm out of the library.

"She's pissed," Grey says.

"We really screwed up," Jing moans.

"Give her some time," Ava says. "It'll all be okay in the morning. Unless you're Matthew."

The library door closes behind me, and I don't hear the rest of their conversation.

I spend the next hour studying alone in my room, but it's hard to focus. I can't believe those idiots would jeopardize my entire future over petty jealousy. If Matthew can be friends with Jing and Ava, he shouldn't have a problem with me having other male friends. And my platoon leader? I can't even with them.

I hear Ava's small knock on the door, warning me that she's about to come in. The door opens a crack, and a plate of spaghetti and meatballs slides through.

"Are you ready for company yet?" Ava asks from out in the hall.

"Yes, you can come in," I concede, "but you better have garlic bread."

Ava enters with just one plate, but doesn't close the door behind her. I narrow my eyes suspiciously. Another plate glides through the opening, piled high with bread.

"Not just garlic bread, but *cheesy* garlic bread," Jing's voice calls out. "And chocolate cake."

"Fine, you can come in, too," I say with a sigh.

Ava sets my plate of spaghetti down on the table and returns to open the door wide for Jing, who's pushing a cart full of goodies into the room. We eat mostly in silence until dessert.

"I'm really sorry I hurt your feelings, Harper," Jing finally releases.

"And I've never seen you stay quiet for so long!" I return.

"Okay, okay. Harsh, but I deserve that." Jing laughs. "I hope you know that I was pissed off on your behalf. I was so worried that moron was going to embarrass you that I ended up doing it myself."

"I know you didn't mean to," I say. "I'm still not *happy* about it, but I know you didn't mean it. That other dumb-dumb, though."

"Yeah, he seemed like he was *trying* to cause trouble," Ava says. "Boys are so stupid sometimes! He really couldn't think five minutes into the future to figure how that might hurt his case?"

"His brain isn't developed enough yet," Jing says through a mouthful of cake.

"What?" she says to our dumbfounded stares. "We learn about it in our medical classes at the hospital. The prefrontal cortex in your brain isn't fully developed till you're like twenty-three. Teenagers make stupid decisions sometimes because we actually can't always think five minutes into the future."

Jing shrugs and keeps shoveling cake into her mouth.

"Well . . . okay," I reply. Ava doesn't speak at all.

"What? You've never made a stupid decision without thinking about the consequences?" Jing asks us.

"No, we've made plenty," Ava answers, and I can only assume she's remembering sneaking into the town meeting just a few months ago like I am.

She turns to me. "Is this what I sound like when I talk about birds?"

I make a face and nod emphatically.

"Probably," Jing agrees. "Add that to the list of things you do without thinking about it first."

We burst out laughing, and I'm thankful to have my friends back. We don't ever have to stay mad because we take the time to talk things through.

Matthew, though? I don't know if I'll be ready to talk to him any time soon.

22

PRAYER

Maggie and John knelt in the square beside the Aarons, heads bowed in deference as Father Cowan led all the townsfolk in morning prayers. After three weeks, each of them knew the daily call-and-response ritual by heart, beseeching the Sovereign to forgive their sins and teach them humility once more.

"And now I invite you to offer your own personal prayers aloud," Father Cowan called as he lifted his eyes toward the sky.

The Aarons' former neighbor, Frank Sheffield, got to his feet and spread his hands out, palms up before he spoke. "Almighty Sovereign, we thank Thee for allowing our crops to begin to grow in spite of our wicked ways. I confess that I myself behaved unrighteously, treating my neighbors' Orphan as a real human child."

At Frank's words, Anna let out a low hiss. Eying her in the periphery of her vision, Maggie noted a sour look on her friend's face, but the woman kept her head bowed and remained knelt on the ground.

Mr. Sheffield's prayer continued, growing louder with every word. "I was led astray by the blasphemers and believed the lies that they told about You, but now I know the truth—that You, *oh Blessed Sovereign, have chosen the Orphans for a higher purpose, and they are not ours to keep. They are spiritual beings who belong only to You. Forgive my arrogance, and bring Mr. and Mrs. Aaron and the rest of their ilk to repentance."*

A feral growl formed on Anna's lips upon hearing herself and her husband specifically named in the public gathering. Only Maggie's sudden, firm grip on her wrist prevented her from hurling herself at the man in fury. Anna glared at her friend and attempted to pull away, but Maggie shook her head abruptly, an urgent warning in her eyes. She maintained her grasp on the other woman's arm as the other villagers took turns offering loud, ostentatious prayers of repentance. Some begged only forgiveness for themselves and their loved ones while others followed Frank's example of naming others who were more guilty than they.

Finally, the bells sounded, signaling the end of prayers and the beginning of the day's work. Maggie rose swiftly and hooked her arm happily through Anna's, practically dragging her away from Mr. Sheffield. "Come, my dear Anna, and bring your little ones along. We've bread to bake for the week ahead, and it's a perfect opportunity to show you that new recipe I've been telling you about."

Anna raised an annoyed eyebrow at her friend as she grabbed her youngest child by the hand. The others followed behind, forming a chain of adorable hand-holders that never even registered the way their mama was being tugged across the grassy lawn. Without answering Anna's gaze, Maggie began singing at the top of her lungs, a joyous hymn of the goodness of the Sovereign.

When the pair of women reached the safety of Maggie's tiny new home, Anna was finally released from her friend's death grip. Rubbing her arm furiously, she stared daggers at the other woman. "What was that all about?"

"Now, children," Maggie began, ignoring the question. Bending at the waist with her hands on her knees, she looked the small troupe of children in the eyes. "I have jobs for each and every one of you. Annabeth, take your sister and gather whatever you can of these ingredients." She handed the eldest Aaron sister a list.

"Peter, take your brothers out to the garden and clear the rocks away for me. Your mama and I will begin planting tomorrow. And you," Maggie said, lifting an apple-cheeked toddler into the air and resting her on her hip, "will stay here and help your mama and me."

Maggie blew raspberries on the baby's belly while the children scattered. Only when the last one was out of earshot did she finally address her friend. "You must be more careful. You simply cannot air your grievances in public during prayer, especially over calls for your own repentance! What do you imagine would have happened if you had pummeled Frank in the middle of the square this morning?"

"What right has he to pray for my repentance? The nerve!"

"He has every right, given to him by the new Council." Maggie adjusted the toddler on her hip. "Do you want to go to the gallows? Leave your children motherless?"

"One of my children already is!" Anna retorted.

Maggie sighed. "You did what you could for Matthew. You've got to start thinking about the ones who are still with you."

"Maggie, you just don't get it."

"Don't I? Both my children were taken from me. Both of them! But I have enough sense not to mope around and get angry with every single person who still blames me for what happened. It was my fault after all!"

"Don't say that!"

"And why not?" Maggie sat in one of the two newly built chairs in front of the fireplace, hugging the littlest Aaron child to her chest. "I was the one who called the secret meetings. I was the one who changed everyone's minds. If I hadn't convinced the village to end the Sending, you would never have gotten attached to him, just to have him ripped from your arms. The Sovereign would never have come back to our town. No one would have suffered any of this. Whose fault could it be, if not mine?"

She sagged in her chair, defeated. A tear dripped off her chin, landing on the collar of her dress. Anna's face filled with compassion. She leaned over and wrapped her arms around her friend. The toddler slid off Maggie's lap, and Anna handed her a carved wooden toy from her pocket. Pulling the other chair up close to Maggie's, Anna took both of the other woman's hands in hers.

"What good does it do you to blame yourself?" she asked quietly.

"About as much good as it does you to get yourself killed," Maggie replied with a shrug, "but you can't blame the rest of the people for thinking what they do. And they're right. You saw the message. We have to repent if we want to survive, whether we like it or not."

"You really believe all that?"

"Don't you?"

The two women bent their heads and prayed together, prayers of true repentance for their blasphemy and requests for forgiveness and for prosperity to return to their community. When little voices could be heard shouting and giggling outside, they said their amens and wiped the tears from their cheeks.

"All right, I'll be more careful," Anna said.

23

ROME

I haven't spoken to Matthew in a week, even when we had a final together or were at dinner with everyone else. I don't know what a conversation with him would look like.

Besides, with everything that's happened between us, maybe what we need is a little distance. Everyone else already has their apprenticeships, but Matthew, Ava, Jordan, and I will all be starting ours in the fall. Maybe it's time we started getting used to a little bit of separation.

"Hey, Rome!"

I jog to catch up with my platoon commander, hoping I can finally talk to him privately and try to make things right.

I think he's been avoiding me.

"Rome! Hey, Rome! Wait up!"

When I reach him, he stops stiffly, eyes darting around for a chance to escape. There are too many people around right now for him to run away from me. I was counting on that.

"What can I help you with, Private Moss?" he asks, refusing to meet my eyes.

Wonderful. We're addressing each other by rank now.

"Could we talk privately, *Lieutenant Markos*?"

He looks at me now, hurt and surprise flooding his brown eyes. I guess he didn't think I'd follow suit.

"Of course. Let's see if there's a meeting room available."

"I know somewhere much closer," I say. "Follow me."

He does as he's told, probably because he knows he doesn't have much of a choice unless he wants to make a public scene. That would be a bad look for an officer-in-training. Once we reach the dormitory halls, though, he sings a different tune.

"Harper, where are you taking me?" Rome grabs my arm. "I can't go back to your room with you. This isn't appropriate!"

"Oh, so it's Harper now, is it, *Lieutenant*? Yes, I'm taking you back to my room, and it's not *inappropriate*. I just need to talk to you, and I don't think either of us wants everyone listening in."

"Fine," he replies through gritted teeth, "but you'd better hurry up while the dormitory halls are deserted. No one can see me go in with you."

I roll my eyes as dramatically as I can possibly muster. "Yes, sir!"

We're around the corner and at my door in no time. Rome glances around in paranoia the entire time, but no one appears anywhere. He refuses to go in with me, insisting that we talk here in the hall.

"Would you relax? They're all at lunch."

"Exactly where we should be. What if someone notices we're missing?"

"What if they do? The way you've been acting lately, no one would even imagine that we're together."

Elysium

Rome blushes again, all the way to his ears. "Yeah. Sorry about that."

"No, I'm the one who's sorry," I tell him. "That idiot and I broke up two months ago, and we had barely even been dating. I don't even want to date anyone right now, but he's so crazy with jealousy that he thinks anyone who's even remotely nice to me must be my new boyfriend. Matthew said some really rude things to you, and I haven't spoken to him since. I don't think you're trying to date me, and neither does anyone else apart from him."

"Wow." Rome runs his hands through his hair. "He really is an idiot."

"Believe me, I know."

"And you're really not interested in dating me? Because that wouldn't be okay. I'm your commanding officer."

"I'm really not interested. I never even thought of you that way, to be honest. I have more important things to worry about. I'm really sorry for how uncomfortable that whole thing made you. I don't want you to worry that you'll get into trouble because of me. I don't think you're flirting with me, and I'm not going to cause you any problems. Okay?"

Rome nods, his dark eyes clouded.

"Can we just be friends?"

"Yeah, we can be friends. I'd like that." He sounds relieved.

"Good," I sigh. "Now that we're friends again, I have a favor to ask you."

"Wow, favors already? You're really pushing your luck today, Moss."

I roll my eyes yet again. "You *are* my commanding

officer, and I need to turn in my apprenticeship application this week. I need a letter of recommendation. Would you write me one?"

"Of course! That's hardly a favor. It's my job to write those letters. What are you applying for?"

I swallow hard. I haven't said it out loud to anyone yet, even though I know Ava's seen what I've been working on.

"General Yarrow's office—Secret Service and Covert Ops."

Rome's eyebrows raise, but he doesn't sound surprised when he speaks. "Overachiever. You know they'll probably stick you in a surveillance office first, right?"

"I know, but I'm hoping I can at least get into officer training."

He narrows his eyes in appraisal. "You're crazy-smart, right?"

I laugh. "You know I am. And fast and strong. General Yarrow practically offered me this job herself. I'd be crazy not to apply!"

"Wait, what?"

"Oh . . . I don't really tell people about it. The day they placed me in S&S, General Yarrow came to meet me personally. She told me she wanted me to do Black Ops, that she knew *I* wanted to do it, too. I guess she's been watching me, and she thinks it's right for me. And I think I agree with her."

"Wow. General Yarrow recruited you personally? That doesn't really happen."

I nod. "I know."

"Well, yeah, let's get you that letter. What else do you need?"

"I could use some help with the acceptance exams and the physical fitness tests. I'm so much further behind than anyone else applying for officer training."

Rome shakes his head. "I'll help you study, but I don't think you need any help with the fitness test. I've seen you in action, remember? I took all those tests not too long ago, and I'm positive you'll be fine. Besides, they won't let you get out of shape over the summer. Even though most other pathways get a long break, S&S still does drills every day."

"Yeah, but I'll want to squeeze in some extra training sessions anyway. I have to be the absolute best one in my year if I want to have a chance of working with General Yarrow."

"You're not wrong," Rome says. "General Yarrow hasn't taken an apprentice in . . . well, ever, I don't think. The more I think about it, the more I realize you're probably right. You'll be taking summer classes already, right?"

"Right," I nod. "Mostly science and history, but I want to take some extra S&S classes, too, to help me get ready."

"That's a good idea. Like you said, you're already behind the kids that started when they were twelve. I'll put together a training and study schedule for the summer. Did you get your exam scores yet?"

"Yep, straight As."

"Awesome!" Rome checks his watch.

"Look, I gotta get back, but I'll get you that letter soon and figure out the things that'll be most helpful to you for your entrance exams. Let me know when you have your summer schedule so we can fit in all the extra training and studying."

"Thanks, Rome! I really mean it."

"Yeah, I'm happy to help," he says as he turns to head for lunch.

24

SUMMER

Summer in Elysium is very different than it is aboveground. For one thing, Matthew and I are still in school, studying our butts off to be caught up and ready for our apprenticeships to start. For another, there's no enjoying the sunshine, roaming through the trees, or hiding out in the Stronghold. There are enough adults with enough technology that we don't have to help out with the crops, either.

No detasseling corn or walking beans for us. It's a good thing, too, because between actual classes and Rome's training and study schedule, I don't know how I'd squeeze everything in. I barely have time to eat and sleep as it is, except that Rome is pretty strict about those things. I have to keep to a specific calorie intake each day, track my nutrient macros to ensure optimal performance, and log at least eight hours of sleep each night. He checks every day, too.

"I don't like to micromanage you, Harper," Rome says during my weekly weigh-in, "but you're gonna have to get used to living like this if you want to be on a Black Ops team. Those are some serious soldiers."

He pinches my stomach, arms, and thighs and

measures them with a weird little device. "Your body fat percentage is right where we want it for an elite female soldier, but you're not gaining muscle mass fast enough and your weight gain has leveled off. We're gonna have to up your protein intake again. I think you might have to go low-carb for a little while. How were your macros this week?"

I start to sigh and—

"And don't roll your eyes at me again, please. I hate this just as much as you do. You know how many times a week I have to check in with your nutritionist? You wouldn't even *have* one if you hadn't been accepted into your fall program. Most of us don't get this kind of one-on-one attention, you know."

Matthew and I were both provisionally accepted into our top-choice apprenticeships for the fall—Matthew in the Ministry of Technology (Ava told me) and me with covert operations in General Yarrow's office. We have to work overtime this summer to show we can handle those assignments. Each of us is completing a full load of advanced coursework in addition to the regular courses we need just to catch up, and we have to take several achievement and performance tests over the course of the summer to ensure our learning is on target. If we don't score in at least the ninety-fifth percentile on any one of those tests, we'll be dropped from our program and placed in a lower-level apprenticeship.

For me, that doesn't just mean taking written tests in a classroom. I have a fitness test every two weeks. I've had to take marksmanship tests on a multitude of different weapons, all of which I have to be able to dismantle and reassemble in a shockingly short amount of time. By the end of this month, I'll have to negotiate a hostage situation with no loss of life, shoot my way out of a siege situation with no backup, and withstand twenty-four hours of actual physical torture.

By the end of the summer, I'll need to pass some very specific sniper requirements, command an actual battalion of soldiers in about a hundred different military formations through actual historical battles, and navigate my way through the whole of Elysium in broad daylight without civilian detection while evading an entire team of pursuers. Luckily, all the shooting in my performance events is just pellets and beanbag rounds. They still hurt, but don't usually do any permanent damage through full body armor.

They're extending the foreign language requirement to the end of my first year of apprenticeship since I've had only a few months of exposure to other languages. I do have to pass the Level 2 exam in at least Spanish and Mandarin by the end of the summer. By the end of the first year of apprenticeship, if I make it that far, I'll need to be fully trilingual to continue to the second year. Covert ops officer training is no joke!

If I had selected just one or the other—Covert Ops *or* officer training—it wouldn't have been so bad. It still wouldn't have been a picnic, but I wouldn't have felt like I was dying every night when I sink into the hot tub with Rome drilling me on languages, weapons, or military formations from a lounge chair. On the bright side, being this busy has given me the space I so desperately wanted from Matthew. Ava tells me he and Amari are thick as thieves when Matthew actually manages to have any free time.

"My macros were fine," I tell Rome, trying not to sound too exasperated, though probably not as hard as I should. "I hit all my numbers exactly. It helps that you have my nutritionist send a meal plan to the kitchen every week."

"You and I both know you don't have the discipline to follow this diet on your own yet," Rome reminds me. "Last time we tried that, pancakes slathered in butter and maple syrup were your idea of healthy carbs and fat."

He shakes his head at the memory. He must have the patience of an absolute saint. I complain all day every day. He's constantly having to find ways to stop me from breaking the rules. The only thing he's done all summer is find ways to keep me on target, yet he still seems to have a smile on his face.

"I don't know how you put up with me," I say during this brief moment of clarity.

"It's not the easiest thing I've ever done," he replies with a grimace, "but I was sort of in your position just a couple years ago."

"You were?" I ask.

"I mean, obviously not your *exact* situation. I've lived here my whole life and was mostly prepared for my apprenticeship, but when I decided to take it up a notch, I did it all at once, just like you are. I was actually fourteen, too, working lower security, and I decided I wanted to go for it. I applied for officer training and covert ops placement, and I had a coach who got me through it. I wouldn't have made it here without him, and I want to return that favor. You don't get this far ahead this early without help."

"Besides," he adds, "you're probably the most gifted

soldier we've ever seen here, and being your training officer'll probably land me another promotion."

He winks at me, and I chuck his body fat calipers at him.

"Ow, hey!"

"Are we done here?" I ask impatiently, all clarity apparently gone.

"Yeah, we're done. Get to class."

The rest of the day and week passes like usual—class, lunch, workout, study, weapons practice, sparring, dinner, study in the hot tub, flash cards with Ava, and bed at nine. Then it's up and at 'em with early morning drills and my check-in with Rome. Day in and day out.

The summer somehow passes at a painstaking, agonizingly slow pace yet disappears so quickly that I hardly know where the time has gone. By the time August 30 rolls around, I've had enough space to last a lifetime. I'm ready to see my friends again—*all* my friends.

"Harper, your alarm clock has been going off for five minutes. You have to get up now. I can't take it anymore." A bleary-eyed Ava shakes me awake.

"Just hit the snooze. I need sleep."

"No, you can't sleep now." Ava's voice grows intense as she shakes me harder than ever before. "You have tests. You have to *go!*"

I swear and sit up fast, rubbing my eyes. Ava shuffles back to her bedroom, where she promptly collapses without even closing the door.

Seven after the hour. I've only lost a few minutes. Good thing I shower before bed instead of in the mornings now. I rush to the bathroom and pull my hair back sloppily while I use the toilet. I'll fix it after drills. I dress in my military fatigues. Then, it's a quick tooth-brushing and a swipe of deodorant, and I'm out the door. Today is a very big day. I can't afford to be late.

Drills with the rest of the platoon go fine. Everything seems totally normal until we head to the locker room to change, and all the other girls start wishing me luck. I know this was a difficult path to take, but apparently it's so difficult that almost no one ever even attempts it. In fact, Rome and I are the only ones to do it in at least the last twenty years, and he was the first one to accomplish it in something like fifty.

To say I'm nervous would be an understatement. I keep thinking I'm either going to throw up or soil myself, and as much as I appreciate the sentiment from the other girls in my platoon, I could do without the constant reminders of what comes next.

"Hey, Ace!" Rome calls as I walk down the hallway toward our daily check-in.

I turn and make a face at him. "What?"

"Ace," he says, as if he's explaining it to a toddler. "That's your new nickname since you're about to ace your exams."

"I don't think so."

"Okay, okay, not a fan of Ace. What about Hulk? You're gonna smash it!"

"I don't even understand that reference."

"You've never checked out any of the old comic books from the library?" Rome looks at me quizzically.

I keep trying to keep my insides *inside*.

"Not a comic book fan, either. Got it. How about Assassin, since you'll knock 'em dead?"

I'm sure my expression is pained.

"Not in the mood for a nickname today. We'll keep workshopping it. Once you get in, you're gonna need a real call tag."

"I'm more likely to need a bathroom," I moan.

"Yeah, you are looking a little green this morning. I didn't want to mention it, but that was part of the reason for the Hulk suggestion."

I glare at him before opening the door to the office we borrow for our check-ins.

"One last weigh-in," I sigh, trying to clear my head.

"Nope," Rome says. "No weigh-in today. No body fat checks or macros, either. Today, we focus on how far you've come, and get that mind of yours at peace."

"Can we at least study for a few minutes? I need to get these extra conjugates down. I want to place higher than Level 2. And I know I can shave a few more seconds off my Dragunov assemblage if I take a few more tries at it."

Rome shakes his head serenely. "No. You've worked harder than anyone I've ever seen all summer. You've earned this more than anyone who has ever achieved it. You're going to be fine."

"But I just need to—"

"I said no, Moss, and I meant it. Take a minute to look at your stats with me. You've cut your body fat in half, tripled your muscle mass, and worked yourself down to a four-and-a-half-minute mile. You've learned seventy-five new weapons, which I can personally guarantee you've mastered, and I'd say you're pretty close to fluent in both Spanish and Mandarin already, even though you only needed to know basic nouns and verbs. You've set new all-time records on every physical training course and achievement test there is. I am not exaggerating when I say that there is literally nothing I think you can't do."

Rome spends a few more minutes inflating my ego before making me sit quietly in the dark, doing mindfulness exercises. I hate to admit it, but it actually makes me feel a little bit better. I'm so relaxed that I'm getting sleepy, but I'm also thoroughly calm. That was something I really needed.

"How do you feel, Moss?"

"Fine, about the same as before."

Rome makes a face, and I can tell he knows I'm lying. I'm not going to admit it out loud. He's been right about too many things, so I won't give him this one.

"Well, you have about ten minutes until your test. I'd say it's time to get moving. You have plenty of time to get there, so please don't rush. You'll just get right back into that stressed-out mindset if you do. Think about your hard work and your accomplishments. You have everything you need."

Rome was right again.

I enter the exam room with three minutes to spare. Matthew is already here to take separate, but equally important, exams. I smile at him for the first time in over three months, and he smiles back hopefully. He almost looks like it might be a trap. I chuckle a little and take my seat on the opposite side of the room.

Multiple test examiners stand at the front of the room, looking important. One of them wears an earpiece. He must be here for me. I doubt anyone from technology would need one of those. I scrutinize him, trying to determine exactly which S&S department he works in and how important he is. Judging by the dark suit, I'm guessing he's here directly from Secret Service or Covert Operations.

I'm still watching the Covert Ops Agent carefully when he puts his hand up to his earpiece and speaks in hushed tones. He looks immediately concerned. He gathers the other test examiners into the far corner of the room, where they begin whispering urgently. Mr. Weiss, our academic advisor for just two more short days, becomes agitated and appears on the verge of shouting.

"No," I hear him say, "we have to tell them. They're wrapped up in this now, too. They have a right to know."

Suddenly, Matthew is beside me.

"What do you think's going on?" he whispers to me.

"Nothing good," I say.

"Fine, Bob," the man in the black suit finally says aloud. "But since you're the one who wants to share classified information, you get to be the one to tell them."

25

DISCOVERY

It wasn't the child's crying that woke her, but the loud barking cough that accompanied it. Anna's husband stirred beside her, swinging his legs over the side of the bed to get up.

"No, Benjamin, I'll get her. You better rest up for the morning."

"Are you sure?" he asked. He was such a good husband and father, never leaving her to handle everything alone like some of the other men.

"I'm sure," Anna replied, kissing his stubbled cheek. She deftly made her way to the hacking two-year-old, hoisting the child up from her pallet on the bedroom floor.

"Oh, poor sweetie. Mama's here," she cooed, slipping her feet into her boots. She threw a blanket over the arm that held the baby, then pulled it over her other shoulder to wrap around the both of them.

"Here we go, baby. Out into the night for a little walk, okay?"

"Mama," her little Cynthia said into her shoulder, "it hurts." Each word was punctuated by more coughing.

Anna rubbed her youngest's back, whispering comforting words to her as they ventured out into the night. Though the weather turned warmer each day, they were lucky that the *nights remained cool enough to soothe the remnants of their little one's late-spring cold. She bounced the baby gently on her hip and sang her a little lullaby as the pair moved slowly about their new, much smaller family home.*

After a while, the cough began to fade along with the tired mother's remaining energy, but Cynthia seemed to become more and more awake. She tugged at her mama's hair, poked at her eyes, and began to sing her own songs.

"Izzy, bizzy spi-dah . . . wa-wa-wa spow!"

The exhausted mother sighed. "Mama's so glad you're feeling better, baby, but it's time to go back to sleep now."

"No!" the child yelled, "Wah!"

Another sigh, heavier still than the last, and Anna hoisted the child higher up onto her hip. "You want to go for a walk?"

Cynthia bobbed her little blonde head. "Wah!"

"Okay, baby, let's walk. Tell me what you see."

Mother and child walked through desiccated houses, weaving in and out to lengthen the distance. The toddler shouted, "How!" pointing gleefully.

"Yes, a house! What color?" Anna replied with feigned exuberance.

"Why!"

"That's right, baby, it's white. What else do you see?"

"Tee!"

"Trees—good job!"

And on and on they went, bouncing as they walked through homes that gradually became larger and nicer, though not newer, on this side of town. Soon, they came to a line of trees that had sectioned off the old Orphan Home, protecting it from prying eyes and sanctifying it within the community.

Anna shrugged and said, "No one lives here anymore. What harm can it do?"

The toddler on her hip yawned and lay her head on her mother's shoulder. "Tees," she declared mildly as they passed through the tree line. Her mother continued to bounce her lightly, hoping she'd drift off soon. By the time they reached the clothesline behind the Home, the baby's breathing had deepened and a light snore escaped her lips.

Anna's relief was cut off by the sound of voices nearby. Who would be out at such an odd hour? The workday wouldn't begin for hours, not until morning prayers were through.

Checking that the baby was truly asleep, Anna moved closer to the abandoned Orphan Home, careful to keep her steps light. When she neared the back of the house, she bent as low as possible without waking her toddler, cradling the child's head in one hand to keep her steady.

Swathed in darkness, she peered around the corner of the house. Several men were moving in and out of the building, hauling crates and furniture from a fleet of wagons parked in front.

"All right, gentlemen," a voice shouted. It sounded like Elder Prewitt. "We've only an hour until sunrise, and this place needs to be livable. Put your backs into it. Let's get this done!"

The sounds of men grunting with effort filled the air until another man spoke, more quietly this time.

"Will it be ready in time for this morning's hangings?" Elder Samson asked.

Hangings? Who were they going to hang?

"Looks that way," Prewitt replied. "They don't have much left to unload. The women can stay behind and continue preparing the space when we go to prayers."

Anna stifled a scream. She couldn't be found eavesdropping here or she would certainly be next. Holding her child close to her chest, she ran as quickly as she could without waking the toddler, all the way back to Maggie's house. She pounded frantically on the door, shouting as loud as she dared.

"John? Maggie? Maggie! Wake up! Something's happening!"

26

BREACH

"Mr. Weiss, what's happened?" I ask.

"There's been a breach," he declares unceremoniously. "A prison break."

"On Thirteen?"

Mr. Weiss grimaces. "Fifteen, actually. It happened in the night, and it was under control until about an hour ago. Somehow, they found a way through the barricade, maybe through the air duct, maybe through tunnels. We don't really know. What we do know is that they've taken up residence in the Ministry offices, where they're holding General Yarrow and Minister Travis hostage."

Matthew looks completely lost right up until Mr. Weiss mentions hostages.

"That's not good," he swallows.

"No, it's not. The entire city is on lockdown, and unfortunately, the individuals who would normally handle the situation are indisposed."

"Indisposed?" I ask. "What could possibly be more important right now?"

"They're locked in this room with you."

My eyes flick from Mr. Weiss to the very important-looking men and women gathered at the front of the classroom.

"Well, what are you all doing?" I shout at them. "Override the locks and get down there to save the general!"

The man with the earpiece rounds on me, his eyes wild and hungry. "Who do you think you are to give us orders? Don't you think we'd all be up there right this minute if it was possible? One of the prisoners is a former technology administrator-turned-traitor."

"Wait—this is Briscoe? *Dan Briscoe* broke out of prison?" Matthew asks in awe.

"Yes, and he's taken control of the city's entire security system from top to bottom. We can't get out of this room."

"Seriously? There's no backup plan for this kind of thing?" I shout. "Who the hell designed this place?"

"That is an unacceptable way to speak to a senior officer—"

"But she's right," Matthew interrupts. "There are fail safes in place for situations like this. I just need to be able to tap into the system's wiring."

"And how do you propose to do that without making your presence known to Briscoe?" an Indigenous woman in a purple pantsuit demands with crossed arms.

"That's just a matter of skillful encryption. I could—"

"Look, do you want to sit around and listen to him talk about it, or do you want to let him actually *do* it?" I say.

The woman uncrosses her arms and gestures to the security panel next to the door. "Be my guest."

Matthew brings his bag and his tablet over to the door, gesturing for me to join him.

"What are you doing? You know I can't do anything

more complicated than plant a bug or hotwire a car."

"I need somebody to assist me, and I'd rather it be somebody who believes I'm as smart as they are."

"Fair enough," I reply. "What do you need me to do?"

He dumps his bag out on the floor beside me and grabs some kind of cable, a flashlight, and a set of tiny screwdrivers. He hands all three to me, taking one screwdriver for himself.

"I'll need you to light up the inside of the panel once I take the cover off and hand me anything else when I ask for it."

"Sir, yes, sir!"

"Shut up," Matthew says playfully, turning to his work. He unscrews the panel on the wall, and I click the flashlight to life. He adjusts the angle of my hand so the light shines directly on a small circuit board toward the back of the compartment.

"Try to keep it right . . . there."

I nod but don't speak, trying to keep my attention on the task at hand. Matthew nudges a few other pieces out of the way, making a little extra space to work.

"Can you find me the wire strippers?"

I hand him a small tool that looks similar to a pair of pliers. He uses them to strip the casing from several sets of wires, exposing the bare metal beneath. He untwists some and combines them with others. Then, he reaches past me and rifles through his pile of seemingly random junk until he pulls out a contraption connected to another larger circuit board.

He wires this new piece of equipment into the door's control panel before he asks me for the cable. This he connects to his tablet on one end and to the contraption that's hardwired into the door on the other. He opens an app and types in a few strings of code, and then the tablet takes over, running line after line of green code over the screen.

"What's that?" I ask him.

"Encryption. It'll hide my attempts to unlock the door."

"That's it? You're just unlocking the door?" one of the adults asks impatiently.

"That's all I can do from this room. We'll have to get to the floor's main control panel to access the actual security system."

A few more moments of silence while the encryption runs, and then Matthew opens another app. He works in this one longer, but I don't understand much of anything I'm seeing until he presses his palm flat against the screen. I hear a small click as the lock disengages.

"I've managed to reset all the locks on this floor to open with my handprint. What now?" Matthew's eyes bypass the adults in the room and land directly on me.

"We'll need a plan," I say with confidence. This time, I feel exactly how I sound. "Where's the main control panel?"

"It'll be in the workrooms in the middle of the floor, near the custodial closets."

The man with the earpiece attempts to take over at this point. "We'll need to get there without being seen. They could have people on every floor looking for dissidents."

"They'll certainly be watching the security footage carefully," another woman chimes in.

"Right," I say, "so we'll need to time it exactly right. We'll have to go in two groups of four. There won't be time for more than that to clear an area before the footage cycles through. I'll head up the first team, and Earpiece, you take the second one."

The man does not look pleased, but he doesn't argue either.

"The cameras move in six-second intervals. The trick will be figuring out when this one is pointed away from the door, so we can follow behind its cycle."

I pull a tiny camera from my satchel and slide it under the door. I'm able to view the hallway camera on my tablet and time its exact cycle until I'm sure I have it. Then, I set a repeating timer on my watch that follows the cycle. Earpiece follows my lead and syncs his watch to mine via Bluetooth.

We divide up into our teams, but before my group leaves, I sketch out a map of this floor and review the plan with everyone.

"You'll enter the ventilation system here," I draw an X on the map at the end of the next hallway where there's a large floor grate. "I'll get it open before your team arrives. Remember to wait at least two full minutes after we leave before you try to head out."

Earpiece nods more agreeably than I anticipated, but I'm in no position to question miracles. I add a few capital Bs on the map in select locations along our path.

"These are camera blind spots. The cameras don't see anything at all in these places. They're not very big—only about four floor tiles square—so you'll have to be very careful how you position yourselves. Make sure you stay together. The most dangerous thing you can do is split up more than we already have to."

"How will you have enough space to get the floor grate

open if the blind spots are that small?" Purple Pantsuit asks me.

"The blind spot at the end of that hall is quite a bit bigger. It's just dead space back there, so I guess no one realized the cameras don't extend that far. The rest of my group will hang back in the corner while I work the grate in the next hall between camera sweeps. Matthew, I'll need to borrow some of your tools."

Matthew hands over his backpack, which I immediately strap on after shoving my own satchel inside.

"Anybody else have an earpiece so we can communicate if our teams get separated?"

Another one of the women pulls hers out of her inside jacket pocket. "Here. Use mine."

"Thanks," I say, stuffing the wire and radio pack down the back of my shirt before I try the earpiece. "Any questions about the plan?"

Everyone looks around and shakes their heads.

"Great, let's get this done."

Earpiece and I double-check that our watches are still synced to one another and to the security feeds. Very carefully, I time my team's exit into the hallway.

"Go, go, go!" I whisper. "Go now, go now!"

I head up the rear as my three teammates rush down the hallway together.

"Stop right there!" I tell them as loudly as I dare. "That's the first blind spot!"

They all come to a halt, crashing into one another. I monitor my watch and the cameras with one hand in the air. When my timer buzzes, I bring my hand down hard.

"Go!"

We turn a corner between blind spots. I see them

hesitate, checking that there's no one there.

"Keep moving! Only two seconds to get to your blind spot!"

They race like they're being chased by Death himself. I've never seen adults move so fast outside military drills, but we make it by the skin of our teeth. We've literally only run for twelve seconds, but the old folks are struggling to catch their breath.

I briefly wonder if it was a good idea to leave Matthew with the other team. He hasn't had any physical training, and if his team is as out of shape as mine . . . I couldn't bear it if anything happened to him. I just have to hope and trust that he'll be okay. Surely, Earpiece still does drills on the reg. I give my team an extra twelve seconds to catch their breath before spurring them on again.

When we reach the end of this hallway, we run right past the floor grate and into the large blind spot. The team collapses onto the floor. Without even looking at them, I know they need a scolding.

Never even taking an eye off the timer, I lay into them in a stern whisper. "What do all of you think you're doing? Get up off that floor! You need to be ready to move at a moment's notice if someone comes around this corner. And be quiet! They can probably hear you moaning and groaning all the way up on the second floor. Get your asses up! Now!"

My team hustles to their feet. I don't check to see if they have the good sense to look ashamed. I unscrew three corners of the grate between camera sweeps with the lightweight drill in Matthew's bag. I don't have time for the fourth because a voice crackles to life in my ear.

"Team Two incoming. Shit, we've got company!"

Three loud pops echo through the corridor. I slap my hand over Purple Pantsuit's mouth before she can cry out and pull a miniature pry bar out of my own belongings. I position it beneath the edge of the floor grate and wait for the right time. Matthew comes racing around the corner with Earpiece nipping at his heels. No other teammates emerge.

The man pulls a handgun from his blazer and begins to fire behind him as two burly men in prison orange barrel toward him. I lay all my weight into the crowbar, and this side of the grate gives way. It scrapes loudly over the floor as I pull it toward me, using the fourth intact screw as a hinge of sorts.

"Drop down!" I command Matthew. He throws his feet out in front of him and slides the remaining distance, landing directly in the floor tunnel. The others drop down behind him one by one. I smell the sulphuric odor of gunpowder just as Earpiece slides into me, leaving a wide streak of wet redness in his wake.

He's been shot three times in the chest. There's nothing I can do, and we both know it. Instead of trying to change the inevitable outcome, he hoists his weapon and aims down the hallway.

"Get the others out of here! I'll hold them off. Maybe even take them down with me."

I give the briefest nod and drop down into the vent backward, sliding the cover back over above me. Something lands on top of me just before I close the gap. It's an earpiece.

As I'm replacing the screws in the grate, a frightened voice behind me asks, "Where's Chuck?"

"He didn't make it," I reply, watching his body slide over

the grate above my head. Gunshots ring out, deafening my left ear. "You need to get moving. Matthew, lead the way. I'll catch up."

"Why? What are you going to do?" he demands.

"Make sure they can't get in after us. Earpiece—uh, Chuck—is on top of the grate now, but they'll move him soon enough. I'm setting a charge that'll go off if they drop down into the tunnel on top of it. I need space to work, so it doesn't explode on me instead."

They don't need me to tell them twice. I hear them scurrying away on hands and knees, bumping loudly as they go. I've just about got the charge in place when the sound of gunfire comes to a halt.

"They went down into the vent. Help me move the body."

It'll take them some time to get the grate off since it's screwed on from underneath. I'd like to be as far away as possible before they figure it out and blow themselves up. I make my way back to the others as quickly as possible in the cramped space.

"Harper? Harper!" Matthew's voice calls out in the darkness.

"I'm here! They're in for a big surprise if they try to follow us."

"Harper, I don't actually know where I'm going. You're the one with the ventilation system memorized."

"I'm coming."

Though these vents are big enough to crawl through, they are definitely only wide enough for single-file travel. When I catch up to the line of terrified adults following Matthew, everyone has to lie down so I can sidle past them. It is uncomfortable, to say the least. The worst is when I reach Matthew. I keep my eyes up instead of looking at him.

After several minutes of extreme awkwardness, I finally take the lead of our woefully diminished group. Matthew managed to lead us in the general direction of the custodial workrooms where the main control panel is housed, even if he didn't know the most efficient route. It's lucky he didn't get us lost.

We spend the next thirty minutes or so bumping around the ventilation ducts. I pause periodically at vents to listen for voices, but there's nothing. I wonder where they think we'll emerge. Surely they're setting a trap for us somewhere.

"I think we're here," I announce as quietly as possible. "Matthew, I'm gonna need you to get my liquid nitrogen and my crowbar out of the bag."

He crawls up close behind me, and I feel him rifling through the backpack.

"What's the nitrogen for?"

"Just watch."

Holding the tiny flashlight in my teeth, I spray liquid nitrogen into each of the screw holes holding this grate in place. Then I try the pry bar in the side, but the grate barely budges.

"Okay, I'm gonna need a small, long screwdriver or even a drill bit if you happen to have one. And something I can pound on it with."

I reach my hand back and within moments, Matthew has already come through. In my hand I find the perfect screwdriver and a small hammer.

Why in the world does he carry this around with him?

That's probably a silly question from the girl with

liquid nitrogen in her bag. I spray more into the holes to make sure the screws are good and brittle. Then I stick the screwdriver in until it makes contact with the bottom of the screw. As quietly as possible, I hammer the end of the screwdriver until I hear a cracking sound. I repeat this process three more times until I'm able to lift the grate.

"Everyone stay here, and be ready to go back the way we came if I say so," I command as I lift myself out of the hole in the floor.

I shine the light around the dark workroom and gradually make my way around corners and equipment until I'm certain I'm alone.

"It's clear," I call quietly into the vent shaft.

One by one, the other four climb out into the room. It's just me, Matthew, Purple Pantsuit, Mr. Weiss, and another man with a large curly mustache whose voice I haven't heard yet. Once everyone's out, I place the grate back over the hole.

"Everybody grab a corner of this filing cabinet. We need to move something with some weight over the opening in case they find a way to follow us."

As carefully as possible, we work together to move not one, but two insanely heavy filing cabinets onto the grate. I briefly assess our small crew, evaluating who is capable of accepting new responsibilities and whose nerves are shot as the weight of three deaths begins to set in.

Mr. Weiss has clearly never dealt with this level of trauma before. He's not freaking out, but he looks numb, unable to focus. Purple Pantsuit is on the verge of hyperventilating. Mustache may not have nerves of steel, but his eyes suggest he still has more to give. I pat him firmly on the shoulder.

"I need you to assist Matthew while I guard the door. Mr. Weiss, Pantsuit, you can sit this one out. Get a little rest, but be ready to move or fight if it becomes necessary. I think we're in the clear for at least a few minutes, though."

Pantsuit collapses into a heap on the floor, but Mr. Weiss still has at least some of his wits about him. He chooses the desk chair and stares off into space, positioning himself with his back to the wall. Matthew moves toward the control panel and raises his flashlight.

"Wait," I tell him, pushing his arm back down. "Not yet."

I nod toward the camera in a corner near the ceiling.

"What do we do?" he asks, less panic in his voice than I would've expected.

I scrutinize it carefully. "It doesn't have night vision. It won't see us as long as we keep the lights off."

"I can't do this in the dark," comes the reply. "I have to be able to see what I'm doing."

"Then we'll just have to keep rearranging the room. What do you think are the chances Briscoe's familiar with the preferred furniture layout of the tech room on the school floor?"

"After ten years in prison? None."

"Perfect. You—Mustache—watch the door for a few minutes."

Ten minutes later, Matthew and I have built a suitable blind around the control panel, just big enough for two people and Matthew's supplies. I close them in and toss a broken-down cardboard box over the top to stop the light from escaping. At this angle, the camera shouldn't pick it up.

"Everyone else, stay as still as possible. The little bit of light that gets out won't illuminate you enough to be noticeable, but they'll definitely see movement."

I position myself next to the door and slide my camera underneath, watching the empty hallway on my tablet. I hold my breath as the two prisoners who killed our compatriots turn a nearby corner and head this direction.

"Everyone quiet! Get ready!" I whisper.

God, I wish I had a real weapon with me. Even if this had happened during tomorrow's performance event, I would have only had a paintball gun.

Thankfully, they don't give this room a second glance and stroll on by. I don't breathe again until they disappear from view.

"They're gone," I whisper into the darkness.

Several more uneventful minutes pass before Matthew finally announces that he's tapped into the security feed.

"They're stationed all over the city! Harper, you have to look at this."

"Cover your screen and turn off the flashlight before I come in."

"Okay, we're ready."

I move some furniture and trade places with Mustache, who closes me in and makes sure the box blots out as much light as possible. Matthew turns his tablet screen back on and shows me a rotation of four feeds at a time.

I swear under my breath. They're in all the most important places, guarding every elevator and every major entrance and exit within floors. This will be almost impossible.

"You've been training for this all summer," Matthew whispers, noticing my expression.

I take a breath to steady myself. He's right. This is exactly what I've been training for.

"I just didn't expect to have live rounds fired at me while I was doing it," I tell him.

"I can't really argue with that, but honestly, how many paintballs have you taken in the last month anyway?"

I grin. "None."

"Thought so. Have you seen everything you need to?"

"Yeah, let's get out there and make a plan."

He shuts off the screen, and we emerge from our hiding place to find ourselves face to face with two hulking prisoners pointing guns at Mr. Weiss's and Purple Pantsuit's heads. Mustache lies on the floor, either dead or barely breathing.

27

SELF-DEFENSE

My training takes over; I barely even think about what I'm doing. I pick up a large wrench from the table beside me with my right hand and shove Matthew back into our control panel blind with my left. I hurl the wrench at the prisoner farthest from me, simultaneously throwing a roundhouse kick at the closer one.

A crunch. A clatter. Shouts, and the metallic smell of blood. Both guns lie on the floor. The prisoner hit by the wrench lies crumpled on the floor, cradling a bloodied and probably broken jaw with both hands. Mr. Weiss picks up a gun while the prisoner who remains standing charges at me.

I duck beneath his advance, then stand up quick and strong, burying my shoulder in his gut and flipping him over my back. He lands face-up on the concrete floor with a thud, the air knocked out of him. Before he can recover, I step my combat boot down on his throat. Keeping my eyes on the prisoner, I hold my hand up in Mr. Weiss's direction, and I feel cold steel pressed squarely into my palm within a second.

Applying pressure with my boot as the prisoner

beneath begins to struggle, I turn my attention and my sidearm toward the other. To my surprise Purple Pantsuit is holding him at gunpoint, though he looks seriously disinterested in fighting back now. The firearm shakes in her inexperienced hands, but she stands her ground. Confident that she'll shoot if necessary, I train my weapon back on the prisoner, who continues to squirm beneath my boot.

"Mr. Weiss," I say, "check Mustache's pulse."

The haggard teacher tries Mustache's wrist and his neck. He checks the man for any sign of breathing before he launches into several minutes of futile CPR. He keeps checking for a pulse, for a breath—any sign of life—before launching back into his life-saving efforts.

"Mr. Weiss," I say. Then louder, when he ignores me, "Mr. Weiss. Bob!"

His head snaps up, staring at me with glistening saucers for eyes.

"It's not going to work. He's gone," I say more quietly.

Purple Pantsuit stifles a sob. Matthew is suddenly standing next to her, one arm wrapped around her tall, bony frame. He takes the gun from her trembling hands, and she lays her head on his shoulder to weep. He trains the weapon on his prisoner uncertainly.

"Nothing you can do," the broken-jawed prisoner says with agonizing, muffled speech. "Briscoe knows about you. They're coming."

The prisoner beneath me lets out a strangled but cruel laugh. Without looking away from his comrade, I shoot the man three times in the chest. It's a good thing they stole silencers, or it would've drawn their backup to us. Everyone but me jumps with each gunshot.

"Harper," Matthew says, wild-eyed, "you . . . you shot him. He wasn't even armed."

"What did you want me to do—knock him out so he could tell everyone where we went when he wakes up?"

Matthew shakes his head, silently staring at the dead man whose windpipe is still crushed beneath my boot.

"No? Maybe tie him up and wait for them to find him or for him to free himself?" I offer.

Silent tension permeates the room until Broken-Jaw starts whimpering, then screaming. I do what I have to do and put a bullet in his chest, too. Blood erupts from his wound, splattering on Purple Pantsuit and Matthew's legs and shoes. They both stare at me, terrified. Clearly no one expected this from the fourteen-year-old girl. That's one of my strengths actually—looking far less dangerous than I actually am.

I sigh and place my gun in the back of my waistband. "I don't like it either, but in this situation, it's his life or ours. It's not like we could take him with us. It's self-defense."

"She's right," Mr. Weiss interjects. "There wasn't any other choice, and she's probably the only one of us with the training or the stomach to do it. What's next, Harper?"

"You're not gonna like this, but we need to empty their pockets. They might have extra ammo or other useful items."

Mr. Weiss rifles through Broken Jaw's pockets while I check the other guy's. They each carry two extra mags. One has a radio that was switched to silent, probably to allow them to sneak up on us. There's also a lighter, a pack of gum, and a small brick of C-4.

What were they gonna use this for?

"Mr. Weiss, I need you to get on this walkie and say these exact words in a gravelly voice: Targets neutralized. Checking out their escape tunnel to make sure we didn't miss anything. Going off-grid temporarily. Over."

The reply comes back quickly, "Copy that. Let us know when you resurface. Over."

Better hang onto this. I clip the radio to the left strap of my tank top, right in front where I can hear everything they say over their frequency.

"Do any of you know how to handle a weapon?" I ask my shrinking group. All three shake their heads.

Mr. Weiss speaks up again. "I think Matthew should have it. Neither of us knows how to do any of the technological stuff that'll get us out of this situation. You two have the best chance."

Purple Pantsuit's eyes widen and stare at the floor, but she nods in agreement.

"Me?" Matthew asks incredulously. "I don't know how to do this. I don't want to shoot anyone!"

"You may not have to, Matthew," I reassure him, "but you may not have a choice. You'd be surprised what you can do when your life is on the line."

I put the two adults to work dumping three dead bodies into the tunnel we used to get here. Then, I take a few minutes to teach Matthew how to use a gun. I show him where to find the safety and how to switch it on and off. I have him practice dropping a mag and reloading until he can do it without his hands shaking.

"Feel a little more comfortable?" I ask, pressing my palm across the barrel of his gun to lower it for him.

"I guess, but I still haven't tried to shoot at anything."

I shrug. "People are pretty big targets. We can't afford to waste ammo on target practice."

"Do you think we'll really need it?" he asks nervously.

I tilt my head sympathetically, as if talking to a child who genuinely believes there's a Lorax living in the forest on the surface. I don't have to say a word.

"Oh," Matthew says, bowing his head in dejection.

"I mean, maybe not." I try to sound positive but come across as manic. "But probably. Sorry."

"I knew it before I asked," he says, but that thought doesn't seem to cheer him up.

Mr. Weiss grunts with the effort of sliding the floor grate back over our makeshift grave. His shirt is soaking with sweat. Purple Pantsuit has given up her blazer, losing much of her previous resemblance to a giant eggplant now that she's down to a white cami. The two of them move to replace the filing cabinets over the grate.

"That's probably not necessary," Matthew says. "We already know they didn't follow us through the ventilation system, and file cabinets on top of a grate is going to make it pretty obvious that there's something down there if someone comes in through the door."

"He's got a point," Mr. Weiss tells Purple Pantsuit.

"Oh, thank God," she sighs, collapsing into the office chair. "What's next?"

"Next is getting to the elevators," I announce, "which isn't going to be easy."

"Could we distract them with something?" Matthew asks.

I shake my head. "I've been figuring out the timing and pattern of their patrols. I think we can get down the hallways if you can watch the security feeds for incoming threats while we do it. Could you make that thing wireless?"

"Yeah, actually. Just give me a few minutes."

In reality, it takes him maybe thirty seconds. He's that good at what he does. He emerges from the control panel blind with his tablet in hand.

"Just had to change a couple things up. I got it all put back together, so no one will be able to tell we messed with the control panel. And now"—he fiddles with something on the tablet—"all the security feeds are set to repeat the same cycle of empty rooms and hallways. It's encrypted pretty heavily, so it should take them hours to find it, if they find it at all."

"Great work, Matthew." I smile at him.

"What's the plan once we get to the elevators?" Mr. Weiss asks grimly.

"I take out the guards. They won't expect us to have weapons, and they think we're all dead."

"By yourself?" Pantsuit stares in disbelief.

"It's just two guys—no more than what I took care of a few minutes ago. Only this time I'll have the element of surprise. It'll be a piece of cake."

My three companions look back and forth between one another and come to a silent consensus. Apparently, they've agreed that I can handle my part of the plan.

"What do we do once you clear the elevators?" Mr. Weiss asks.

"Okay, look . . ." I tell them the rest of the plan with the aid of the map I drew earlier. We collect our supplies and head out into the empty hallway.

28

INFERNO

Matthew guides us through the halls safely by watching the unaltered surveillance feeds on his tablet. Occasionally, we duck down a side hall or into a room to avoid detection. We make it to the elevators without incident.

As we get closer, Matthew taps my shoulder, and everyone stops silently. I take a few moments to watch the feeds. Looks like everyone nearby is mercifully headed in the opposite direction for now. I creep toward the next corner, around which are two guards.

Matthew signals me when their backs are turned. I rush out behind them soundlessly, grabbing one around the neck, putting him in a sleeper hold until he blacks out. The other turns around, reaching for a handgun in the waistband of his pants. I shoot him twice before he gets the chance.

Matthew protests killing the unconscious guard, but I know what has to be done. We stash the bodies in a nearby closet and clean up the blood as quickly as possible before we enter the elevator. As soon as the doors close, I get to work.

"Matthew, gimme a boost."

When the elevator dings and the doors slide open, the small compartment is empty. The prisoners guarding this floor enter with their guns raised, clearly bewildered by the elevator's unexpected arrival. One silenced shot rains down on each of them, and they drop where they stand.

I hop down through the elevator roof and hold the doors open. Matthew and Mr. Weiss follow and help Pantsuit get down. Checking the security feed, Matthew signals that it's safe to disembark. We drag the bodies to a nearby maintenance closet and stash them inside.

"All right, it's just down this next hall." I turn the corner with Matthew right on my heels.

"Harper," Mr. Weiss says urgently.

I spin around on the spot, concern filling my face. He stares at me from around the corner, blood-covered hands clutching at his side.

"Mr. Weiss, we have to get you out of here!"

"No," he tells me, and his eyes say he means it.

Purple Pantsuit goes down behind him, two bullets in her back.

"Harper, you and Matthew have to get to the general. You're the only ones who can stop this. I'll hold them off."

"Here," Matthew hands Mr. Weiss his gun. "Make 'em fight for it."

Mr. Weiss nods, turns, and charges toward our assailants. As Matthew and I make a desperate sprint for the hidden Secret Service entrance, gunshots fire. I pull a fire extinguisher off the wall and place my hand on the scanner hidden beneath it. A panel pops open to the left. I shove Matthew through it, desperately thrashing at the button on the other side. A bullet whizzes by just as it seals itself.

"Do you think he made it?" Matthew pants as he slides down the wall onto the floor.

I shake my head with true remorse. "Someone was shooting when I closed the door."

"Worst. Day. Ever."

"You can say that again."

We allow ourselves to rest for a few minutes and feel our loss. We really didn't know Earpiece or Mustache or Purple Pantsuit or whoever those other people were, but Mr. Weiss is a serious blow to my confidence. I had thought I could keep them all safe. I had thought we could save Elysium. If I couldn't save anyone else, I can at least save Matthew. We've been through too much. I'm not going to lose him, too. I stand up all of a sudden, taking even myself by surprise.

"I guess that means you're ready?" Matthew asks.

"You're not coming with me."

"What?"

"I can't lose another person. I can't lose you."

Matthew stands now and wraps his arms around me. I burrow my face into him, breathing him in. Even now, through blood and sweat and tears, he still smells comforting. I pull my head away and look him dead in the eyes.

"I need to know you're safe. I can't do this if I'm worrying about you. Give me your hand."

He holds one hand out, palm up, and I drop my extra earpiece into it. He raises an eyebrow.

"Earpiece gave me this before he died. You'll be able to watch out for me from here."

"Harper," he says sternly.

"No." I shake my head at him. "I'm not letting one more person risk their life. You can help me from in here, where I know you're safe."

"At least let me go with you a little farther. I'll stay behind when it gets dangerous."

"I think I can live with that."

We walk together in silence as I navigate the covert corridors. Within ten minutes, we've reached the National Security wing—just enough time to formulate this final part of my plan. Matthew seems satisfied with my ideas, so I don't hesitate when we reach the exit to the hallway just outside General Yarrow's office.

We check our earpieces to ensure we can hear each other properly. Matthew monitors the security feeds for additional threats.

"I wish you had some Kevlar right about now," Matthew says.

"You and me both," I say. "But these guys aren't exactly trained commandos. They're not as tough as they think."

"Good luck out there," Matthew says, kissing me on the forehead. "Your real job is to come back."

I squeeze his hand. "Copy that."

I rush headlong out of my hiding place, taking out the convicts guarding the general's door before they have time to register my presence.

"Did anyone hear that?" I ask through the mic on my earpiece while dragging the bodies out of the way.

"I'm not registering any movement," comes Matthew's reply in my ear. "Sealing the National Security wing now."

"How many are still in this wing?"

"Looks like four." He swears. "They're all headed your direction, about to cross paths right where you are. Can you handle four at once?"

I roll my eyes. "Course I can!"

"I can still see your eye rolls through the cameras, you know."

I stick my tongue out at the nearest camera and show it my middle finger.

"Nice, Harper. Real classy. You better get moving. They're almost there."

I step out into the main hallway as if I don't have a care in the world. I walk all the way across, pretending I don't know anyone's around. Then, I back up and do a double take in each direction, making my most frightened little mouse face. As grown men and women reach for their weapons, I hit the proverbial dirt and let them shoot each other.

When the smoke clears, only one is still moving. I put her out of her misery from a distance before I start dragging bodies back to the general's atrium. A heap of six is pretty impressive for little old me.

The voice in my ear congratulates me. "Harper, that was awesome!"

"I thought you didn't like me killing people."

"Technically, they mostly killed each other."

"I knew you'd come around," I say, smiling at the camera. "Have you locked down the elevators yet?"

"Yep, just as soon as you took out the first pair of thugs. No one should be able to get to you."

"Perfect," I say as I unclip the pilfered walkie from my tank top. "It's showtime."

Into the radio, I say, "Dan Briscoe. This is Harper Moss,

Elysium Safety and Security. We need to talk."

A few minutes of silence follow. I imagine the crews of prisoners all over the building arguing about what's going on. I don't wait too terribly long before I speak again.

"Dan Briscoe. Harper to Dan Briscoe. I have something you want."

The radio crackles to life with a guttural voice. "How did you get this frequency? I don't even know you."

"Maybe you didn't know me before, but you definitely know me now," I say. "I have something you want. Are you watching the security feeds?"

"Yes, and you're nowhere on them. Hiding, are you, little princess?" the voice on the walkie growls.

"Keep watching."

Matthew should be switching the feeds right now. The walkie explodes with shouted orders.

"Mr. Briscoe," I say calmly. "Mr. Briscoe, can you hear me?"

"What?" he barks back.

"They can't do any of that. You'll find that the elevators are locked down, far beyond your reach, as well as the doors to the National Security wing."

A string of swears erupts from the radio, some of them quite creative.

"You'll also notice that every one of your henchmen who was in here with me has been neutralized. No one can stop me from getting to you now."

"Is that supposed to scare me?"

"Look around the city, Mr. Briscoe. I've taken out more than just these six today. Six more are missing. If I can handle twelve of your men all by myself, what makes you think I can't handle one of you?"

"There's more than just me in here, though, young lady. Maybe we let you in so you can find out."

"Maybe you do, Mr. Briscoe. I'd love a chance to chat face to face. Unless you'd like to go ahead and surrender now."

A rumble of laughter bursts from the walkie. While Briscoe is distracted, I give a command through my earpiece.

"Now, Matthew."

"Okay . . . go!" comes his reply.

I race back into the secret passageway, rushing past Matthew who works diligently on his tablet. I take a sharp left, sprint down one hall, another left, another sprint, and another left, where I find myself standing at the hidden entrance to the back of General Yarrow's office. I hear an explosion on the other side of the door, and that's my cue.

I burst into the office, prepared to shoot or pummel any enemy I spot through the smoke. What I find instead is a sea of government officials holding their ears, taking cover behind various pieces of furniture, and spraying fire extinguishers. I rush toward the blown-off office door, searching desperately for Briscoe.

How did he get away?

"Matthew, which way did he go?"

"What? Who?"

"Briscoe! He's not here. Where did he go?"

"No one left the office, Harper. He must still be in there somewhere."

A large man stands up amidst the chaos and starts to speak. Before he can get a word out, I kick him squarely in the gut. He doubles over, shock and pain plastered on his face.

"She's here!" someone shouts, and now there's music playing and colorful paper drifting through the air. Someone slams into me with their arms wrapped around my waist. I assume a defensive posture when I hear a familiar voice.

"Harper, it's me! Stop it!"

Ava?

I pull away, trying to understand what's happening. Ava's standing right in front of me with my whole gang of friends. She was the one hugging me.

Ava was hugging me?

"What are you doing here? Did they hurt you?" I demand, examining her for injuries.

"What?" She makes a face and swats my hands away. "No, nobody hurt me! Where's Matthew?"

"He's—" I stop short, noticing that Matthew has emerged into the hallway and is standing next to—

"Mr. Weiss? What is going on?" I demand of no one in particular.

General Yarrow appears, thoroughly unabused, though she looks about to burst into laughter.

"Harper, this was your test, and you both passed!" She pats me on the back.

"*This* was the test?" I gawk at my immediate surroundings, trying to make sense of things. "This was the test."

Rome appears as if from nowhere and scoops me up into a hug so massive that my feet no longer touch the ground.

"You did it, Ace!"

"I think I need to lie down. And I thought I said no to Ace."

"You still need a call tag," Rome replies affectionately as he sets me down and releases me. "What about C-4? Detonator? Everyone's pretty impressed by your use of explosives, even if they do have to do some serious construction on General Yarrow's office now."

I shake my head, mentally reviewing the day I've just had. "What about Inferno?"

"I like it," Rome nods in approval. "You know this means I'm not your commanding officer anymore."

"Yeah," I say, noticing the discomfort on Matthew's face as he watches us from across the hall.

"Maybe I could take you out on a date to celebrate," he says.

"Oh, I uh . . . there's something I have to do first. I'll get back to you."

I leave him standing there, staring at me as I walk away.

29

THE ORPHAN HOME

He struggled against them as he watched his wife, a former Elder, being dragged onto the platform to be hung. The gallows had loomed over the village all these weeks, a constant threat to their safety, and yet, they had never been used again. They had grown complacent, perhaps on some level believing the Council wouldn't dare. They had spoken too loudly and too often about missing the child who was taken without taking care of who might be near, listening. Today, there would be no more.

He wasn't a small man; it took four others to restrain him. One on either side kicked him firmly behind each knee, bending his legs and sending him crashing to the ground. The cry of pain and surprise that might have escaped his lips was stifled by the rag that had been tied around his head shortly after he and his wife were arrested not twenty minutes ago. Forced to kneel in the dirt, he still fought them until the cold steel of a blade touched his throat.

"That's enough of that, Mr. Johnson," the Elder's voice growled from behind him. "You don't imagine you could actually save her, do you?"

Mr. Johnson stiffened behind the knife, beads of sweat forming across his brow. Men with rifles flanked the gallows *and surrounded the people in the square, ensuring that no one could fight back. Most were too stunned to try anyway. Mrs. Johnson struggled against her captors until they slipped the noose over her head and her eyes met her husband's. Tears began to leak down her cheeks as Father Cowan read the charges against her, his voice choked and broken.*

"Mrs. Johnson, you are charged with . . . refusal to uphold . . . the sanctity of the, the . . . Sending. Witnesses have heard you speak of the personhood of your Orphan and of your desire for her to return to your home. The Council has found . . . has found you . . . guilty of . . . religious insubordination with a punishment of—"

Father Cowan faltered. A slight shift several feet to the left of his podium showed a gunman taking subtle aim at his head. He looked into the waiting crowd for reassurance. He must have found what he sought because his gaze steadied before he cleared his throat and continued.

"—punishment of death by hanging." He looked into the crowd once more and gave a slight nod. The men holding Mrs. Johnson threw her from the platform. When the rope pulled taut, her neck snapped instantly, throwing her head into an unnatural, gruesome angle. A strangled cry went up from the crowd, and her husband slumped over. Mr. Johnson's face had turned an awful shade of purple. The men who had restrained him were forced to release him, no longer able to support his weight. He fell onto his side, dead.

"Well," declared Elder Samson, shattering the absolute silence as he sheathed the knife he had held to the dead man's throat, "I suppose that saves us from another hanging. String up the bodies, so they don't forget. Father Cowan, I believe you have further business with the people."

Father Cowan's eyes had grown wide, his face pale. He

shook himself and shivered. "Uh, yes. If you'll bring the child to me."

The hook-nosed man held his arms out, and Mrs. Prewitt delivered an infant, no more than a few months old, into his arms. "Our gracious gods, the Sovereign, we pray a blessing over the Johnson Orphan. Watch over her in her parents' absence and sanctify her continued presence among our people. As of this moment, we commit her soul to Your care. She shall no longer be one of us, for she belongs to You. Guide her and keep her in Your grace so that she might not fall into the footsteps of her forebears but may be worthy of Your good Name. Amen."

A chorus of tear-choked and mournful amens followed, but with much less gusto than would normally be heard at morning prayers. Father Cowan returned the baby to Mrs. Prewitt's arms, turning to face the people once again.

"This morning marks the reopening of the Orphan Home. It has been prepared in advance for our first Orphans, who have been under the community's care until today. New Caretakers await them there. As the community which they protect, it is our duty to see them to their new home and to pray blessing over it. We shall hold our morning prayers at its front doors after the blessing. I admonish you, as followers of the Sovereign"—the look the father gave the crowd was pointed, dripping with meaning—"to repent, in both word and deed. Repent, for the Sovereign know our sins, and we will be held accountable!"

30

MOVING ON

Before I reach Matthew, I'm intercepted by Earpiece, who's intent on congratulating me. Apparently, I completed my tasks in record time and, in a real-life situation, would likely have had a much lower mortality rate.

I don't hear much else he has to say after a cute, petite blonde girl approaches Matthew. I can't deny that she's adorable. I also can't deny the way they look at each other. Something's happening there, and I'm not sure how to feel about it.

"What do we think of the new girl?" Ava asks.

I realize I've been staring at Matthew and his new friend so intently that Earpiece gave up and wandered off. Ava now stands beside me, glaring across the hall in solidarity.

"She's cute," I reply solemnly.

"Right. I hate her, too."

"No." I shake my head. "Please don't hate her. Maybe she's really nice. Maybe she'll be good for him."

"Better than you were?"

I sigh. "It was my choice to end things, remember? I don't have any say in what he does now, but that doesn't make my feelings any less complicated."

"What do you mean?" Ava asks.

"We were together for the first time in months today. We spent the whole day together, getting through life-or-death situations."

"Fake situations with actors," Ava points out.

"But we *thought* it was life-or-death. It felt real. We did this together. I realized that I can't be okay without him in my life. We had this moment just before the end." I wipe a tear from my cheek. "He kissed me on the forehead. I held his hand for a second. I thought maybe things could go back to how they were, but I was wrong."

"Maybe things *could* go back," Ava offers, "if he knew how you felt. You should tell him."

"I don't want to get in his way. He deserves to have a life of his own. And I do, too."

"What's that supposed to mean?"

"Rome asked me out on a date, and I kind of wanted to say yes."

Ava's eyes widen and she giggles. "Really?"

"I was gonna talk to Matthew first, but now it seems like maybe I don't need to."

"You should still talk to him," Ava advises, wise beyond her years. "And he obviously has some things he needs to talk to you about, too."

"True."

"But you wanted to say yes to Rome?"

"I think so. I mean, he's really cute and nice and funny. And he totally gets the S&S life. He understands me in a way Matthew probably never could. It makes a lot of sense."

"You think too much," Ava says, pulling a face.

"I know," I say. "I just need to talk to Matthew and get it over with, except Blondie's still over there. What do I do about her?"

"I don't think it makes much difference now," Ava replies. Matthew must've seen us staring at him. He's headed our direction.

"Hey, Harper," he says when he reaches me. "Can we talk?"

"Yeah," I gulp. "Of course."

I stare at him expectantly, but he looks like he's waiting for something.

"Somewhere more private?" he suggests.

"Yeah." I try to shake the fog from my head. "Yeah, where should we go?"

Matthew leads me down the hallway, out of National Security, and into an empty conference room in Technology.

"You saw me talking with Amelia," Matthew says.

"Oh, is that her name? I was just wondering where you know her from," I say, attempting to sound nonchalant.

A pained expression crosses his face. "She's in Tech, too. She's got a good apprenticeship, but not quite as good as yours or mine."

I struggle to stop my eyes from rolling.

"We've been hanging out a lot this summer. We're not dating or anything but—"

"But you're thinking about it," I finish for him. "I could tell you like her. She likes you, too. She'll say yes if you ask her."

"So, you think I should ask her out?"

"If that's what you want," I say, my face a mask of indifference.

"It's just that . . . earlier, it felt like there might still be something between us."

"I can't ask you not to be with someone you really like, Matthew. It wouldn't be right. I want you to do what makes you happy, no matter what it is."

"Oh, right," he says. I'm having trouble reading his expression. "Okay, uh, I guess that clears things up for me. I'll . . . I'll ask her out."

"Rome asked me out, too. I'm thinking I might say yes," I blurt.

"Oh, good. You two are good together."

Matthew starts to stand, but I stop him by putting my hand over his on the table.

"I just want you to be happy," I say, softer than before.

"That's what I want for you, too." He leaves me there to sit in silence and wallow in my mixed-up emotions.

31

AUTUMN

If I thought life would slow down once I was accepted into my apprenticeship, I could not have been more wrong. For the past two months, my daily schedule has been about as insane as the one Rome had me following during the summer. I start with five o'clock drills with the other National Security apprentices, followed by a shower and a breakfast that continues to be managed by a nutritionist. Then, I have two hours of indoor patrols with Public Safety and another two hours of outdoor perimeter checks with Reconnaissance before lunch.

In the afternoons, I continue taking specialized classes, including Covert Tech, Field Medicine, and Advanced Demolitions Training. When classes are over, I go to my after-school job with the Secret Service, where I rotate throughout the various government ministries: Education on Mondays, Technology on Tuesdays, Health and Research on Wednesdays, Agriculture on Thursdays, and Safety and Security with General Yarrow herself on Fridays. Occasionally, the general throws in a night guard shift to test my constitution and build character.

Hooray for character.

I'm thoroughly exhausted, but at least I get Sundays off every week. I desperately miss the one week of vacation I had between my entrance "exam" and actually starting my apprenticeship. I hung out with my friends every single day, and Rome and I went on a date every night. He was always kind during training and as a commanding officer, but he was tough, too. He had high standards and expected me to rise to them.

As a boyfriend, Rome's unbelievably romantic. He took me to candlelit dinners every night. He arranged a private showing of his favorite movie of all time, *The Princess Bride*, from long before the Global Devastation. He surprised me with my favorite foods and favorite flowers. He brought me books he thought I might like, and we traded favorites that we'd discussed the next night.

And talk about a gentleman! He never touched me without my permission. By the end of the week, I was dying to kiss him, and he was still so sweet about it. Even once we had kissed, he never tried to come into my room with me. Two months later, I've still never been inside his apartment.

Since my apprenticeship has kept me so busy, I mostly see Rome at work and for a date night every other weekend. He's joined our little friend group for the rest of the time because he didn't want me to feel like I had to choose between him or them. He's practically the perfect boyfriend.

Rome walks me back to my room after tonight's date. Tomorrow starts a whole new schedule, and I've been trying not to think about how nervous I am. Every new thing makes me crazy-anxious. Sensing the butterflies trying to burst out of my stomach, Rome takes my hand, intertwining his fingers in mine while we walk.

"So, how are you feeling about the new digs tomorrow?"

"Nervous," I say. "But what else is new?"

He laughs easily, never a care in the world despite a schedule that's every bit as grueling as mine. "So it's on to surveillance and interrogations next, right?"

I nod.

"Well, we're here," my sweet boyfriend tells me as we reach my door. "Better rest up for tomorrow."

I lean into his warm, strong body and breathe him in. "I don't want to. I just want to cuddle with you all night."

Rome wraps his muscled arms around me, but I already know he won't budge. "I'd never sleep again if it meant spending every minute with you, but we both know you have more important goals for yourself than that."

"I know," I sigh, pulling away and making a grumpy face at him. "I just wish we had more time together."

"I do, too," he tells me before kissing me again, this time long and deep. "But I don't ever want to get in your way. There'll be more time before long. I'll be given my permanent assignment once I turn seventeen, and I have a feeling you're going to rise through the ranks even faster than I have. Just a little while longer, and we'll have so much time you'll start getting sick of me."

I push against his chest playfully, and he tickles my sides. My friends say we're disgusting. They're obviously jealous of how adorable we are.

"Okay, I guess you're right. I need to sleep. But I'll see you tomorrow, right?"

"Always," Rome says, winking at me before wandering off toward his apartment.

The next morning starts much like any other with five o'clock drills and a quick shower in the locker room. I exit into the hall at seven-forty wearing fresh fatigues and a sleek bun on the back of my head with just enough time to grab a breakfast to go from the cafeteria.

By the time I hit the thirteenth floor, it's nearly eight, and my anxiety about being late on my first day is sky-high. I've never been on this floor before, but I know a lot about it. It houses interrogation rooms, surveillance units, several offices, the headquarters of various classified projects, and the upper prison wing. Because of all that, security's pretty tight.

But I don't know what any of it actually looks like. The elevator doors open into a small room with a metal detector, upright X-ray machine, and two heavily armed guards.

"Clearance?" one of them grunts at me.

I yank my badge from my neck and hand it to him. He scans it and checks his computer.

"ID number?"

"YR-6893.72-9," I recite from memory. We do this dance to verify our identities before entering secure locations. The guard grunts and hands me back my badge before pointing me to the metal detector.

"Place any weapons or metal items in the buckets." He sounds incredibly bored. I doubt they get a lot of visitors down here.

I don't have anything on me except my coffee mug and a standard-issue sidearm, both of which I dutifully place in the bucket. I walk through the metal detector without incident. The guard removes the lid from my coffee mug, unscrews the bottom, and sends the poor dismantled cup through the X-ray machine as his partner scrutinizes the picture on the monitor.

"Looks safe, Ed," she tells him before turning her attention to me. "Step into the X-ray, please."

I step into the machine and raise both hands above my head. Its whirs and spins around me for a few moments before they dismiss me.

"She's clean."

Ed grunts again and points me toward the double doors behind the desk.

"Retinal scan," he barks.

I search the wall beside the doors for a moment, and then I spot it. There's a small panel to the right that almost looks like a touchscreen. I step up to it and center my right eye in front of the panel. I stare into darkness until a bright red light shines directly into it. There's a loud beep, and the doors open. I take a step back, blinking away the floaters in my vision.

"Looks like you passed, Lieutenant," the female guard says. "They should be waiting for you. Go straight down the hall and take the second left. Surveillance will be the first door on the right. You'll have to scan your badge again, but the hard part's over."

I nod my thanks before pushing the doors open. A never-ending bright white corridor stretches out before me with doors lining each side. Nothing is labeled. I wonder how anyone finds what they're looking for down here. I make my way to the correct hallway and find the door to Surveillance, but the handle doesn't budge.

Right, scan your badge. Stupid.

I swipe my badge next to the door, and it clicks open. I'm astonished to find myself standing face to face with someone entirely unexpected.

"Matthew!"

"Oh! Hey, Harper," my old friend says as he struggles with an enormous bag that looks to have been torn apart by security.

I side-step him carefully and bend down to pick up odds and ends of things that have fallen on the cold concrete. Several surveillance officers wearing headsets sit behind large screens, oblivious to us. Screens cover every inch of the walls, with command center after command center filling the enormous room.

A middle-aged man wearing civvies sits in the far corner, examining lines of code at an entirely different, not to mention disorderly, workspace. He glances our direction and waves exuberantly. He starts to shout across the room but seems to think better of it. Instead, he walks over to us.

"Matthew, right?" he says, shaking my friend's hand. "I'm Andrew, the tech who'll be training you. And you're Harper?"

I shake his hand. "Yes, nice to meet you. Can you tell me who's in charge of the officers?"

"That'll be Genevieve."

I feel my mouth twist into a disapproving frown. "Genevieve."

"Major Thalhammer, actually," a voice behind me says.

I spin on my heel and salute as quickly as possible.

"At ease, Lieutenant Moss," my new commander says easily. "I'm looking forward to showing you the ropes around here. You're already a bit of a legend after crushing Captain Markos' record for the final evaluation with only a fraction of the training."

Trying not to blush, I reply, "Captain Markos did oversee my personal training over the summer."

"I appreciate your recognition of a superior officer's assistance, but I'd be cautious about giving others credit for your outstanding accomplishments," the major says somewhat sternly. Lowering her voice, she adds, "Especially the men. No matter what help you may have received, you're the one who smashed those records and came out on top. I doubt Rome would hold it against you."

"No, he wouldn't." I smile.

For the rest of the morning, Major Thalhammer explains how the surveillance room works while I take copious notes. I knew Elysium and the village above were under surveillance, of course, but I hadn't fully processed just how little privacy there truly is. Miniature drones buzz along through the fields, forest, and village. There are even hidden cameras in most above-ground homes and businesses, no doubt watching for signs of illness.

My afternoon is spent observing interrogations, though there are few enough problems in the city that true interrogations are rare. Major Thalhammer pulls already-convicted prisoners from their cells to demonstrate various techniques for extracting information.

Over the next several weeks, I gradually take command of Elysium's surveillance efforts under Major Thalhammer's watchful eye, running mock interrogations in the afternoons.

Matthew is my constant companion, ensuring both

software and hardware are running smoothly and guarding against potential hacking threats. Working together each day has brought us closer again. It's different from the Orphan Home, now that I understand him better, but it still feels the same somehow. We trust each other implicitly, creating a smooth flow to some of Elysium's most classified internal workings.

32

REQUEST

"They hung another one today, Mags," John said as he entered their little shack at the edge of the woods, hanging his winter coat on a nail beside the door.

Maggie sighed. "I've lost count of how many that is."

John opened his mouth to speak, but his wife spoke first. "Please don't tell me. Things have gone from bad to worse around here."

"I don't think it'll get any better, either. What have we gotten ourselves into?"

Maggie got up from her place knitting beside the fire and wrapped her arms around his woefully thin frame.

"Maybe if they'd give everyone appropriate rations instead of keeping extra for themselves, they wouldn't have to keep 'disciplining' people," she told him. "Everyone's just so hungry, and the Elders keep getting fatter."

"They've let the power go to their heads. Chose the wrong men for the job." John sighed. "Wouldn't be surprised if they're killing people just to get their hands on the extra rations at this point."

A knock at the door interrupted their conversation. When Maggie opened it, there was no one there, but a basket full of *canned food, fresh bread, and dried meats sat on the doorstep.*

"Another basket?" John asked.

She hoisted it up and turned to show him in answer. "Don't they understand how dangerous this is? Anyone who gets caught skimming will just be added to the body count."

"It's the only way most of us are getting fed, Mags."

"I don't want anyone else dying for me," Maggie replied with a huff.

"Either they die of starvation or they die from hanging. The one's a whole lot slower than the other."

"Doesn't matter. I won't be the cause of it. We need to give this back."

"Give it back to who?" John asked gently. "We don't know who's been leaving it, and if we take it back to the storehouse, we'll just stir up more trouble for ourselves. They'll send you straight to the gallows for theft."

Maggie sighed. "You're right, of course, but they need to stop."

"You know, the best way to figure out who's doing it would be to join them. Maybe you could help make it safer?"

"I don't want to get involved, John. I only make things worse for everyone."

"They don't seem to think so," John said with a jerk of his head toward the back window. There in the dark stood about fifty villagers waiting to speak with her. She opened the door and stepped outside, knowing so many people would never fit into their meager home.

"What are you all doing? You can't be here. What if someone sees you?"

Anna Aaron stepped forward, the spokesperson of the group. "We'll be quick, Maggie, and then we'll leave the same way we came—in shifts. No one will know we were all here together."

Maggie let her guard down a bit, but it didn't stop her from glancing around frantically in the dark to make sure no one was coming. "What do you want then? Out with it."

"The Council is taking things too far. They've turned us all against each other, pointing fingers and laying blame to keep ourselves off the gallows. They're killing people every day and taking their rations for themselves. They're even starting to target those who've fallen ill, calling sickness a sign of lost favor with the Sovereign.

"You've seen what we've been able to accomplish so far with your extra basket each week. We're keeping the entire village fed, and no one's the wiser. But we need your help."

"What could I possibly do?"

Another woman stepped forward—Mrs. Prewitt. "No one supports the Council anymore, Maggie—even myself and the other Elders' wives. We've worked together to mete out the rations more fairly, but we're unable to convince the men to rule justly. We need you to help us deal with them."

"Have you all lost your minds?" Maggie accused. "This is dangerous business. You all saw what happened! You saw the message the Sovereign left. The Council is in power because I failed you. You'd all be better off to live quiet lives in humble submission. We have to atone for our sins. There's nothing I can do to help you except to say this: Stop working against the Council and accept your lot. The Sovereign will have mercy on who they choose, and the rest of us will rightly pay for what we've done."

Maggie shoved the basket of food into Mrs. Prewitt's arms, slamming the door in her face as she left. While the crowd grumbled outside, she returned to her knitting. John sat quietly beside her for several minutes before he finally spoke.

"Are you sure this is what you want to do?"

Maggie nodded, though tears glistened on her dark cheeks. "I've nothing to offer anyone anymore. I won't be responsible for anyone else's deaths."

33

BLACK OPS

"You wanted to see me, General?"

I'm standing in the doorway of General Yarrow's enormous office. She's talking on the phone, so I'm left to stand here and wait. She glances up and waves me in. I close the door behind me and take a seat at her conference table where she can sit beside me. As I've gotten to know General Yarrow over these past months, I've learned she doesn't like barriers between her and the people she's talking to, physical or otherwise.

The general ends her call and seats herself next to me. She sets a white file folder down. On the cover, the word *CLASSIFIED* is stamped in red letters. I reach to open it, but she places her hand over mine. My brow furrows, and I look up at her quizzically.

"Harper, you've done some excellent work for me these past months. You've surpassed your peers at every level despite missing years of formal training that should have put you at a disadvantage. I'm extremely impressed with your progress."

"Thank you, General."

"I've known you had talent for a long time, but it's been

really impressive to see you in action. You've gone above and beyond every expectation. I think it's time we started giving you some special assignments. Are you prepared for this level of responsibility and confidentiality?"

I smile. "Yes, ma'am."

"Good." General Yarrow's hand lifts from mine. "Go ahead and take a look."

Practically salivating, I lift the front cover of the file. I've been waiting for this almost since the first day I met General Yarrow. The first sheet is a reminder that this is an "eyes only" document, meaning it contains highly sensitive information that cannot be accessed by just anyone. Files like these are so confidential, in fact, that they are not even kept digitally.

There are three copies, each kept in a fireproof safe inside an indestructible vault within one of three ministries: Safety and Security, Technology, and Health and Research. This is obviously the Safety and Security copy, which will not leave this office except in the general's hands, and then only to be returned to its secure location. I was granted my security clearance months ago, but this is the first chance I've had to use it for something more than standard surveillance.

The second page details the medical history of a surface villager titled Subject IB-7586.047-5. It appears to be a young woman who has given birth to three children. She has a history of minor illnesses and injuries, like chicken pox, colds and flus, sprained ankles, and the like. She has no history of any of the major illnesses the villagers tend to catch since losing access to vaccinations centuries ago, which is no small miracle. The next page details the shorter histories of three more subjects, IB-7586.047-5's children.

The mission is relatively straightforward—infiltrate the village in the dead of night, enter the subject's home undetected, and bring back DNA samples from all four subjects. The samples are to be delivered to Dr. Tori under guard no later than one hour before sunrise. The lab studies the DNA of living villagers to assist in finding a cure for the mysterious illness that ravaged Earth during the Global Devastation.

Everything I've learned from Jing and Ava suggests that they need to study this woman's blood for specific immunities, probably based on her surprisingly mild medical history. Her children's samples will probably also be studied to determine specific immunities, as well as identifying any genetic components that may be responsible. When I finish reading the file, General Yarrow is watching me closely.

"Seems simple enough," I say, sliding it back toward her.

"Excellent. Rome is the commanding officer for this special mission's unit, and you'll be his second in command. He practically begged to let your first mission be in his unit. But if we catch you two making out, it'll be your last—so be careful." Yarrow grins, and we both laugh.

"I'd probably be more likely to mutiny," I say.

The general roars with laughter. "Let's not have a mutiny, either. Rome is just assembling his team this morning. He'll be briefing all of you in the conference room in a few minutes, so you better head over to collect your assignment."

"Yes, ma'am," I say with a salute.

"And Harper? Do well out there, and it won't be long before you're the one in charge. Without a mutiny."

"Yes, ma'am," I reply, ducking out. The ma'ams aren't strictly necessary between the general and me anymore. We feel more like friends than soldier and commanding officer, but using the formalities keeps my head from getting too big. You can't afford to be too friendly with your commander-in-chief or you might forget your place.

Rome is already in the conference room when I arrive. Out of habit, he starts toward me for a kiss, but I give him a pointed look and wave him off. Instead, I salute him.

"Captain Markos."

"Lieutenant Moss," he returns, winking at me.

Three other soldiers enter the room—two specialists and a corporal. They're all older than Rome and me, but few soldiers rise through the ranks as quickly as we have. Rome begins his briefing by explaining the objective, the subjects, and the location of the house we'll be infiltrating. He shows us the equipment we'll be using to extract the samples. Having already received specialized medical training, apparently more than other soldiers, I'm already quite familiar with how to accomplish our task.

I'll do the brunt of the medical work and ensure the samples are collected correctly to avoid a repeat mission. Rome will stay with the chopper and perform remote surveillance and tactical support. The corporal will guard the home from outside, and the specialists will accompany me inside. We'll gas the occupants of each room before collecting samples to keep them from waking. Then, I'll collect the samples, pass them off to my comrades, and we'll be on our way without leaving a trace. Easy peasy.

"All right, everyone, it's gonna be a long night. You've all been given the afternoon off, so get some sleep if you're able. You'll have the morning to rest, as well, after we've returned home."

Once salutes have been exchanged and the other soldiers have gone their separate ways, Rome closes the blinds and pulls me in for a long kiss. I can't help but giggle with delight.

When I finally pull away, I ask him about being assigned to his team. "General Yarrow said you practically begged to have me on this mission."

"I wouldn't say *begged*." Rome looks amused. "But she *did* want to get you started in Black Ops missions, and mine was happening now. It took a little convincing, but I managed to persuade her that we can be professionals."

"Oh, yeah, the closed blinds and secret kisses scream professional," I tease.

He waves away my ribbing. "A small risk, but tonight it's all business. I'll be your commanding officer, not your boyfriend."

"I totally agree. General Yarrow is already watching us closely. Neither of us wants to be disciplined."

He shakes his head. "Or court-martialed."

I stare at him with wide eyes. "Is that an actual possibility?"

"It is," he replies grimly. "We have to be extremely careful and consummate professionals. Nothing can go wrong tonight. But if all goes well, you may be looking at a promotion already."

"General Yarrow hinted at that. Do you think it'll really happen?"

"I can't be sure, but I've gotten that impression. Yarrow believes in you, and so do I. At the rate you're going, you'll outrank me before long."

34

INTERROGATION

I roll over and squint at my alarm clock: twenty after eight. I've only been asleep a couple of hours when something slaps me in the face and I realize Ava's in my bed with me. I yawn and huddle under the blankets, trying to go back to sleep.

"Are you awake yet?" Ava whispers.

"Mmm," is all I can manage.

"How did it go? Was it amazing?"

"It went great, Ava, but I'm really tired. Can I go back to sleep now?"

A heavy sigh sounds in my ear. "I guess. I have to be in class soon, but you'll tell me all about it when I get home?"

"No, I will not tell you all about it. It's classified, remember? All I can say is I had my first mission as an officer, and everything went exactly as planned. Got it?"

"Got it." She sounds disappointed, and I remember that there's still some little girl in her. Probably in me, too, but it doesn't get to come out to play very much anymore.

I hear my door close, and I know Ava has gone to finish getting ready. She's been drawing blood and swabbing cheeks in her Health Sciences class, but today she gets to start looking at cells under the microscope. It's kind of a big day for her.

When the phone starts to ring in the next room, I shove my head under my pillow and pull it down over my ears. The next thing I know, my door is opening again.

"Um, Harper?" Ava asks quietly.

"Must. Sleep," I say.

"General Yarrow's on the phone."

I sit bolt upright. "General Yarrow's calling our apartment?"

"She says it's urgent. Can you go to her office now?"

I take the phone from Ava's hand and press it to my ear. "General Yarrow, this is Lieutenant—"

"Yes, yes, Harper, I know who you are. Just get down here as soon as possible, okay? I'm sure you haven't had any sleep, but we've got a situation, and I need you to handle it. I'm on Thirteen."

"Yes, ma'am. I'll be there right away."

"Come in your pajamas if you have to," she says, and the line goes dead.

Little does General Yarrow know, I'm still in my mission blacks from last night. I dropped my Kevlar, helmet, weapons, ammo, and all my other equipment on the floor of the debriefing room last night and came straight back here to crash. I'm even still wearing my combat boots.

I pull off my bonnet and hastily tie my hair up in a bun. It's not great, but it'll do. I grab a muffin on my way out the door.

"What's going on?" Ava asks.

"Dunno. Some kind of emergency," I say, stuffing my

mouth. "Good luck today!"

I race through the corridors and catch the elevator door just before it closes. I press Thirteen and do my best not to look completely frazzled. The couple waiting beside me looks mildly amused. Based on their uniforms, they're headed to work in the factories on Eleven. Their expressions become much more serious when they notice my military-issue boots and the security badge slung around my neck. They casually put a little more distance between us until we reach their floor.

When the elevator opens on Thirteen, I'm greeted by Ed and Addie, the usual morning security officers. We know each other well by now. They don't make me check my weapon or run anything through the X-rays. They swipe my badge and hurry me to the retinal scanner.

"Looks like your security clearance was upgraded slightly this morning," Addie tells me. "I think something big is happening. General Yarrow's waiting for you in Interrogation C. Good luck."

I nod my thanks before I push the doors open. Even though the rooms don't have signs, I know the interrogation rooms by heart. I locate Room C with ease—third door on the right.

I swipe my badge across the reader on the wall. A short beep and a green light indicate the door is unlocked. I pull it open and find myself standing in the viewing portion of the interrogation room. Two Secret Service guards turn, hands on weapons, but they relax when they recognize me.

"What's going on?" I ask.

Without saying a word, the guard on the left, Marlo, shakes her head and points at the one-way glass in front of her. I peer through and see General Yarrow seated at a stainless-steel table with Secret Service personnel on either side. I don't imagine she handles interrogations personally under ordinary circumstances. Opposite the general, with his back toward me, is another soldier. It only takes a moment before I recognize the back of his head and gasp.

Rome!

Marlo presses a finger to her lips. The message is clear: Shut up and listen!

"You expect me to believe that you were in the woods, over a kilometer from your assigned location, because you had to take a leak?" General Yarrow is incredulous. "Is there any particular reason you couldn't do it where you could still supervise your people?"

Rome's ears turn red. When he speaks, his voice is barely loud enough to hear.

"I was embarrassed. You were right: I couldn't handle having Harper on the mission."

"So a villager who could've been gassed and given a memory agent died because you didn't want your girlfriend to see you pissing?"

He hangs his head low but doesn't speak.

"Well, it's certainly clear that you can't handle being her superior officer, but can you withstand being *interrogated* by her?"

My jaw nearly hits the floor. Rome's head pops up and turns to peer at his own reflection, as if he can detect me on the other side. I'm too busy gaping at him to notice the door to interrogation open. I jump when General Yarrow taps me on the shoulder. When I turn to face her, she hands me a file.

"Brief yourself and get in there," she says. "You were the next highest rank on this mission. It falls to you."

I swear under my breath, but I take the file from her. The details are basically what I just heard. A review of drone surveillance after this morning's debrief showed that at 0200 hours, Rome abandoned his post and headed west into the forest. When the breach of protocol was discovered, soldiers were deployed to investigate his unexplained disappearance. What they found was a dead village girl, strangled and left behind to rot. After discovery, the body was brought back to Elysium for an autopsy. Time of death was estimated at 0215, shortly before drone footage showed Rome return to his post. The bruising matched his handprints on file. All other Elysians and villagers were accounted for at the time of her death.

"This doesn't make any sense," I say, shaking my head at the general.

"It does if you think about it hard enough," she replies gently.

"What are you trying to say?"

Yarrow gives me a pointed look, but says nothing.

"And you want *me* to interrogate him?" I choke on the words.

"As I said," the general explains, stroking my back, "it falls to you. You were at your posting and couldn't have stopped it, but now that Rome's been arrested, you are the commanding officer of this unit. You've done interrogations before."

"But not on this level. Not *classified* interrogations. Not as Internal Affairs Police. Not my *boyfriend*. I can't!"

Yarrow removes her hand from my back as her

expression hardens.

"You can and you will," she says sternly, our friendship fully dissolved. In this moment, she is only my commander-in-chief. "You have an advantage here. You have a power over this young man that no one else does, and I expect you to *use it*. He's not your boyfriend, not right now. And you may want to rethink that label after this anyway."

Shit. I swallow hard.

"Collect yourself and get in there," the general says through gritted teeth.

She's losing her patience. It's exactly what Rome and I discussed after his pre-mission briefing yesterday. At work, we're not dating. I'm a soldier, a commanding officer, a highly skilled interrogator. Rome is not my boyfriend. I am not his girlfriend. I'm a soldier with a mission, and I will get the truth.

I take a breath and steady myself, formulating a plan. General Yarrow must see it in my face.

"That's my girl," she says with one firm pat on my shoulder.

When I enter interrogation, I am steely. I am strong. I am a warrior. And I have no personal attachments. Exactly who Rome trained me to be.

I toss the file at my boyfriend, who appears to be in danger of coming utterly undone.

"You wanna tell me what happened last night?" I ask nonchalantly, ice in my veins.

He steels himself, a soldier trained to withstand interrogation. "I already told the general—I needed a little privacy to relieve myself."

"Since when are you embarrassed about your bodily

functions?"

Rome doesn't answer.

"And the girl in the woods?"

"She snuck up behind me. Curious about who was out there, I'd guess. She startled me, but I didn't kill her."

"What happened when you saw her then, if you didn't kill her?"

"I gassed her, and I gave her the memory agent, just like I was supposed to. She should've been taken back to her bed by the recon team after we were gone."

"Then how'd she end up dead?"

"I don't know, Harper. I don't. Someone else must've been out there with us. I have no idea what happened out there."

"General Yarrow seems to have a theory."

Rome raises one eyebrow, curious but miserable.

"Maybe something else was going on entirely," I offer sweetly. "Maybe you met that girl on another mission. Maybe you were friends, or maybe you were having an affair. Whatever your relationship was, she knew you'd be there last night, and you went out into the woods to meet each other. You thought everyone else was busy with a simple mission and nobody would notice. But something went wrong, and she paid for it with her life."

Fear flashes across Rome's face. His eyes race back and forth, trying to formulate a plan.

"Look at me, soldier!" I scream, slamming my hands down on the table. I don't even know who I am right now. Or maybe I do. I am an Elysian officer, and I will do whatever is necessary to complete the mission.

He looks up at me, his eyes red with tears.

"Who was she?" I ask.

"No one important," he replies, collecting himself. "Just an asset who provided intel from time to time."

"So you did know her then," I accuse.

"Yes, I knew her, but it wasn't an affair. I followed the usual protocol."

"The usual protocol," I mimic. "Except for abandoning your post and supervision of your unit during a Black Ops mission. Except strangling that poor girl to death!"

"I didn't strangle anyone," Rome hisses through clenched teeth. His eyes shift back to the table. I grab his chin in one hand and jerk his head up, forcing him to look at me. Our eyes are inches apart.

"Tell me. The truth." My words drip with venom.

"I can't," he says. "I can't tell you anything else."

"Can't? Or won't? While you were out there murdering your other girlfriend, your team was left in the field unsupported. What if something had gone wrong?"

"It was a simple field op with no risks. Nothing was going to go wrong. I was just foll—" Rome cuts himself off.

"Just what? Following your heart? Your instincts? Or just committing an *act of treason*?" My temper is rising, and Rome, calm as he usually is, can't fully withstand this from me. Yarrow was right about that.

"It wasn't like that," he moans.

I punch him in the face, knocking him out of his chair. Sprawled on the floor, he turns himself over and skitters away from me, pressing himself against the cold concrete wall.

"You left . . . your soldiers . . . alone," I growl. "For an affair with some surface girl?"

"Yes! I did. I left you alone. But I wasn't having an affair with her!"

I pull my chair out and sit down casually, trapping Rome in his little corner. "Then why did you kill her?"

He goes stone still and doesn't speak. I can see that he's trying to fabricate a story I'll believe. But I know him, and I know when he's lying.

"You don't understand," he says quietly. His voice drops so low I can barely hear him, low enough that the mics in the room won't pick it up. "There was another mission. I had orders."

I stare at him in shock, scrutinizing his face. *Is this the truth?* His face is pained, and I don't know what to believe. *Something isn't right, but is it with Rome?*

"Your handprints are bruised all around that poor girl's neck, and you have the gall to tell me you didn't kill her?" I growl, making up my mind. The evidence is irrefutable.

Rome sighs miserably. The fight drains out of his body. He initiates intense eye contact, sending a message I can't quite decipher. Without looking away, he makes his monotone confession. It almost sounds rehearsed.

"I killed her. She wanted to come to Elysium with me. I had let some information slip, and she threatened to tell the village everything she knew. I didn't know what to do. A memory agent wouldn't be enough to wipe out everything she'd learned, and I panicked. I choked her and couldn't make myself stop. The next thing I knew, she was dead. I had to get back to the chopper before the rest of the team and didn't have time to clean up my mess."

I nod and stand, making my decision. "You violated protocol, divulged classified information to an unauthorized non-citizen, went AWOL during an officially sanctioned operation, and have admitted to murder. Confessed acts of treason are punishable without a trial. By confessing to these acts, you have waived your right to counsel. You will be remanded to solitary confinement in military prison until the commander-in-chief hands down your formal sentence."

Two guards pick Rome up off the floor, one under each arm. They zip-tie his hands behind his back and place a black bag over his head. He doesn't even fight as they drag him out of the room.

35

COVER-UP

"General Yarrow, it's done."

"You secured his confession?"

"I did. The video should be on its way for you to review. I remanded him to solitary until you execute a formal sentence."

"I expect you'll be cleaning up his mess."

"Affirmative. I'm going in alone. I don't want more people knowing about this than absolutely necessary."

"I'll make a call. The girl's remains will be waiting for you on Twelve, Captain."

Just like that, I've earned my promotion. I navigate my way through the labyrinthine floor until I reach a little-known secondary armory. I suit up in full tactical gear, changing to brown camouflage to match the season on the surface. Once I've suited up, I find my way back to the front elevators. Ed and Addie eye me cautiously, likely due to my change in attire and the large weapon I now carry.

I step onto the elevator and make my way up to the next floor. Dr. Tori greets me when the doors open onto Twelve.

"It's good to see you, Captain Moss," she says.

That got out quickly.

"Good to see you, too, Dr. Tori. You have something for me?"

"Right this way."

I follow her down a long corridor and through a hidden door. A large duffel bag lies on a stretcher in a deserted exam room. Surgical tools adorn the steel tables. It smells of disinfectant and decay.

"Everything you need is in the bag," Dr. Tori proclaims.

That bag will be heavy. I sling my weapon over my back and take hold of the stretcher, rolling it toward the door.

"I don't recommend you take it out the front." Dr. Tori points me in the opposite direction. "Use the secure elevators at the back."

I nod silently and make my way to the elevators, swiping my badge and succumbing to another blinding retinal scan before the doors open. Then I press the H at the top of the column of buttons and wait in adrenaline-fueled silence for my ascent to be over. Finally, the doors slide open, and I push the gurney out onto the helipad. The pilot races forward to help me, but I've already hoisted the duffel off the stretcher, carrying it in one hand and my weapon in the other.

I haul the bag to the helicopter and toss it inside with a grunt. Then, I climb in and grab the copilot's seat.

"Are you it?" the pilot asks.

"Just me," I say. "I'll need you to get me as close to the GPS coordinates as you can. Has surveillance checked in with you yet?"

"Yes, ma'am. No one's that far out. It was strange she was out there in the first place, don't you think?"

"Not really," I answer grimly.

The pilot shoots me a quizzical look, but I don't say anything else. Instead, I click on my radio.

"This is Captain Moss checking in for Operation Wounded Eagle."

"Copy that, Captain. Recon here. Secure line has been established and live surveillance is a go."

"10-4, Recon. We're hitting the air. Is our GPS signal intact?"

"Confirmed. You're good to go."

The ceiling above opens to blue skies, and the propeller starts to spin. I pull on the headset that will allow me and the pilot to talk to each other over the noise. We take flight.

It's unusual to complete an air-based mission in broad daylight, but we have to do what we have to do. If Rome hadn't murdered this girl and tried to cover it up, we wouldn't be in this mess. We'll just have to avoid being spotted. A voice crackles in my ear.

"Captain, I have heavy drone coverage. You should make it to your destination free and clear. Closest subject is three miles from your destination."

"They have any transpo?"

"No transpo. Just kids playing in the woods."

The pilot lands as close to the edge of the forest as he can manage. We never come this close for fear of being seen, but this'll be a quick job once I get in there. I disembark and grab the bag from the back. Carrying this thing all the way into the woods isn't going to be pleasant, but like General Yarrow said, it's my mess now.

I haul the duffel through the trees, taking care not to leave any trace that a person has been here. I was always pretty natural at this, but my training has made me that much better. By the time I reach my destination, I'm slick with sweat in spite of the cold early-winter air. It would've been faster if I could've left the girl at the scene of the actual crime, but since it's so rare for villagers to come out this far, she might never have been found. That area has already been wiped anyway. Instead, I've had to trek much farther than Rome did last night in his stupidity.

I set the duffle down on the ground and unzip it, the smell of decay bursting out. I try not to picture the poor girl's face from the last time I saw her at school as I unwrap the plastic sheeting and carefully unpack her dismembered corpse. I scatter the pieces I've been given deliberately, making it look like she was mauled by a bear. The rest will be in a classified research lab in Elysium.

I use some specialized tools to leave animal tracks. Then I spray the entire area with pheromones to attract some actual animals to finish the job. I make sure I leave some identifiers tangled in the brush nearby—her hair bow and a scrap of torn fabric, undoubtedly from her dress. I say a brief prayer over the body before picking up my gear and heading back.

This girl will have justice for what Rome did to her. Her family will never know about it. They'll think she was torn apart by a far less cunning monster, but at least they'll have closure and most of a body to bury.

36

THE UNDERGROUND

"I'm disappointed in her," Anna said as she replaced the lid on a jar of corn and set it aside to be resealed. "How could she possibly refuse to get involved?"

Mrs. Prewitt shook her head. "Don't be too hard on her, Anna. Think of everything she's gone through."

"Haven't I gone through the same? I lost my Matthew, too!"

"Some of it's the same, dear, but not all of it. She's the one who convinced the rest of the Council to turn on Samson and Isaac. She's the one who called the meeting and provided the evidence that ended the Sending. Can't you see that all the blood spilled so far is on her hands?"

"Refusing to help will only add to it," Anna replied, scooping another spoonful of corn into a fresh jar. She had filled more than a dozen new jars just this morning by taking an unnoticeable amount from the existing jars in the storehouse.

"She doesn't see it that way, though. I'm afraid she never will."

"Well, we'll just have to keep taking care of things ourselves then, won't we?"

"You've already solved the food crisis. Brilliant idea having the Council wives supervise the storehouse shifts, by the way.

Our husbands take our loyalty for granted. We're totally above suspicion—for now, at least."

"Food crisis," Anna mocked. "That's what happens when only men are in charge."

"Well, they couldn't have any women on the Council anymore, what with our nurturing instincts making us think Orphans are children and all. Maggie showed them just how dangerous we are."

"If only she were still willing to be dangerous."

"Maggie aside, what else do you have in mind?"

"We'll have to put precautions in place for all those on our side. There can't be any more hangings."

"I'll speak to the other wives," Mrs. Prewitt decided. "We'll siphon Council information to you to help keep our people off their radar."

"That's perfect," Anna replied. "We'll make sure they follow all public expectations to the letter, but in private."

They smiled together as if enjoying an inside joke.

"The next step will be to pull away the Council's supporters."

"Shouldn't be too hard. They'll starve to death without the extra food we're providing."

"Don't bite the hand that feeds you," Anna said. "We'll just have to make sure they understand whose hand that is and how easy it would be to remove it."

Mrs. Prewitt nodded. They worked the rest of the day in the storehouse, recanning rations to create more equal portions and plotting their underground network of spies. Other women came and went, picking up rations while dropping off tidbits of information. Now that they controlled the storehouse, each basket contained a much healthier portion, and the Elders were none the wiser.

37

NIGHTMARE

By the time I finally sink into bed, I feel like I could stay there for the rest of my life. Yet how do you sleep when you've just found out that your (now ex) boyfriend is a murderer? My military training has taught me a lot of calming strategies to calm my body's processes, but I'm too emotionally drained to make the effort. Instead, I pop a couple sleeping pills and drift off to dreamland.

I'm traipsing through the woods, carrying a heavy duffel bag full of murdered-girl body parts. Voices drift in on the breeze. *Who's this far out here?* I should be alone. Drone surveillance didn't spot anyone.

"Recon, what's the surveillance status in my general vicinity?"

Silence.

"Recon, do you copy?"

Static answers back. I check my battery, but the radio is fully charged.

"This is Captain Moss checking in. Recon, do you copy?"

More static. Then, a voice crackles to life in my earpiece.

"Harper? Harper, is that you?"

"Maggie?"

"You can call me Mama if you want to."

"Mama, what's going on? What are those voices? Who's out here with me?"

The voices grow louder. A man and a woman. She's giggling. Now, Matthew comes on the radio.

"I never liked him. I knew something was off."

"Matthew, what are you talking about? You shouldn't even be on this frequency!"

The voices grow louder still. The woman is yelling, and the man sounds angry. She starts to shriek, but the sound is cut off, replaced by a strange gurgling. I creep closer and peek around a tree trunk.

Rome is strangling a village girl. She's wearing a cream-colored dress with a high-necked lace collar and dainty buttons all the way up her back. Her black hair trails down her neck in beautiful curls. Her dark arms extend from the gorgeous puffed sleeves of my barn dance dress as she claws at the hands choking the life from her. Her body goes limp, but it only spurs Rome on. He squeezes even harder now. Her head lolls to one side, and I finally see her face.

It's me!

I gasp loudly, and Rome startles. He drops her—my—body, and it falls to the forest floor like a sack of wheat. He turns to face me with a wicked, sharp-toothed grin. He's no longer just Rome. He's half-beast, and he wants to tear me apart. Saliva drips from his chin as he inches closer.

I hurl the bag of body parts at him and take off running. I hear the bag drop to the ground with a dull thud, and then footsteps pound behind me. My own feet strike the soft earth as I race through the darkened forest, weaving in and out among the trees in an ardent endeavor to evade my pursuer. My breath comes in shallow gasps; I can hear my heartbeat in my ears, even louder than the one who gives chase.

In the distance, I see it—the Stronghold! But the beast Rome is too fast. I'll never make it in time. I glimpse a hollow tree log off to my right. I dive for it, sliding deep down into it. Menacing growls surround me, but they gradually die off. I must have lost him.

Just when I think it's safe to crawl out of my hiding place, a pair of evil red eyes appears at my feet. The growling starts up again, louder than before, and a clawed arm reaches in to grasp my leg. I kick at it and struggle, but its claws dig in, tearing the flesh from my body. Finally, one kick makes contact, and the hand loses its grip.

I scramble out of my prison and race for the Stronghold. The ladder dangles from the opening in the floor. I climb as fast as I can, but my hands are slick with ice-cold mud. I can barely hold on. I hear the creature gaining on me. I make it to the top and pull the ladder up just as Rome reaches for it. It slides beyond his grasp, and he paces angrily below, spitting and growling and wrenching the bark from the tree with his claws.

I close the door in the treehouse floor and cover it with everything I can, hoping it will be too heavy to open if he finds a way up. I hide in a large wooden chest. If I can just survive until morning, he'll have gone, and everything will be okay.

But everything is not okay. A sharp whistle sounds in

my ears, followed by the thud of metal scraping into wood. I know that sound. *A grappling hook!* I hear Rome grunt as he climbs over the windowsill. His boots thump against the wooden floor as he nears my new hiding place.

THUD!

THUD!

"Harper," Rome's monstrous voice croons. "Come out, come out wherever you are. I have orders."

Orders? What orders?

Maybe if I stay completely quiet, he won't find me.

But then my radio sounds again. Ava's voice crackles into existence.

"Harper? Harper, are you okay?"

Then, a sharp crack, and the creature is shaking me violently. Its drool drenches my face.

"Harper, wake up!" Ava shouts.

I blink up at her, trying to make sense of what's going on. My face and clothes and bed are all drenched.

"Issat sweat?" I mumble.

"No, I had to pour water on you to wake you up. How many of these did you take?" She shakes a pill bottle at me.

"Jus' a cuppa," I slur.

"Well, you're only supposed to take one. You were screaming in your sleep, but your heart rate was insanely low. I thought you were going to die. You had me really worried!"

Ava helps me sit up before she returns to scolding me. "You need to stand up and move around. I'll make you some coffee. The caffeine will help get your heart pumping again."

"No, don't go back to sleep." She catches me before I can lie back down. "Don't make me call for backup."

I grudgingly roll myself out of bed and let Ava help me up. I can barely walk, so she puts my arm around her shoulders and helps me into the kitchen. Here, she forces me to sit on a stool while she puts a pot of coffee on.

"I 'on't unnersand. Whussa big dill?" I ask drowsily.

"The big deal is you almost stopped your heart, dummy! You're not a very good sister if you're *dead*."

Just a few minutes ago, my heart was in my throat. I'm not sure how it could be anywhere close to stopping.

"Muh hars fiiiiiide," I declare, though even I can barely make out my words.

Ava stops what she's doing and grabs my wrist. She places two fingers on the inside below my thumb and presses down hard. She growls in frustration, drops my hand, and puts her fingers on my neck instead. I let my arm flop loosely to my side and tilt my head to make my neck more accessible. I toss her a goofy grin, but she's staring at her watch.

"Forty beats per minute, Harper. That's not fine," she declares grumpily.

"'S'fine." I wave my hand at her. "I'm in rully good shape."

Ava glares at me. "Fifty-five is your normal resting heart rate, and you know it. Forty's at least better than the twenty-seven I got before I woke you up. It's so weak I can barely feel it!"

She busies herself in the kitchen for a few minutes, but continues to eye me suspiciously.

"What happened today to prompt this little sleeping

pill experiment, anyway?"

"Jus' hadda badday." I say, starting to realize I don't actually sound right. Bad day is usually two words.

"A really bad day from the looks of it," Ava says. "And the smell."

I grin sloppily. "Haven't showered in a while," I reply, making a concentrated effort to enunciate my words.

"No kidding," she says. She hands me a cup of black coffee, and I take a big swig, barely noticing how it burns all the way down. I drink half the cup before I can even begin. I've sobered up a bit now, and I remember the awful details.

"Rome did something really bad. Really, really bad. Awful, in fact."

Ava looks sympathetic, but waits for me to continue.

"We're not together anymore. But the worst part is, I can't tell you anything about it."

Ava's eyes narrow. "Something . . . *military* bad?"

I nod. "He's in prison, actually. I'm the one that did the interrogation. I'm the one that got the confession. And I'm the one that gave the order to throw him in the deep, dark hole where he'll probably spend the rest of his life."

"Wow. That *is* a bad day. Can you talk to Julia about it?"

"No." I shake my head. "They'll have me talk to a military therapist. I can't share classified information with a regular therapist."

"That sucks. When you took the pills, you weren't trying to . . ." Ava trails off, but concern fills her face.

"No, nothing like that," I answer. "My mind was just racing with everything. I didn't just get the confession and give the order. I had to clean up after him, too. And it wasn't pretty. Once I got home, I just . . . couldn't shut it off. I needed sleep, so I took an extra pill without thinking."

"Well, I'm glad you're okay. You can go back to bed in a couple hours. I just need to make sure you'll actually wake up in the morning."

"Got it, Mom," I tease.

Ava smiles weakly. I can tell she's grateful that my sense of humor's coming back, but she's not exactly in the mood. She must've been completely freaked out when she found me.

"What was all the screaming about?" she asks me.

"I had the world's worst nightmare. It was like a fever dream on acid."

"Sounds fun," she says, raising one corner of her mouth. "You want me to fill everyone in, so you don't have to talk about it?"

"Yes, please," I say, taking another sip of my coffee.

Ava picks up the phone and starts to dial. I hear her say the same story about five times, but I can tell when she's on the phone with Matthew. He asks the most questions and offers to come over about a hundred times. In all this time, there's another thing that hasn't changed: Matthew will always have my back.

38

CODING ERRORS

The blaring sound of my alarm startles me awake at four-thirty, just like every other morning. I want nothing more than to call in sick, ask for a couple days off, but a captain doesn't show that kind of weakness. What happened yesterday was business as usual. I didn't discover my adoring boyfriend of the last six months was also a murdering psychopath; I unearthed treason within my team and handed down a just punishment. Nothing more.

Rubbing the sleep from my eyes, I roll out of bed. Voices murmur in hushed tones outside my door, and I detect the faint smell of blueberry pancakes. If we've got company at this time of day, it's a good idea to throw on a robe and leave the bonnet over the tangled mess of hair it surely covers.

I saunter out of my bedroom trying to look a little more awake than I feel. Matthew and Jing sit at the kitchen table, whispering over coffee. Ava's nowhere to be seen.

"She must've rea—"

"Shh!" Jing scolds, her index finger pressed to her lips.

"Ava's sleeping," Matthew whispers. "She stayed up

most of the night taking your vitals."

Guilt washes over me.

"She didn't have to do that," I say, matching Matthew's soft tone. "She'll be exhausted at work today."

Jing shakes her head. "Took the day off. She figured she'd be more likely to rest today than you. Looks like she was right."

"I made pancakes," Matthew says, pushing a plateful toward me.

"Can I take them to go? I'll throw up if I eat before drills."

"No problem," he replies, grabbing a plastic container from the cabinet. His voice sounds cheery, but he looks downtrodden just the same.

"We were really worried about you last night, Harp," Jing says.

"I know Ava was worried I was trying to hurt myself, but I swear I wasn't. I didn't realize how strong those pills are. I figured taking an extra one would just put me to sleep faster."

"Well, it did," Matthew remarks grimly. "Almost permanently."

I flash him a dark look without responding.

"How are you feeling this morning?" he asks, changing the subject slightly.

"Emotionally or physically?"

"Both," my friends respond in unison.

"Physically, dry mouth and eyes and a bit of a headache. Sleeping pill hangover, I guess." I grab a bottle of water from the fridge and drop in an electrolyte tablet.

"And emotionally?" Jing probes.

I take a deep breath before answering. "Not the best

I've ever felt. I just keep reminding myself I don't want to date someone who could do something like that anyway."

"Dumped him, huh?"

"Something like that. I'll never see him again." I shrug. "Sorry, I don't wanna be rude. I know you guys came over here to check on me, but I'll be okay. I gotta get ready for work."

The two of them go back to their whispering, though they seem slightly quieter before, like they don't want me to hear what they're saying now that they know I'm awake. I brush my teeth, pull back my hair, and throw on my training fatigues before stuffing my after-work clothes in my gym bag. My uniform's in my locker at work, but I'll change into these at the end of the day.

When I emerge with my gym bag slung over my shoulder, the whispering in the kitchen stops abruptly, and I discover that Amari's here now, too. *Gotta love it when your friends are saying things about you that they don't want you to hear.* Even if they're just worried, it's not the best feeling in the world. They'll get over it, though. It'll be easier for them; they don't know what Rome turned out to be capable of.

Amari, who's so far into medical school now that he's started his surgical rotation, forces me into a chair despite my protests that I'll be late for work. He slaps a pulse ox on my finger and takes my blood pressure on my other arm. Then, he takes a pen light from the pocket of his white coat and checks my pupils.

"Take off your shoes and socks," he commands me.

I cross my arms over my chest, pouting like a toddler.

"Harp," he says sternly. "You have to be cleared for

duty. I can either do it informally at your kitchen table, or I can fill the military doctors in on the situation."

"Fine," I say, kicking off my shoes. "Can you just be quick, please?"

I know my friends mean well, but they're just being so annoying. I'd really like to get on with my life and pretend this never happened.

I cross my arms again and continue to pout as Amari checks my reflexes and the neural responses in my feet and legs. It feels just like waking up from my coma in the hospital wing almost a year ago.

"I swear I can feel my arms and legs, doc." I cringe as he drags something sharp across the sole of my foot, making my toes curl. "I'm walking fine, aren't I?"

"Doesn't mean you don't have nerve damage," he says absently as he continues his work. Jing notates every result on a medical chart with precision until they're both satisfied that I haven't done any permanent damage.

"They'll have you talk to a psychologist, right?" Amari asks me.

"Yes," I say impatiently. "Probably today. It's standard procedure after a dispo— after yesterday's mission."

Oops, it wouldn't have been the best idea to say *disposal*. Good thing I caught myself. "I'm sure it's already on the books," I reassure my friends. Finally, they agree to let me get on with my day.

As I say my goodbyes, Jing jerks her head toward me in what I think is supposed to be a covert gesture. *Does she not know I can see her?* I hurry out the door before I have to watch them patronize me any more. When I'm about three doors down, I hear Matthew's voice calling out behind me, "Wait up!"

I turn and wait, head cocked and eyebrows raised.

"Yes?" I stretch out my single syllable with mock patience.

"I need to grab something from the office. We may as well walk together."

"*You* need to grab something from the office at five? Your day doesn't start for almost four more hours."

"No, it's . . . I needed to go in early for, uh," he sputters.

"Jing and Amari asked you to babysit me and make sure I get to work safely." I put one hand on my hip.

He looks at his shoes and nods. "Well . . . yeah. Everyone's worried about you. What if there are side effects?"

"Did Amari *say* there could be side effects?"

"Not exactly, but . . . well, they'll be pissed if I go back now."

I exhale loudly. "Fine. You can walk me to the locker room. But I don't need an escort home unless we're actually leaving the same place at the same time, okay?"

"Okay," he agrees. We walk in silence until we reach the elevators.

"So . . . uh . . . bad breakup?" Matthew asks awkwardly.

"You don't have to seem so happy about it," I tease, laughing.

He doesn't seem to catch my sarcasm, putting his hands up and shaking his head. "What? No, I'm not happy about it. I'm disappointed for you. I know you liked Rome a lot."

"Matthew, it's fine. Seriously. He didn't turn out to be who I thought he was."

"I'm sorry."

"Me, too. But not everyone is exactly who they seem

to be, are they? It's part of life. I'll be okay."

"Okay." He nods.

Matthew and I make small talk the rest of the way to the locker room, where we separate. I dump my stuff in my locker and head out to drills. When the Elysian military says "classified," they mean it. No one has any idea about what happened with Rome, and I'm thankful for it. I won't have to tell anyone here what he did or who he turned out to be. Or what I had to do to deal with the whole big mess.

"Hey, Rome out sick today or something?"

"Something," I answer.

"He okay?"

"Yep."

"Where's Rome this morning?"

"Rome's not gonna be doing drills with our squadron anymore."

"Transferred out, huh? You guys break up?"

"Yep."

"Wanna punch something?"

"Do I ever!"

Kickboxing and sparring do me a world of good this morning. Nobody worries about my emotions or my deep-seated trauma. Nobody asks me if I'm okay. They understand. I let loose and release all my rage through physical activity. All the adrenaline that tried to build up in my system, that I trampled down with sleeping pills last night, is spent—and then some. The crushing weight that's been building in my chest for the past twenty-two hours starts to dissipate.

"You were on fire today, Inferno!" one of my buddies calls as we head to the showers.

"No joke! You really kicked my ass!"

It feels good to be joking and laughing with people who aren't worried about what happened to me yesterday. They don't know what happened, but even if they did, they'd get it. We've all had to follow orders we didn't like. We've all gone on a traumatizing mission or two. I'm not planning to talk to them about this; I couldn't even if I wanted to. But if I did, it wouldn't be an issue like it is with my civvy friends. These soldiers aren't my all-time best friends, but we share a bond that no one outside here will ever understand.

After drills, I shower, fix my hair and makeup, and don my uniform. When I arrive in the surveillance room, it's rounding on eight o'clock. The skeleton crew from the night shift is just closing up shop for shift change.

"Hey, Gary," I say as I pop my container of pancakes in the break room microwave.

"Hey, Moss. Didn't see you around here yesterday. Everything okay?"

"Emergency mission," I reply.

Gary nods knowingly, then raises an eyebrow. "The fun kind?"

"Not remotely."

I chit-chat with a few more of the night shift soldiers while I microwave my pancakes. They're steaming and drowned in maple syrup when I stride into the surveillance room. I just about drop the whole thing on the floor when I spot Matthew, sitting in a swivel chair and staring at a computer monitor as lines of code drift by continuously. He stops every few seconds to jot down notes on a legal pad. He doesn't even notice I'm here.

"So did you really have something to do in the office

this early, or have you just been sitting here waiting for me? Stalker."

Matthew jumps, flinging his pencil across the room. I catch it before it lands in my pancakes.

"S'pose you wouldn't have jumped that hard if you were here for me. What are you working on this early in the morning?"

"This?" He gestures with his pad. "It's nothing. Just a project Travis gave me with a serious deadline. Figured I'd get some work done on it since I was awake and down here already."

"Okay, I'm a better liar than that, right?" I wink.

"What?"

He's getting defensive. I must be on to something.

"Come on, Matthew. We've known each other since we were like three. I know you."

"Seriously, Harper, I'm sure it's nothing. I just need to be sure before I can let it go."

"You've never been very good at letting things go. Neither have I, for that matter. You know you'll have to give in eventually. Just tell me what this is all about."

"Look," Matthew says as he stares me dead in the eyes, "if you'd have caught me here a week ago, I would've told you. If you'd have caught me *yesterday*, I would've told you. But this isn't the right time for it."

"Why? Because my boyfriend's a mur—" I stop myself mid-word, but it's too late.

"Did Rome kill somebody?" Matthew asks, stunned.

"We're soldiers," I say. "We've *all* killed somebody."

"Somebody he wasn't supposed to?"

"You know I can't talk about it," I say, pressing my lips together firmly.

"Wait," he scrunches up his face. "You've *all* killed somebody? Does that mean you've killed somebody? Like, for real?"

I shrug one shoulder and finally sit beside him, stuffing my face with pancake, letting syrup drip down my chin.

"You're getting syrup on your fatigues," he says absently, knowing I've clammed up for good.

Matthew swipes his pencil from my hand and turns back to the monitor. He looks like he's counting something. I have a basic understanding of a lot of different kinds of code—I need to be able to use it on the job from time to time. But I'm not exactly a hacker. Matthew, on the other hand, he's the best there is. He clearly sees a pattern I'll never be able to pick up on.

"Fine. No, I haven't killed anybody. Not yet, anyway. But I'm trained to, and I'll probably have to sooner than later. I won't *like* it, but it'll be the only way to stay alive someday. I'll do what I have to do, and I'll get to come home because of it. Happy?"

Matthew eyes me cautiously in his peripheral vision, then turns his attention back to his monitor. He puts the end of his pencil in his mouth, the way he used to do in school when he was trying to come up with the solution to a really tough problem.

"Matthew," I say quieter, gentler, "I'm fine, I swear. Yesterday was awful. Everything about it sucked, but I did not try to kill myself. I worked out my anger and frustration in drills. I'll talk to the department therapist, too. It's on my schedule for 1500 today. I don't like what happened, and I never will. But I can accept it and move on. And as for Rome, good riddance!"

"I never liked him in the first place," Matthew mutters

without looking at me.

"I know." I smile at him. "So, what are you looking for? I can handle it. Might be nice to have something new to think about."

He sighs and points at the monitor with the tip of his pencil. He appears to be waiting for something.

"See this?" he asks. "Right here! This!"

His pencil starts tracking a line of code up the screen until it disappears. I shake my head.

"Sorry, I don't know what I'm looking at."

"I know. It's hard to spot at first. That's why I'm tracking it."

We wait in silence until it comes around again. And again. And again. He's right; something about it looks off, but I don't have the expertise to understand what.

"It comes every three minutes, like clockwork. But it doesn't *belong* there. It's not part of the program."

"How do you know that?" I ask with disbelief.

"Because I wrote it," he says with much more humility than anyone else would have about that fact.

"You wrote it? The whole program?"

"Well, yeah. It was my thesis. It's how I got such an important apprenticeship. I actually revolutionized our surveillance systems with this program. But somebody's done something to it, and I'm sure it's not working the way it was intended anymore."

"Well, what—" I start but can't decide where to go next. "How's it *supposed* to work, and what's wrong with it now?"

"Okay, in layman's terms, it's sort of a revolving AI surveillance system. It tracks what every camera, every drone, every *everything* sees constantly, both inside and outside Elysium, constantly. And it *interprets* it. It doesn't need human eyes to tell it what's a threat and what's innocuous. It has facial recognition for every person both here and above-ground. It knows who everyone is and what everyone's doing all the time. It even reads your vitals to determine intentions. It's the reason *you* get a vacation on the holidays now."

"Wow, what a brilliant piece of programming and spectacular invasion of privacy!"

Matthew punches me in the arm, a little harder, I think, than he would have a couple of years ago. I don't even flinch. I just laugh.

"Okay, I get it," I tell him. "It was designed to keep us safe, so we can continue the research that will ultimately save the population of the whole world. But what's wrong with it?"

"That's what I'm struggling to figure out. No matter how long I look at it, I just can't figure out exactly what this piece of code is doing here. It's genius, really. It's so well-written. But it fundamentally alters some function of what we're seeing in the surveillance, and I can't figure out what it is."

"Wait, it's altering how *we* see the surveillance?"

Matthew nods.

"But not how the *program* sees it?"

"Yeah, it's like it goes through some kind of filter before it reaches the surveillance monitors. Why would someone do that? It doesn't make any sense."

"Probably to hide something from the people watching it."

"What would they be trying to hide?"

"More importantly, who's trying to hide it?"

39

SURVEILLANCE

When Ava and I were little and living in the Orphan Home, Maggie used to send us on "secret missions." We prided ourselves on being chosen to deliver gift baskets and messages. We were thrilled to pick up items from the market. We were convinced that we were Maggie's spies, her eyes and ears around the village, even though she never once asked us about what anyone said or did.

I'm not a little kid anymore. I go on real missions now. They're all packed with the adrenaline I craved as a child, but now I know not all missions are full of fun and excitement. General Yarrow has been sending me out more and more over the weeks, placing more and more trust in me. After Rome's arrest, she waited a while before sending me back out, but she has gradually assigned more sensitive work to me and my team.

"Harper, you've shown yourself to be trustworthy and loyal to Elysium's cause," General Yarrow says. "Although our city is full of hardworking people devoting themselves to finding a cure for the blight on the surface, there are some among us who no longer believe that a cure can be found. They would see us abandon this great calling of our founders and let the illness run rampant.

"Because of the great loyalty and skill that you've shown, I want you to ferret out the insurgents in Elysium. A specialized surveillance team has been collecting intelligence for weeks." She slides a two-inch-thick folder across the table to me. This one is black.

I swallow. Black files signify the highest level of security. No one of my age has ever held one before, to my knowledge. I pick it up, feeling the weight of it.

"Don't worry: There's a summary page on top," the general reassures me. "I don't expect you to read the whole thing with me watching."

A nervous chuckle escapes my lips, and Yarrow grins. "Go ahead and open it."

"A black file," I say, relishing in the gravity of the moment. I inhale deeply as I open the front cover. Just as General Yarrow said, there's a summary on the very top, right after the warning about highly sensitive, eyes-only information.

The file contains activity logs for several Elysians whose movements and activities have been repeatedly flagged as suspicious by Matthew's AI surveillance program over the past three months. All are marked with their identification number rather than their names. Their phones, homes, and workplaces have been bugged and their communications have been logged. Detailed reports follow, which explains the thickness of the file. A team of intelligence analysts has reviewed the surveillance in depth, determining that this particular group of Elysians have engaged in intentional sedition, the dissemination of anti-Elysian propaganda, and conspiracy to commit sabotage against the Ministry of Research.

I let out a low whistle. "Hefty accusations."

"Concerning that there are citizens who would take these kinds of actions against their own people," General Yarrow replies.

I shuffle through the rest of the papers, attempting to scan each section of documents quickly. "There've been no arrests? No preliminary hearings?"

"Not yet," the general answers. "Arrest warrants will be obtained, but the surveillance we've collected so far may not be sufficient for conviction in civilian court."

"And that's why you're assigning a trained operative. You want me to collect irrefutable evidence—to catch them in the act."

"Top of the class," General Yarrow beams. "You're being reassigned to lead a classified surveillance team, effective immediately. Your team will answer directly to me."

I'll have private access to the entire city's surveillance records every single day. Exactly the opportunity Matthew and I have been waiting for.

"You'll be surveilling the activities of the group at all times and will be responsible for infiltrating their ranks. You now have the authority to call together a team of specialists on a whim, to make civilian arrests, to order Black Ops missions—essentially, do whatever it takes. Every action you take from this moment is officially sanctioned. No questions asked. Just catch these bastards."

I nod gravely. "I'll need a top security clearance."

"Already done," the general remarks.

"And a technology consultant."

"Take your pick. You can choose any team you want."

"Thank you, General."

"There's a little more to this, Harper. Keep reading."

A pair of villagers from the surface is involved—a husband and wife. The surveillance collected on them is damning, and as non-Elysians, they have no right to trial. They've been making plans to rebel against the agreement between our two communities with the goal of infiltrating Elysium and setting our research labs ablaze.

"Insurrection on the surface," I say. "How common are these kinds of actions?"

"We've put down a rebellion or two over the past few centuries."

"Yes, I've read the military histories, of course. But if those are the only incidents, then these kinds of behaviors must be relatively rare?"

"Historically, yes," answers the general, "but the knowledge we shared after bringing you here seems to have emboldened the villagers to revolt against us. Some would rather not aid in our research, choosing to believe there is no infection. They don't believe it to be a worthwhile cause, nor do they understand that our technology is what allows them to continue to produce the materials they need for survival."

"It looks as if the two groups are on the verge of discovering one another," I say thoughtfully.

"And therein lies the problem."

"If Elysian insurgents collaborate with surface revolutionaries—"

"It could spell disaster," Yarrow finishes for me.

"All our research could be lost. We could end up back in the dark ages, like the villagers."

"Exactly," General Yarrow agrees.

"This isn't good," I state plainly, as if it wasn't already obvious.

"You have free rein over this mission, Moss, but I recommend eliminating the surface targets."

"Elimination" is military speak for assassination. Murder. I don't like it, but I don't have any better ideas. Elysium uses non-lethal means whenever necessary, employing gas or sedatives and memory wiping agents, like in my Taking.

Memory agents, though, only wipe the past twelve hours or so at the highest doses. That wouldn't be effective in this case. Extraction would only supply these villagers with more opportunity to come into contact with the Elysian insurgents. It would be difficult, but if they're connected to anyone with clearance, they could make it happen. We don't know how deep this thing goes yet. That's not a risk I'm willing to take.

"I agree, General. Elimination is the only logical course of action. I'll make it happen."

"You'll also be responsible for ensuring there is a logical explanation for their deaths in the village," Yarrow explains. "We can't have more questions popping up."

"Understood, ma'am."

40

ANNA

Over the past several months, Maggie had noticed the increased weight of her weekly ration basket. Knowing that asking questions would only lead more to the gallows, she had held her tongue. At morning prayers, she began to notice the Elders slimming down little by little. Still, no one seemed suspicious. If anything, the people appeared far more pious and content than before, especially Anna.

Since the gathering outside Maggie's back door months ago, Anna had barely spoken to her, except to exchange the most righteous public pleasantries. Though the village had seemed to be faring well for some time, the atmosphere had shifted in recent days. The air was electrified at prayers, leaving the hair on Maggie's arms standing on end. There was a gentle murmur through the crowd, as if the entire village could sense it. The Elders appeared smug, giving each other knowing looks but saying nothing. She didn't know what it was, but something was happening.

When John came home, Maggie practically jumped at him. "Any news?"

"Only one candle was lit in Widow Martin's kitchen window."

Maggie sagged back into her chair with relief. "So, all is well then. The underground haven't received any intelligence."

John had noticed weeks ago that the Widow Martin's candles seemed to be lit in multiples when the Council was planning to take action against the village. Only on uneventful days was there a single flame, and a single flame had been lit for quite some time now.

"So it would seem," John replied. "No new bodies in the square, either."

"I only hope they haven't been able to catch onto the signal as easily as we have." Maggie wrung her hands. "Something was off this morning. I could feel it."

As John reached out to comfort his wife, their front door crashed open, and the oldest Aaron boy after Matthew was standing beside them.

"What is it, son?" John asked, seeing the frantic look in the boy's eyes.

"They have my mama. Mrs. Prewitt tried to warn us, but it was too late. She sent me to fetch you. Come quick!"

The boy turned and ran like a bolt of lightning. John started after him, but Maggie put a hand on his arm.

"What can we do about it, John? We'll just be two more bodies in the square."

"We can stop her husband from getting himself hanged alongside her and sending those kids to the Orphan Home," John replied. She knew he was right, and so she ran after him and the boy.

When they arrived at the square, Anna Aaron was being dragged up onto the gallows with her hands and feet tied. Her husband was held back by two hulking men who were loyal to the Council, but he continued to fight. More and more people appeared out of thin air, but none knew how to stop what was happening. The Council's men stood nearby with rifles, something that had been taken from the majority of residents long ago.

When John and Maggie reached Mr. Aaron, they stood in front of him, trying to block the gruesome scene from his view.

"No! Let me see my wife! I need to see my wife!"

"You can't stop it. You'll only end up hanging, too," John said quietly.

"You have to be brave for her babies," Maggie crooned, putting one hand on his face.

"What's she accused of? Tell me what you think she's done!" Mr. Aaron shouted.

Father Cowan ascended the steps of the stage to read the charges against Anna, as had become his unfortunate responsibility. After the last hanging, he had cried in Maggie's sitting room for three hours before he could bring himself to go home. He felt so responsible, but he was no more to blame than the rest of them. He was trapped.

"Anna Aaron," he called out, his voice threatening to crack, "you stand accused of poisoning Mr. and Mrs. Sheffield and orphaning their children. Their unexplained illness has been traced back to a meal you prepared for them on the night of their deaths, while their children were in the company of friends."

"That's not true!" Mr. Aaron was screaming now, going blue in the face. "She didn't do that! We ate the same meal!"

Mrs. Aaron, for her part, stood on the stage before the gallows with the utmost composure. She looked her husband in the eye before she spoke.

"Please. Stay alive. Take care of the children."

When he didn't stop shouting, she implored their friends. "John, Maggie, save him from himself."

Maggie met her eye and gave a solemn nod. John placed a hand over Mr. Aaron's eyes while Maggie covered his mouth. Nearby women snatched up her children, burying their heads in bosoms that would protect them from the horror of seeing their mother's untimely death.

Anna didn't wait to be pushed. She stoically stepped to the edge of the platform and leapt right off. The rope snapped tight, breaking her neck immediately. She didn't struggle, and she didn't suffer. She had known how this would end, and she chose a quick death, one that would torment her family less than slowly strangling over several hours' time. She wouldn't torture them more than necessary.

"She was so much braver than I," Maggie said through tears. "Come now. Let us take you and the children home. She wanted you to survive this, to keep the children from the Sending."

She uncovered his mouth. When he looked about to shout again, John said, "Don't make this worse than it already is. They don't need two dead parents."

Mr. Aaron nodded, tears streaming down his face. The town's women approached with the Aaron children, a brood of hens protecting the fallen mother's chicks. The group blocked the view of the Aaron mother's swinging body from the rest of the family. They didn't need to remember her this way.

They spent several hours in the Aaron family's home that night, clucking over them. They gave baths, fixed meals, and comforted the grieving family. After they had put the children to bed, they gathered in the Aarons' substandard sitting room.

"The bloodshed must end," Maggie told them with more resolve than she'd felt in half a year. "I've finally had enough. Help me spread the word. This is what we must do."

41

ANOTHER BREAKUP

Before I reach up to knock on Matthew's door, I realize there's shouting inside his small apartment. Ava and I exchange a look, and she puts her ear up to listen. I smack her lightly on the arm, but she brushes me away.

"You're gonna want to hear this," she whispers.

I hesitate for a moment before deciding that Matthew doesn't have any real privacy in this place anyway. I shrug and position my own ear about an inch from the door.

"—can't believe you would do this to me!"

"I'm not doing anything *to you*," Matthew's voice replies. "I've just been reassigned."

"Reassigned by your ex-girlfriend. To work with her every single day," Amelia snaps back.

"I've already been working with her every day. When did this become a problem?"

"It's always been a problem, Matthew. You're obviously in love with her, and I can't compete!"

"In love with her?" His voice sounds incredulous. "Who ever said I was in love with her?"

"I did!" Amelia is not happy. "You do anything she asks at the drop of a hat. You always have stories about some great new thing she's done. You don't think it's weird that you're always talking about her to me?"

"I thought it was normal to talk to my girlfriend about my friends."

"Not when that friend is your ex it isn't. It isn't normal to be friends with her at all!"

"We've known each other since we were in diapers," Matthew replies, hurt. "I won't just abandon her because we decided not to keep dating after we went to one dance together."

"Well, I'm uncomfortable with this situation," Amelia says. "I don't want you working with her, and I don't want you spending time with her anymore. It's Harper or me."

"What are you saying to me? Can you even hear yourself right now?" Matthew asks her.

"I want you to refuse the assignment. Say no, and then don't see her anymore."

"I can't do that. You don't refuse an assignment like this. It's the opportunity of a lifetime."

"Then I think we should break up," Amelia says, her voice quavering.

"Fine, maybe we should," Matthew says, his anger now boiling over.

Ava suddenly looks up at me, alarmed, and yanks my arm, dragging me back across the hall into our room. She shuts the door as quietly as possible, then turns and stares out the peephole. I can't see anything, but I hear a door slam in the hallway and the sound of running feet.

"She's gone," Ava says. "Can you believe that just happened?"

"Why would she think Matthew's in love with me?" I

ask, making a face.

"You're kidding, right?"

"No."

"You're ridiculous," she replies, flipping her golden hair.

"How am I ridiculous?"

A knock on our door interrupts us, though she didn't look like she was going to answer me anyway. It is pretty absurd to think of Matthew being in love with me. We dated for like three hours a year ago, and we've both been with other people since then. Ava and Amelia are the ridiculous ones.

Grey and Amari stand in our doorway.

"Have you guys talked to Matthew yet?" Grey asks.

"No, why?" I reply.

Our two guests glance at each other before Amari speaks. "We just ran into Amelia in the hall. She broke up with him just a few minutes ago."

"Yeah, we could hear their fight from over here," Ava says with raised eyebrows. Not entirely true, but I guess it sounds better than telling them we were eavesdropping at the door.

"She thinks Matthew's still in love with me just because we work together," I say, almost shouting, my eyebrows drawing together.

"Yeah, well," Grey says, kicking at the ground.

"Yeah, well, what?" I demand.

"Nothing," Amari says briskly. "We just gotta make sure our boy's okay, that's all. Can we get you guys to skip out on tonight? If she was hassling him about you during their breakup, he probably doesn't need to spend his evening with you staring at him. And try to pretend you don't know what happened when you see him at work tomorrow, okay?"

I nod. He's totally right. Matthew needs a guys' night and probably a break from me. He'll have other things to be unhappy about when he finds out about our first mission in the morning.

42

ELIMINATION

"I just don't understand why you have to *kill* them," Matthew says, standing in my cozy new office. I kicked everyone else out when I noticed how agitated he was becoming.

"Because there's no other way to stop this threat. I've already explained it to you. Memory agents won't work, and bringing them here is too great a risk."

"So, you'll sentence them to death just based on a folder the general gave you? You won't even give them a chance to explain themselves?"

"They're not citizens. They have no right to a trial," I say quietly.

"But they're still *people*, aren't they? You of all people can't pretend that being from the surface stops you from being human."

"Yes, Matthew, they're obviously people, but I don't have any other way of dealing with a threat that could result in the entire population being wiped out. Sometimes saving hundreds of lives is worth losing one or two."

"Sort of like giving up Orphans to save a whole town?" he retorts.

"I seem to recall you being pretty willing to make that sacrifice yourself!"

"That was my choice!" he shouts back. I wonder how soundproof these walls are. "You can't sacrifice innocent people who don't even know what's happening to them!"

"Innocent? *Innocent?* These aren't children, Matthew, and they're far from innocent. These are full-grown adults who are sentenced to death for crimes endangering the entire human race!"

"I thought you said you only killed people in self-defense, when there was no other way to stay alive," Matthew spits.

"That's exactly what I'm doing. Except they're not only putting my life in danger. They're endangering you and Ava, all our parents, Jing, Amari, Gray and Jordan, literally *everyone*. It's my responsibility to stop them, and that's what I'm going to do."

"I hope you have the guts to do it yourself then."

"Don't worry about that," I say, sitting back down behind my desk.

Matthew stands there glaring at me. He looks like he's about to hurl another argument at me, but I've had enough. Without even looking at him, I wave him away.

"You're dismissed."

"Harper—"

"I said you're dismissed. Go. Now," I say with finality. He tromps away, slamming the door behind him. I get up and tear the cushions off my couch to use as punching bags. Maybe working with my childhood friend wasn't a good idea after all. And a civilian. *How's he ever going to let me be in charge?*

Once I've worked out some of my aggression, I'm

finally able to finish reviewing the plan with the rest of the team. Matthew is nowhere to be found. I suspect he took a walk to cool off.

"Go do what you need to do to relax a little before the mission. Be back here in one hour. Dismissed."

The room clears, but my soldiers all wait until they're out of my office to resume normal conversation. I lock my door behind me and head for our private surveillance room. I shouldn't be surprised to find Matthew here, but I honestly expected him to go a little farther after our argument. I rest my hands on the back of his chair.

"I know you don't like it, Matthew," I say quietly, trying not to startle him. "I don't like it, either, to tell you the truth, but I don't see a way around it."

"I don't either," he sighs. "If the intel is right, they're putting everyone in danger. But I don't like the idea of killing anyone. I don't suppose we could just talk to them and change their minds."

"The general would have my job," I say. "Or my head."

Matthew nods. "This sucks."

"Yep," I say, sitting beside him. "But at least we get to check out your AI program."

"True," he replies. "Should I pull it up now?"

"Let's worry about the mission first. I'll give the team tomorrow off to rest, and you and I can take a look then, okay?"

"Okay."

"Are you gonna be all right doing surveillance for a mission you disapprove of when you're already feeling crappy?"

"I've never watched anyone die before." Matthew gulps.

"It won't really look like dying. I'll just give them an injection in their sleep, and they'll gradually stop breathing. Painless and uneventful. It'll cause some splotches on their skin that mimic illness so no one questions it, but they won't feel a thing. I thought I could at least give them that. And you."

"So I won't even be able to tell?"

"No, it won't look like anything is happening at all. And you'll have other monitors to watch and drones to control anyway."

"I can't believe we never realized they have cameras in everyone's houses above-ground," Matthew says. "You'd think we would've noticed them at some point."

"We wouldn't have known what we were even looking at if we did."

"Good point."

"All right, I've got a mission to lead," I say, rising to my feet. "You got everything pulled up?"

"Yes, ma'am, Captain Moss, ma'am," he says, and I know he's already forgiven me.

The mission goes off without a hitch. Matthew's surveillance is spot-on, and my team gets in and out without a trace. I've heard some soldiers get a sort of thrill from killing. It's almost like they're adrenaline junkies, getting a high from doing the most terrible thing they can imagine.

It's not like that for me. I used to know these people. Some of them were my neighbors. My team gassed four young children to keep them from waking while I went into Mr. and Mrs. Sheffield's bedroom. They didn't wake, which was a small mercy. I gave each one an injection between their toes, where the healers wouldn't think to look, and I stayed with them while their skin mottled and they breathed their last breaths. It was peaceful for them, if not for me, but there was nothing thrilling about taking a life.

I made four new Orphans last night. Better than thousands dead, but no matter how I try to rationalize it, it continues to eat at me. Four new Orphans who will surely be taken in nine years' time. How do I live with that?

When I finally fall asleep, I'm tormented by beast-Rome chasing me down, insisting that he has a mission and is only following orders. I race out of the woods into the nearest house, slamming the door behind me and shoving furniture up against it. I turn to find a family of six watching me suspiciously.

"It's okay. I'm not here to hurt you," I try to reassure them, but when I look down, I see that Rome has scratched my arm. It's a deep wound, but it isn't bleeding. Instead, it turns a sickly green as hair starts sprouting from me everywhere. I feel an animal urge and attack the parents, killing them viciously. Then, I pick up the children and carry them out into the night, howling alongside Rome, who helps me deliver them to captivity.

43

CONSPIRACY

I can barely keep my eyes open. Last night's mission still haunts me. Matthew startles me awake in front of the computer screen I've been staring at incomprehensibly for what seems like hours.

"I think I've figured it out!" he shouts.

I nearly fall out of my chair.

"Sorry," he says with a grimace. "Didn't get much sleep after the mission, huh?"

"Elimination missions don't exactly make for restful nights." I yawn broadly.

He puts a hand on my shoulder but doesn't push the topic. Instead, he points toward the monitor and explains the work he's completed while I failed to keep myself awake. I don't understand much of what he says until he exclaims simply, "It's a deep-fake!"

"Wait, a deep-fake? What is—the surveillance footage?"

He nods enthusiastically. "Yes! They took my program and embedded a line of code that enables some programmer somewhere to deep fake literally anything they want into the footage."

"But what purpose could that possibly serve?"

"I'm not sure yet, but it looks like they back up the

original footage to a secure server. Not so secure that I can't access it," he says, giving me a sideways grin, "but it'll take me a little while."

Just then, my phone rings.

"Captain Moss," I say. Amari is on the other end, and he sounds frantic.

"Slow down, Amari. What's going on?"

"I found something weird that you need to know about."

Jing and Ava shout wildly in the background.

"Are Jing and Ava with you? I can't understand a thing anyone's saying over all the noise."

"Yes, they're with me. They found some documents in the research labs that, combined with what I've got, don't look so good. We need you to come up here right now."

"Amari, I don't understand."

Ava comes on the line. "Harper, we can't explain it to you on the phone, but it's about Mama. And you. You *have* to come up here right away."

"And make sure no one sees you," Amari adds. "This is big."

Matthew chimes in. He's been eavesdropping. "I'll take care of it, Harper. You better go."

"All right, guys," I say. "I'm coming up. I'll meet you in Amari's office in ten minutes."

Matthew and I establish a secure line, each of us wearing a headset just in case.

"I've set you a clear path with the feed on a loop, just like in our final eval," Matthew tells me. "I want anyone who looks to think you're still down here working. I'll be watching you on the feed while I work on accessing the originals of the deep-faked security footage. Whatever they found up there, it could be connected."

"Thanks, Matthew. Better get going then."

"See you soon, Harper."

My trek to the research floor is fairly uneventful. Matthew redirects me a few times to stop me from meeting up with anyone. When I near the surgical intern offices, Amari is pacing back and forth nervously in the hall. He ushers me inside his tiny office, where Jing and Ava are waiting, and locks the door behind us.

"What's going on?" I ask, looking from one friend to the other.

"Hang on, don't talk yet," Matthew's voice says in my ear. "I need to sweep for bug feeds."

"Wait," I say, pressing one finger to my lips and setting my earpiece on the desk so everyone can hear.

"All right, I've silenced the bug. There's no camera in there, so you should be safe to talk now."

"They have my office bugged?" Amari is incredulous.

I fight the urge to roll my eyes. "We live in a military state. Did you honestly think you had any privacy here?"

"I didn't even know we lived in a military state!"

Matthew answers him. "The highest general overseeing the entire military is automatically the president, and you didn't know this was a military state?"

"I don't think it should surprise anybody to hear that they don't teach us about that in school," Jing chimes in. "All we learn about is how wonderful Elysium is compared to the governments of the past. We're supposed to be a utopia that has everything figured out. Doesn't feel so utopian right now, though."

I sigh. "Can somebody please tell us what's going on?"

"I got promoted this morning, and they upgraded my clearance," Amari explains. "I thought I was just going into a more secure lab, but I wasn't expecting this. I didn't know."

"Didn't know what, Amari?" I ask. I've never seen him so upset.

"There were live test subjects," he says.

"Animals?"

"*People.*"

My jaw drops. "People?"

Amari nods. "Villagers, I think. Adults, children. Some of them have been here for decades. They're experimenting on actual people, and it isn't pretty."

That can't be right. It doesn't make any sense. Why would they experiment on live people? The Orphans undergo weekly medical exams, and Black Ops teams perform covert genetic extractions all the time. They should have everything they need. My mind is a whirlwind of information, and I can't make sense of anything right now.

Concern fills Jing's face. "Harper, are you okay?"

"I'm okay," I try to say, but I can barely find my voice. I can't breathe. I feel like I'm being strangled. *Am I hyperventilating?* Someone takes my arm and helps lower me into a chair.

"You still haven't told Harper and Matthew what you guys found," Amari says.

This time, Ava speaks up. "They've got us digitizing and archiving some of the old research records that are more than ten years old. It's really boring, so we were having a contest to see who could find the weirdest or most interesting thing in a file before we moved them all to storage. Well, I found a file on a test subject from about eleven years ago."

She pulls a file from her bag and sets it on the desk. "He was taken just after your third birthday along with his wife. They left diseased remains behind to look like they had died of some illness that had broken out in the village that summer. He was Black, and she was white, and they left behind a little girl."

My heart is beating so hard, I feel like I could pass out. Amari offers me his hand, and I squeeze it tight.

"So I looked up the subject number to see if we could figure out who it was," Ava continues. "The name wasn't familiar. It didn't mean anything to me at all, but the husband had a sister. When we looked up her subject number," she places another piece of paper in front of me, "it was—"

"Mama," I cut her off, scrutinizing the papers they brought.

"It was Mama. And I think her brother was your dad. She's your auntie, Harper."

My ears are ringing, and my vision is going black around the edges. My whole world is upside-down and spinning. *What does any of this mean?*

"Harper? Harper, did you hear what I said?" Amari is on his knees in front of me, staring right in my face and shaking me lightly.

"Is she okay?" Matthew asks, sounding alarmed.

"I think she's in shock," Amari answers.

I shake my head a little and refocus my vision. "What, Amari?"

"Your biological father. I looked up his records, and he's still here. They've been experimenting on him all this time, but he's alive."

"My dad is . . . alive?"

"This is too much, you guys," Amari says. "We need to give her some time to process."

My mind is reeling. *My real dad was also Mama's brother, and he's here? In Elysium somewhere? How do I begin to come to terms with this?*

"Guys, I know we've gotten a lot of shocking information in the last hour, but it's about to get worse," Matthew's voice announces. "I just found the original surveillance footage they've been faking, and it's not good. Harper, can you get back down here? There's no safe way to send it up to you, but you're gonna have to see this to believe it."

44

REVOLT

The village bell rang out loud and clear, rousing many who would normally have been awake by now. They shot out of bed and hurried to morning prayers in the square, where the gallows and the dead loomed over them, a constant reminder of the task at hand. Father Cowan stood on the stage in front of an assembly of glowering Elders. The Council's goons surrounded the villagers to ensure good behavior, but with one stark difference today—they carried no rifles.

Whispers spread among the crowd. The Council had known about Anna, about her secret signals, but they couldn't put a finger on exactly what she was up to. When the Sheffields died unexpectedly, they took it as an opportunity to rid themselves of her. Did they truly believe Anna's death would solve all their problems? Their trouble was only just beginning.

After morning prayers, noticeably unarmed henchmen lugged villager after villager to the town meeting hall to be questioned by the Council. Each one was released within the hour, only for another to be interrogated. Yet, the gallows stood empty.

"It would seem that there's quite the commotion at Town Hall this morning," Maggie mentioned to Mrs. Prewitt, who passed her friend a fresh muffin from the basket she carried.

Fresh baked goods meant that things were going according to plan.

"Yes," Mrs. Prewitt replied with a frown, "someone broke into the armory last night. All the Guardsmen's rifles were stolen."

"Is that so?"

"I suppose you wouldn't have seen anything strange last night since you were leading the prayer vigil," Mrs. Prewitt said, glancing at her own guard. "But do you recall anyone being absent?"

"No, I don't believe so," Maggie replied thoughtfully, "though you know what a firelight vigil is like. It's hard to see anyone who's not standing close to you."

"Well, I imagine they'll want to talk to you this morning. Seems like my husband will be tied up with the investigation most of the day."

"That's a shame, Mrs. Prewitt. Feel free to come around for dinner if he's not home yet this evening. There's no need for anyone to eat alone here." *Maggie patted the Elder's wife on the hand, and the two women exchanged a brief look.*

The Council would be busy and unarmed all throughout the day, too tied up to notice any other goings on around the village.

Later that afternoon, the town bell clanged again urgently. Bewildered townsfolk stumbled into the square from their jobs in barns, shops, and fields that were being tilled for the new year's spring planting. It took quite some time for everyone to assemble.

Father Cowan took his usual place on stage out of obligation, though he appeared just as confused as everyone else. Elder Samson shoved him out of the way to harangue the waiting masses.

"Where is he?" Samson screamed, spittle flying from his mottled purple face. "First the rifles and now Gideon! Who's responsible for this?"

A murmur rippled through the crowd. Gideon was the Council's most feared lackey. Vicious and cruel, he was often the purveyor of the Council's "justice," taking a sick pleasure from kicking the feet out from under the innocents who met the gallows. He stood over six feet tall with arms and legs as thick as tree trunks. Who would have the gall to do anything to him?

Father Cowan was appalled. "Elder Samson," he said, cautiously bowing his head in deference, "what has happened? Gideon is certainly not a man to be trifled with."

"He disappeared from his guard duty right outside Town Hall this afternoon. I want every villager accounted for! See that no one is missing," Samson replied fiercely.

Father Cowan nodded. "I'll see to the villagers, sir, if the Council has other matters they'd like to attend to."

Elder Samson continued sputtering in rage, but he took the Council and went back inside. Father Cowan did exactly as he'd been told and accounted for each and every villager. Only Gideon was missing.

When John and Maggie arrived at the front of Father Cowan's line, he murmured quietly, "I'd be cautious. They'll have your head if you're involved."

Soon enough, they came for Maggie, who had stationed herself in the square with a small group of other women to pray loudly for Gideon's safe return.

"Perhaps Gideon's run off to strike out on his own," she suggested.

"Or perhaps you've something to do with all this," Elder Prewitt said, his narrowed eyes watching her closely. They locked her up, keeping her under constant guard overnight. To

the townspeople, the intention was clear—hang her at morning prayers the next day as a show of the Council's strength.

But when the Council arrived in the square the next morning, the gallows were gone, and Gideon's head, with a bullet hole through his left temple, stood atop a pike that had been erected in its place. Though Maggie was still locked up with a guard inside the room, the man who had kept watch outside the room was now missing. The inner guard had not seen or heard a single thing. The Council shook with fear at what would happen next.

"I love that they took down the gallows," Maggie told John when she arrived back home. "What did they do with them?"

"Oh, I suspect someone'll find them burned in a field when they go to start the planting next week," John remarked with a good-natured chuckle. "And now they can't blame you for the disappearances, can they?"

"They'll still find someone to blame, I'm sure," Maggie told her husband, "but now they know they're losing control. We'll match the actions of the Founder and regain control through fear, if necessary, or they can simply surrender."

The following day, another henchman's head had been erected atop a pike in the square. Anna Aaron's desiccated corpse was missing, along with a few others, and nearly every villager was armed. A message had been carved into the ground to match the one received by the Sovereign nearly a year ago to the day:

WE TOOK WHAT WAS OWED.
REPENT OR FACE A NEW REIGN OF TERROR.

45

DEEP-FAKE

I blink at the monitor and ask Matthew to play it again. The absolute nightmare that has been happening in our village since the Taking is beyond belief. The sheer carnage and devastation—I don't know what to make of it. They told us that the Elders knew. They told us everything was safe and peaceful with only some beginning talk of rising up against Elysium.

They don't know anything at all! The entire community thinks the Sovereign are real, that we were taken by gods for some greater spiritual purpose. They believe they'll be punished if their repentance is not evident enough.

Maggie lost a finger. The lashings, the loss of homes and rations. The kind and gracious Elders stripped of their positions and the ability to do anything good. When villagers rebelled against the cruelty, they were sent to the gallows, their bodies strung up for all to see, their children sent to the reopened Orphan Home. It was only a matter of time before Mama and Papa joined them.

"Matthew, your mama!" I cry out.

He stifles a sob. "It's not your fault, Harper. You didn't know."

"But I'm the one who killed the Sheffields! If I had

listened to you, she might still be alive."

Matthew shakes his head. In spite of his obvious grief, he still can't manage to hate me. "There was nothing else you could do. They were gunning for her. They would've found some excuse no matter what."

I wrap my arms around him, and we cry together. Nothing is right in my world anymore. I thought they were all good—the people in my village above-ground and the leaders of Elysium. I thought they were saving the world. *What even is the point of all this violence? What could Elysium possibly hope to gain?*

Despair drops like a ten-ton weight in the pit of my stomach. "Matthew, can you pull up the current feed on the village? The real one?"

"I think so, yeah," he says, typing frantically through his sniffles.

Before long, a new picture comes onto the screen. Matthew must've left Mama's subject ID number in the drone search when he pulled it up. She and Papa kneel in the dirt, planting what little they can manage in the small garden they've dug between their tiny, decrepit shack and the woods. My breath catches in my throat at the sight of them both alive and well.

A fine mist rolls out of the woods towards them so slowly I almost don't notice it. I gasp and shout as if they can hear me, but there's nothing I can do. Two camouflaged figures in gas masks appear behind them. Mama lays her head on Papa's shoulder, her dark face sleepy. As Papa begins to fade, the masked soldiers place dark bags over each of their heads and zip-tie their wrists and ankles together.

As the fog clears, the soldiers stoop and each hoist one

of my parents over a shoulder. They take off their masks to radio that they've completed their objective and are ready for extraction.

Rome's face stares back at me through the computer monitor with my Mama—my auntie, my father's sister—slung over his shoulder. *Elysium's newest experiment.*

EPILOGUE: TEST SUBJECT

The room was dark and cold. The cells were solid concrete on every side and soundproof. They had spent years tormenting him, performing painful experiments that were meant to test . . . what? Even now, he couldn't be sure. They seemed to test everything from his physical ability and stamina to his mental resolve and emotional health.

He knew he wasn't the only test subject. He'd been subjected to group experiments many times since he was brought here. Though many of the others were from his village, none were his wife. They weren't permitted to speak to each other, so he had been unable to determine if she'd survived.

And his beautiful little Harper. What had become of her? Had they brought her here, too? Were there terrible cells for children and labs where they experimented on them? Or was she at the Orphan Home? Perhaps Maggie and John had taken her in when he and her mother had disappeared. No, that would be unlikely in their village. Unsupervised children were never allowed to live with relatives. They were always deemed Orphans. She would be sent to the Sovereign soon. Or maybe she had already been sent? He'd lost track of the days and the years long ago.

A familiar knock sounded on his cell door, the one that told him to stand back in the far corner. It would be time for a meal delivery, he supposed. He had wasted away in this place, languishing in lost hopes and dreams. He had long since given up imagining an escape or reunification with his family. Now, he only hoped they hadn't suffered as much as him.

He backed up to the far wall of his concrete cage, waiting in the corner with his head down as many an electrified cattle prod had taught him to do in his early weeks here. The door opened. He heard the sound of his lunch tray scraping across the rough floor. Then, the door slammed shut.

Only after he heard the latch slide back into place did he move to pick up his tray. He sat on his hard bunk with it in his lap and began to eat. He rarely knew hunger in this place, but that was more for disinterest than large portions. He had long since lost his appetite, but he ate anyway. If he didn't, there would be more torture.

When he picked up the water cup to drink, he found something stuck stubbornly to the bottom. He carefully peeled it off to find a message.

Pretend this is trash and throw it into your toilet bucket. I know you're alive. I'll get you out. Be ready.

—Harper

He crumpled the paper into a small ball and tossed it into his toilet with disinterest. He couldn't afford to show emotion. The cameras would see.

After they came to retrieve his meal tray, he curled up on his bunk with the book he was allowed to read to keep his mind lucid. It spoke of things he didn't comprehend, but it was all the better right now. He wasn't reading anyway. He would use this time with his face carefully hidden from the cameras to contemplate what he had just learned.

His little girl was alive!

NOTE FROM THE AUTHOR

When I wrote Sovereign, I deliberately left the characters' physical descriptions vague. Harper wears braids. Matthew has gray eyes. Ava has chin-length blonde hair. That was it.

I wanted everyone who read the book to be able to see themselves in the characters, to actually put themselves in the characters' shoes and become them. Every teen who reads the story is Harper and Matthew and Ava. They're not just relatable; they're you.

When it was time to start writing Elysium, I had to think of the Sovereign universe in a whole new way. I needed to know the events that actually created this world and this society. Where Sovereign was insular and isolated, Elysium opens up to the broader world and its history.

What I wanted from this world was something very different than the one we live in today. I wanted a world that had survived beyond racial divisions. I don't know if a world like that will ever exist in reality, but reading one has the potential to inspire future generations to work toward such a world.

Despite having transcended racial barriers, those with power in the world of The Sovereign Trilogy have still found other ways to divide and dehumanize those they classify as "other." We've already seen it happen to the Orphans, and by the end of Elysium, you've seen it happen to other groups, too.

Most of us, I think, picture characters that look like us. In Elysium, you may discover that some characters don't actually look how you pictured them. Because you've already lived one story as these characters, you know that you are more alike than different, no matter what you look like on the outside. You may look different, live different, or love different, but on the inside, we are still the same.

No matter the character in the story or the reader reading it, the message remains: We are all human, and we all deserve love, dignity, and respect.

Never be afraid to speak up for the humanity of those who are different from you.

—AJ

ACKNOWLEDGEMENTS

The journey to writing this book was wildly unexpected. When I wrote *Sovereign*, I had a pretty good idea of what I wanted it to be and some rock-solid inspiration for the characters and the story. *Elysium* was a completely different experience! I had written a beautiful story that was leading . . . somewhere, but I didn't actually know where yet. No inspiration. No preconceived notions. Nothing. My mind was a blank slate.

This was a new challenge for me, and I really felt like I was testing myself. I've read series before where the first book blew my mind, and then every book after that just went further downhill. I did *not* want The Sovereign Trilogy to be one of them. But this time, I didn't have much of anything guiding me. I couldn't depend on a wild dream to tell me what the story was.

You mean I have to come up with this all on my own? Whhhhhhhhhyyyyyyyyyyy????? (Yes, Ricky and Amber, I know that's too many letters and question marks. LOL)

But you guys, *I DID THE THING*. All I had to work from were the words I had already written: "Welcome to Elysium. Your new life is about to begin." I managed to figure out this whole plot that would span two more books, and my publisher still liked it. I'm not a one-hit wonder who can only produce one coherent, halfway entertaining piece of literature. I'm a real author, and I'm finally starting to think I might be good at this.

But bragging about how great it is that I wrote another book isn't exactly the point here, is it? Even though I wrote the thing, I didn't really do it alone.

In fact, I'm fond of telling everyone who ever asks for writing advice that "no one writes a perfect book alone." And so, I'd like to thank the many amazing people who supported me on this journey and helped me see in myself what they've been seeing all along.

I will always thank my husband, Pip, first. You support me in so many tiny ways and in all the huge ones, too. You come to every event. You learned the pitch to sell *Sovereign* well. You had my *Sovereign* earrings made, and you read every single version of every manuscript I've ever written. You are the ultimate AJ Whitney hype guy! I couldn't do any of this without you. I love you more than you could ever know.

Thank you to my mom, Kathy Goranson-Doty, who became my biggest fan and pushed *Sovereign* and then, I'm sure, *Elysium* to everyone she ever met—friends and strangers alike—and we all know you've never *really* met a stranger. In one of the hardest seasons of your life, you still never hesitated to support me, to read what I wrote, and to love every word. You are, beyond a shadow of a doubt, the most supportive mom a girl could ever ask for. I love you!

Thank you to Ricky Treon, the director of publishing at Blue Handle Publishing, who didn't just believe in a single book I wrote one time, but who believed in me and my ability to be a real, live, grown-up author. Of your many gifts, you are the most incredible encourager! You see people not just for who they are right now, but for all the potential they have to be-come more than they ever dreamed they could be. You knew this was more than just one book. I think you might be the person who encouraged and believed in me the most after my husband, my kids, and my mom.

Thank you to my editor, Amber Guffey, for always making me sound better, but also for replying to my author emails, joking around with me on social media, and becoming a genuine friend. You are a sweetheart!

Tammy Walters, thank you for being probably the best beta reader in the history of the world. You are an author's dream and just the most incredible friend.

Shontel Nance, thank you for answering my "stupid white person questions" while in-sisting that they weren't stupid. Thank you for being understanding and for appreciating my, and everyone else's, desire to learn instead of getting annoyed with me. I love your heart! You are the real-life Maggie, for sure.

Nikki Brewer, thank you for always believing in me, for reading my work, and for host-ing my first school author visit. You are such a kind, sweet, and supportive friend!

Thank you also to Maggie Rodriguez, Princess Consuela Banana Hammock, and Sophia for being early readers and giving amazing feedback.

Thank you to Sarah Schmidt and Jacque Lerch for being amazing, supportive friends. Sarah owns at least three signed copies of Sovereign—one for reading, one for lending, and one as a collector's item. Get out there and find yourself a friend who has that much faith in you! Jacque works some of my events with me and gives us a place to stay when an event is too far from home. More importantly, she supports me in my dark times, listens without judgment, and lets me cry on her shoulder, even when I'm being stupid. It doesn't usually have anything to do with writing books, but my life is brighter with her in it. Thanks for always being there for me!

And thank you, thank you, thank you to my readers, my email subscribers, social media followers, and my fans. Who cares if you can write a book if nobody reads it? You guys have made some of my wildest dreams come true! When you fangirl over meeting me and getting a signed book, I try to look composed, but I'm fangirling ten thousand times harder on the inside.

O-M-SQUEE! I love you all!

ABOUT THE AUTHOR

AJ Whitney writes the books she needed as a teen—the kind that get under your skin and won't let go.

A Kansas City author and high school counselor, she spins stories that walk the line between dystopian nightmares and raw, emotional truth. Her debut novel *Sovereign* launched *The Sovereign Trilogy*, a twisty, high-stakes YA series full of secrets, survival, and rebellion.

Whether she's writing or working with teens IRL, AJ's mission is the same: Help teenagers own their weird, ask the right questions, and never settle for silence.

Called "the future of YA fiction" by KC Book Beat, she's here to challenge the rules and remind readers that the only way to the light is through the dark.

www.ingramcontent.com/pod-product-compliance
Lightning Source LLC
LaVergne TN
LVHW032007070526
838202LV00059B/6335